Praise for *Wa[...]*

"Exactly the kind of smart, fast-paced t[...]
night.... A masterful story that will stay [...] is
turned." —Danielle Girard, *USA TODAY* bestselling author of *Up Close*

"The essence of terrific crime fiction: with authentic motivation, a
cinematic setting, characters we can root for, and a gasp-worthy
heartbreaking conclusion. Kristen Bird is an amazing talent, and *Watch It
Burn* is not to be missed!"
—Hank Phillippi Ryan, *USA TODAY* bestselling author of *The House Guest*

"This addictive thriller...will leave you gasping. Every chapter...masterfully
challenges what you think you know as it propels you to its chilling end."
—Darby Kane, internationally bestselling author of *The Engagement Party*

"An enthralling look at how toxic ideologies can impact families and
communities in a way that will haunt you for days after reading."
—Olivia Day, host of *Thrillers by the Bookclub Pod*

"NXIVM meets Southern suspense.... Gripping, timely, and ominous, this
one is not to be missed."
—Allison Buccola, author of *Catch Her When She Falls*

"Atmospheric suspense at its best.... As thought-provoking as it is
compulsively readable."
—Heather Chavez, author of *Before She Finds Me*

"Beneath the rosy surface of progress and prosperity in this tiny Texas
town are secrets, coverups, and manipulation."
—Jennifer Fawcett, author of *Beneath the Stairs*

"A scorching tale of revenge and an unflinching look at what women
will do when pushed to their limits. Bird has a pitch-perfect ear for the
rhythms of Southern life, but be warned, these women are no steel
magnolias. They're raw, real, and mad as hell, and I would follow them
anywhere."
—Polly Stewart, author of *The Good Ones*

"Southern scandal and a small town punctured by violence.... *Watch It
Burn* is fast-paced crime fiction at its absolute finest."
—Chandler Baker, *New York Times* bestselling author of *Whisper Network*

"With intricate plotting, lush, visceral prose, and richly layered characters,
Watch It Burn is a skewering, incendiary examination of a small town's
darkest, most explosive secrets."
—May Cobb, author of *A Likeable Woman*

Also by Kristen Bird

I Love It When You Lie
The Night She Went Missing

WATCH IT BURN

KRISTEN BIRD

mira

Recycling programs
for this product may
not exist in your area.

ISBN-13: 978-0-7783-6969-1

Watch It Burn

For questions and comments about the quality of this book, please contact us at
CustomerService@Harlequin.com.

TM is a trademark of Harlequin Enterprises ULC.

Mira
22 Adelaide St. West, 41st Floor
Toronto, Ontario M5H 4E3, Canada
BookClubbish.com

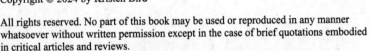

Printed in U.S.A.

For Jessica

So glad we met at that swing set thirty-plus years ago

PROLOGUE

Children and parents, teenagers and grandparents—all lined the banks of the river at sunset, their laughter echoing the delighted squeals of kids who'd once played along this waterfront.

Citizens and tourists—and even the ghosts—awaited the onslaught of black-and-gold floats, rose-laden kayaks, bright lights, and Tejano beats. Every business in Edenberg shuttered when water levels were high enough to hold the Our Lady of the Guadalupe Paddle Parade each Labor Day. Maybe that was why no one noticed the first flicker.

For the people who bothered to look up, the horizon glowed with a faint orange haze not unlike a late-summer sky in the Texas hill country. The thing that finally gave away the secret of the flames was the smell, heavy with the aroma of family pictures curling at the edges before melting to nothing, of heirloom quilts sparking into kindling before dissolving to ash. An out-of-tune piano crackled like tinder, and a beloved plush rabbit lit up in a flash of cotton stuffing.

It wasn't just one building or just one home or just one business that burned that night. It was the entire downtown. The fire didn't discriminate between the hip new wine room and the hundred-year-old bungalow. That was what you got for building an idyllic town in a tight grid with Main Street cutting through the center: the flaming dominoes toppled, transferring the burden of heat from square to tragic square.

Listen, fire safety is key.

Flames double in size every thirty seconds.

Stop, drop, and roll.

Be sure to install smoke alarms in every room of the house.

For the next year, these words would echo in victims' minds as they rebuilt their hamlet brick by brick. For now, as realization dawned, these people—made to withstand rising waters rather than trial by fire—turned their backs on the river that could've saved this place if only Mother Nature wasn't so fickle about when she flooded the banks.

Only one person knew for certain how long the fire had been burning before the first call came through to 911, but she'd never tell. Nine minutes and twenty-seven seconds later, three fire trucks, laden with hoses and brave men, arrived on scene. They met the inferno as a rock meets water, submerged and steadily sinking. *We should be grateful*, the fire chief said, *that only one person died.*

By dawn, no matter how hard they fought, every place of business and historic home in the center of Main Street would be cradled in ash, citizens mourning the markers of lives well lived: a recipe box from a grandmother, the brand-new menus at the local diner, an antique guitar that Willie Nelson might've once played, a handwritten letter from an old flame.

Even the Blessed Mother herself couldn't help them on this fiery night.

PART ONE

"When a woman thinks
that her house is on fire,
her instinct is at once
to rush to the thing
which she values most."

—Sir Arthur Conan Doyle,
The Adventures of Sherlock Holmes

Excerpt from "Welcome to Edenberg" by Marge Pierce
Features Section
September 5, 1988

Some may not realize that Edenberg is known not only for the very first Catholic cathedral to offer an Our Lady of the Guadalupe shrine; we're also known for our wine.

William von Hoffman founded the town in 1849, settling in the hill country and naming his acreage Edenberg. He saw the land as the perfect place to start anew for his family and friends. The climate was mild most of the year, similar to his homeland in Germany, and he was glad he'd brought with him cuttings from his family's winery, Weingut Hoffman.

Unfortunately, for reasons William never understood (according to his diaries), the pinot blanc grapes did not fare well in this new soil, so within five years, his dreams of a Texas winery had shriveled on the vine. At least we still have Our Lady.

Speaking of which, this year's Paddle Parade is expected to be quite the shindig. The band Mariachi Mayhem will perform in the town square at 7 p.m. sharp, and you can come out early for a sampling of some of the finest wine from Messina Hof, our neighbors to the east. We're grateful to them for sharing their wine, since we no longer make our own. Hope to see you there!

1

MONDAY
ONE WEEK BEFORE THE FIRE

NICHOLE

Nichole pulled on purple running shorts before plodding to the bathroom and gulping down four ibuprofen. Last night's whiskey sours had been the wrong libation for the eve before school started.

Without looking in the mirror, she applied moisturizer with SPF and pulled back her straight black hair into a wide cloth headband, banging brushes and bottles as she went. As she made herself a bowl of oatmeal, she created as much racket as possible, hoping all the while that the man in her bed would wake up.

When fifteen minutes passed and he was still snoring soundly, Nichole left him a note saying she'd gone for a run and he should let himself out. Then, she turned her clock radio to the '80s station at full volume, Bon Jovi's "Livin' on a Prayer" echoing behind as she dashed out the front door as fast as her former cross-country legs would carry her. Nichole was a thirty-nine-year-old Korean American woman sneaking out of her own house. It had come to this.

Hot and sticky couldn't sufficiently describe the smothering humidity, like a stack of wet paper towels pasted to her head, as she jogged the path she took every morning—only recently running from the men she'd invited home. This had to be the fourth such morning. Or the fifth. Oh, God, had she actually lost count? She was not supposed to be one of those women. She should've called her best friend, Jenny, like she'd promised to do if ever this situation arose again.

I'm back now. You don't have to grieve alone, Jenny had told her earlier this summer, looking Nichole straight in the eyes. Much had changed since that first day of kindergarten when they'd swung side by side, conversing about the best name for the puppy Jenny's mother had brought home (they'd finally settled on *Bluebonnet Rose Dandelion*), but their friendship had solidified. The next day on those same swings, Nichole had asked Jenny if she wanted to be "booby friends." (She'd heard the term *bosom buddies* on TV and asked her big sister what the first word meant.) When Jenny said yes, Nichole figured she'd made a friend for life, that they'd forever be on the same team. She'd been right so far.

But Nichole hadn't called her oldest friend before that first drink, and now here she was.

She reached the edge of the neighborhood where the asphalt ended and the earthen path into the woods began. As she kept her eyes on the horizon, she tried to recall the sum total she knew about the man she'd left alone in her house.

1. He was mixed race, half Native American and white.
2. He took up much of her queen bed, which meant he was more than six feet tall.
3. She was pretty sure his drink of choice had been a gin and tonic.
4. He worked in…air-conditioning, or maybe he was a mechanic? Something with his hands.
5. He could say the alphabet backward while drunk.

A stirring list, no doubt, but not enough to keep her interested in… What was his name? Oh, shit. *What was it?* She

swiped hard at her brow, either to jar her memory or to punish
herself for this terrible lapse in judgment. At least she'd known
the names of the others.

As her feet padded against the earth, she decided to distract herself by thinking through the day in front of her. After
showering and dressing in her first-day-of-school outfit—even
after nineteen years of teaching, she still selected a special ensemble each year—she would arrive at school and cut the remaining All About Me worksheets into heart shapes for her
students. Then, she would place a special eraser at each desk
and wait for the first bell to ring. It would be a fresh start for a
new year. Still, at the periphery of her mind, something bothered her about this plan.

A few more yards and she remembered the problem: when
she was on her way to the bar last night, she—along with the
rest of the faculty—had received a vaguely worded email from
the head of the board, letting them know a new position had
been created on campus: a curriculum coordinator.

The title sounded appropriate for an educational administra-
trative position, but the last-minute appointment and the description of the role had seemed…*off*. It stated that this person
would be evaluating—and, when necessary, censoring—books
and exercises deemed "inappropriate" or "irrelevant" to "today's cultural climate."

In past years, Nichole would've responded to the email with
a professional series of questions and concerns pushing back on
such a sudden decision; she might've even protested the appointment. As it was, she had no emotional energy for an outcry.

Ten minutes into her run, and her stomach roiled with
the liquid contents of last night's debauchery. She slowed to
a steadier pace, holding hands above her head in an effort to
stem the nausea. It would be fine. Everything would be fine.

When she got home, the man in her bed would be gone,
and she would shower and dress and enter the new school year

without any of the baggage of this lonely summer of men. A new leaf to turn over this fall. That was what she needed. She would embrace her singleness like Cheryl Strayed in *Wild* or Julia Roberts in *Eat, Pray, Love.* She shook her head. No, not Julia Roberts—that was the film. The book was Elizabeth... Elizabeth *Something.*

Nichole took gulps of the dank air and tried to sprint across the slatted bridge hovering over the Guadalupe. She could see that the river levels were low, which meant the Paddle Parade was unlikely to happen this year unless they got a good rainfall in the next week. Rocks cut a jagged course to the other side, the white water shallow but fast as it dodged impediments.

One time when she was a kid and the water had been low like this, she and her sister had taken their neighbor's kayak down to the banks. Ten-year-old Christina, with her fair skin and blue eyes, looked nothing like Nichole, but that made them no less a bonded pair. Christina sat in the stern, gripping tightly to a tree root, as five-year-old Nichole stepped shakily into the bow. When her sister let go, the two of them caught a current that carried their borrowed vessel into the middle of the river, bumping them across algae-ridden rocks and silty divots before eventually hurtling them into a tree growing at the edge of the water and upending the kayak. Nichole had flailed, arms and legs pulsating, as she attempted to stay afloat in the drop-off. Only seconds had passed, but fear slowed time for Nichole, so when her torso connected with Christina's leg, Nichole held on for dear life, climbing her older sister's body like a koala in a bamboo tree.

After the two of them finally made their way to the banks, dragging the boat behind them, they swore never to step foot in those waters again. When fifteen children died in the river a few years later, their pact was solidified. To Nichole, those waters meant danger, even at low levels.

As she ducked under a hanging branch now, leaves scratched

at her shoulder and she remembered the stories kids in her class told about the tragedy that had stolen lives in this river, whispers about how you could hear children laughing on the banks on late-August days.

Nichole shivered despite the feverish heat and forced herself to make a full loop by crossing the second bridge.

As she came closer to the paved road, she peered into the distance, trying to see if the man's Jeep was still parked in front of her house. As she squinted toward home, something colorful caught in her periphery, a typical sight in a river that kept flowing in the same direction day in and day out, all the way to the Gulf. But this wasn't the usual orange lifejacket, bikini top, or beer koozie. It was a pink-and-blue paisley-printed scarf, possibly silk and certainly expensive.

Nichole watched the fabric glide past before turning her face upstream. In the distance she spotted a mound of clothing piled in the center of the riverbed.

She glanced at her watch. It was almost 6:30 a.m., and if she was going to make it to school on time, she really needed to get home. But something about the fabric in the middle of the river wasn't right. She needed to take a quick look.

She navigated the bumpy terrain with precision, and as she crept closer to the bank, stepping around fallen branches and exposed roots, the mound began to take shape. That of a torso, of arms, of legs.

Nichole stopped midstride as she realized exactly what was in front of her: this was a body—a woman, it seemed—face down in the center of the shallow river.

2

JENNY

Jenny grabbed her diamond studs from the counter and scanned the kitchen table laced with waffle crumbs, a dotted trail of syrup, and unwashed plates.

Not my job, not my problem, she reminded herself, using the phrase Nichole had reminded her to say over and over until she actually believed it. The earrings poked her palm as she balled her fist to keep herself from throwing open the dishwasher and piling dishes inside.

"Did you put a snack in each of their backpacks?" Jenny asked, avoiding her husband's eyes.

"Yes." There was an edge in Curt's voice to which only her ears were attuned. "I've got this."

Jenny raised her eyebrows but didn't say a word. He didn't have any of this, and they both knew it.

Curt turned to the kids, his pitch risen to a faux-cheerful note. "It's your mother's first day, too, guys. Tell her good luck—and that we'll be fine."

Little Austen, his mouth full of cereal, gave her a thumbs-up.

Emmy squinted at her daddy as she ran a butter knife across a third waffle. "Do you even know the way to our school?"

Jenny smirked as she lifted the coffee to her lips. A fair question.

"Very funny, Em." Curt reached out and rumpled their daughter's hair.

"Will you pick us up, Mommy?" Emmy asked a moment later, walking a few feet into the living room, brushing sticky hands to purple shorts and fingering a blue shirt that read *Second Grade Smarty*. Aunt Nichole had made it for her.

"Remember that Dad is the one at home now, so he'll do drop-off and pickup most days." Jenny rifled through her purse, displacing the contents she wouldn't need at her new job: markers, an apple sauce squeeze pouch, three crayons, and a crumpled drawing of a giraffe that looked more like a distinctive aspect of the male anatomy.

"That's right," Curt said, making a silly face. "Daddy's in charge around here now."

Emmy giggled, and Jenny saw a flash of the four of them in their tiny kitchen in LA, laughing as they each dipped a spoon in chocolate chip cookie dough and ate straight from the bowl. They were like the poster family for all-American, upper-middle-class white people. But that had been before. She blinked twice to dislodge the memory and stepped into the red two-inch pumps that squeezed her toes, unsure of how long she'd be able to stand wearing heels after living in slip-on canvas shoes for the past few years.

Austen's eyes brightened. "Will we still get ice cream after school?"

"Of course, silly," Emmy jumped in to answer. "We go every year."

Jenny smiled. She loved when her kids spoke as if they'd already lived decades.

In his excitement, Austen flung his hands into the air, and Curt attempted to catch the cup of milk before it fell to the floor. He missed and it tumbled, splattering across the kitchen. Wall-to-wall dairy.

Each person froze, waiting for a yell, a curse, a sigh. Nothing came except the silent resignation that had become the hall-mark of their home as of late.

Jenny turned her head to study the spill pattern. It looked a bit like a Jackson Pollock painting.

Not my job, not my problem.

She looked away, planted a kiss on Emmy's and Austen's foreheads, and picked up her keys. It was her husband's turn to clean things up.

3

NICHOLE

Nichole closed her eyes and opened them slowly, hoping that the image she'd seen had been a terrible vision, the shadowy morning light playing tricks on her. But no, the woman was still there.

Nichole instinctively reached into the hidden pocket of her running shorts to call Jenny, which was ridiculous because, of course, she should first call 911. But it didn't matter because the phone wasn't there. She'd left it in her clutch last night. Damn. She glanced around. No help in sight.

She stared at the figure, motionless and resembling a pile of dirty laundry. Maybe the woman in the river was inebriated, but alive. That was right. Maybe it wasn't just a body, devoid of a pumping heart and breathing lungs.

Oh God, oh God, oh God.

She could not do this, not after… She swallowed and pushed back the thought.

Perhaps someone else had already stumbled across the woman that morning and was calling for help. She often came across other runners on the trail or fishermen out for an early catch.

Still, she couldn't very well risk that no one else was coming. Nichole told herself to calm down, to think logically. She could hurry back to her house or she could step into the terrifying river, but if there was any chance of helping this person, now was the time.

In case someone—anyone—could hear her, Nichole placed her hands around her mouth, filled her lungs, and screamed for help. The first cry came out as a squeak, so she tried again, this time using the air from her belly.

She listened for any sound other than the trickling stream and the warblers in the trees. No response except for cicadas and rustling leaves.

When another few life-saving seconds passed and no one came, Nichole took a deep breath of muggy air and then tiptoed into the river until her tennis shoes and socks were soaked in the frigid water. Good Lord, she hated this river. She hated this moment. She hated that she would have this as another shitty memory to add to this already shitty year.

Nichole reached the figure and hesitated before extending a trembling forearm to touch the woman's back. The fabric was damp and slick, and instinctively, she jerked away. She cleared her throat and clenched her back teeth to keep herself from shivering. No more touching. She would try to simply talk to the woman.

"Hey, hey, are you okay?" Though she felt silly standing alone in the river, talking to a mound of clothes, it seemed strange not to say something, anything, even if the woman was completely unresponsive.

"I'm going to turn you over," she informed the body.

With her foot, she prodded until gravity took over and the woman's lifeless eyes were staring at the sky.

She tried to remember the CPR steps she'd learned at the medical training for coaches last year. She was supposed to have renewed her certification this summer, but what with the drinking and the men, the task had somehow slipped her mind.

She tried to recall the life-saving steps, but all she could think about was the way their school's PE teacher had appeared to be making out with the dummy, Resusci Annie—or "Ranny" as her team had designated the plastic doll. But now, when she needed the information, her mind was blank. Was it breaths and then compressions? Or the other way around?

The splash prickled her calves and sent a domino of goosebumps up her legs as she inched closer. Her breath caught. The older woman's skin was translucent, her lips purple. Without ever having been trained in the stages of death, Nichole knew this person had been gone long enough that she wasn't coming back. She forced her fingers to feel for a pulse. Nothing. She dropped the wrist and looked away. She couldn't face another dead body, even if this time it wasn't someone related to her.

Nichole moved to the feet, and as she did so, her mind rearranged this woman's features into a living person with mannerisms and expressions. After thirty seconds or so, she let forth a gasp. Nichole knew this woman.

She was the wife of Dr. George Hoffman, city superintendent and head of the school board, the man who'd put Edenberg, Texas, on the map. Beverly Hoffman was the woman behind the genius, the silent helpmeet who spoke when spoken to, the afterthought. And now she was dead.

"I'll be back as soon as I can," Nichole whispered before darting out of the water, grabbing at tree roots and clawing at the dirt as she hoisted herself back up the riverbank. By the time she reached level ground, her knees and elbows were muddy and scraped, and grass stained her calves.

When she made it back to Mill Road, Nichole broke into a sprint for the four hundred or so yards to her cottage. Panting, she threw open the door to see the man from last night sitting at her kitchen table drinking orange juice.

"Good morning," he said after a sip.

"Morning," Nichole mumbled, starting toward her bedroom to search for her phone.

The man called out, "Last night was fun."

Nichole ignored him, found her clutch, took out the device, and grimaced. It was dead. She let out a low groan as she knelt beside her bed, searching for her charger.

"I was going to make us omelets, but you don't have much in the way of real food," the man said as he followed her into her room, scrolling on his own phone.

Without a word, she took it from him.

"What—" he started, but Nichole shushed him with a finger in front of her lips as she often did with her second graders and dialed the number.

"911. What's your emergency?" a voice on the other end of the line asked.

"There's a body, a woman. Just past Mill Road and Fifth, in the river." Nichole's eyes filled, surprising her. She hadn't cried since the breakup. She'd assumed she was all out of tears after an already tragic year. "She's…" Nichole wasn't sure if she could finish the sentence.

She's…what?

Eerily white?

Pale with blue lips?

Alone?

The last descriptor was the worst.

"She's dead," Nichole said flatly into the phone.

The man's eyes grew round.

"We're sending someone now," the operator told Nichole.

She dropped the phone and sank to the edge of the bed.

The man moved to her other side and put an arm around her. "I'm so sorry."

His voice was deep and steadying, and despite struggling to remember his name, Nichole buried her head in his chest and sobbed.

4

JENNY

Jenny drove through town, her destination the faded building at the end of a long Main Street dotted with tourist gift shops stocked with everything from oversize rhinestone cowgirl belt buckles to specialty mango salsa to signs that said things like "Remember the Alamo," a location only thirty miles from Edenberg's town center.

Two months ago, as she and her family had pulled into the town proper and inched down Main Street at the now-requisite twenty miles per hour, Jenny had seen for herself that Edenberg had become a full-fledged tourist destination filled with shopping, dining, and wine tasting. The buildings had been spruced up since she left for college two decades ago, and one name had been emblazoned on signs and buildings on every block and at every intersection: *Owned & Managed by Dr. George Hoffman.* This man was touting the fact that he now ran the town.

Since when do we have a city superintendent? she'd asked Nichole last week as they watched the kids play at the brand-new city park.

Since when is Edenberg a full-fledged city? Nichole had responded.

Both good questions.

The newspaper office was quiet when she arrived. No bustling newsroom, not even a phone being answered. So much for a first-day celebration.

She peered into one of the four cubicles and called out, "Hello?"

A toilet flushed from the wall behind her, and a minute later her new editor-in-chief stepped out of the restroom and into the fluorescent light of the empty front desk.

"Jenny," Ed Zimmerman proclaimed cheerfully. He wore skinny jeans, a Western shirt with pearl snaps, and wide-rimmed glasses. A perfect mix of hill country and early-2000s metrosexual.

"Hey, Ed. Where is everybody?"

He rubbed at his bald head with his pointer finger as he glanced at the empty space. "Oh, well, Shonda had to take her kids to school. Marge is grabbing breakfast for the three of us, and Ron is probably in the back fiddling with the press. It's been acting funny the last couple of runs. Good thing this is only a weekly paper, am I right?"

Ed chuckled, the lines in his face crinkling into a soft smile as he led her to a makeshift desk, which was actually a stained table stacked with marked-up printouts of stories, a pile of photos, a bottle of antacids, and someone's reading glasses.

"This is your workspace." He must've noticed the expression on her face because he apologized. "Sorry about the clutter. With only a handful of us, we travel from desk to desk. I was trying to find a usable photo from the town hall meeting, but all of them are crap."

Jenny picked up the stack and leafed through them, turning her head this way and that as she considered. "DeDe White isn't really 'Doing It Right' in these pictures," she said, spoofing the longtime slogan the mayor had used for every election as far back as when Jenny was a kid. The older woman had a constant look of wide-eyed surprise on her face, as if she wasn't quite sure how she landed the job in the first place.

"Who's behind her?" Jenny pointed at the image of a man in his midsixties, a grandfatherly sort who'd retained some of the handsomeness of his youth. His hair was slightly tussled, and he wore a well-fitted blazer but no tie.

"Dr. George Hoffman." Ed didn't sound pleased. "He's behind everything and everyone in Edenberg these days."

She looked closer. "No, that's not him. He was..."

"Younger? Fatter?" Ed lifted one shoulder. "He's an up-and-coming worldwide phenomenon, don't you know? He went and got some kind of makeover after his first *New York Times* bestseller. Haven't you seen the signs around town, the name of his organization plastered on them?"

"Oh, right. Gen—something. Curt's doing a job for them— a contract gig."

"Genetive Inc. Give us your mind, and we'll take your soul," Ed said in a singsong voice that indicated this wasn't the actual slogan. "Senator Riley was recently reelected and gave George all the credit, and some lady who's been taking his classes just landed a minor role in the new Marvel franchise. We get press releases every week from Genetive because that's the kind of breaking news they want us to cover these days."

"I heard about his first big book," Jenny mused. "My mom bought it but never read it."

"Me, too. Along with half of America. It's a load of horse shit."

"Oh, yeah?" Jenny sat on the edge of the table and folded her arms, listening. She'd known Ed ever since she interned here as a gopher in high school. His Jewish ancestry combined with his preference for men were both characteristics that made him a bit of an outsider in Edenberg, but he'd forged ahead, creating a name for himself. That's why she wouldn't have been surprised to hear frustration in his tone. But this... This was laced with animosity.

"What's his book about?"

Ed waved a dismissive hand in the air. "Dictates to work hard. Use your privilege. Be rich, white, and straight by any means necessary."

Jenny chuckled. "Sounds like you're a true fan."

He glanced around as if making sure no one could overhear them. "I'm about the only person who isn't." He pointed at her. "Well, me and your mom." He rubbed at his eyes, either reconsidering his stance or admitting defeat—she wasn't sure which. "I don't know. Maybe he's harmless."

"Maybe?" Jenny tilted her head and studied Ed.

He flipped through a few photos of the mayor. "Maybe," he said again, this time more resigned. "Listen, I'd advise you to keep your ears and eyes open and your mouth shut when it comes to the Hoffmans. That's how I'm keeping my job these days."

Jenny wasn't good at taking this kind of advice. She was a reporter, after all. "Why is his name everywhere in town?"

Ed dropped the photos again and stepped back on his heel. "He's bringing people here, supposedly changing lives. Tourism is booming—we've even had a few big celebrities in town."

"Hard to believe people would listen to him after what happened to all those kids..."

"People forget a lot in thirty years." Ed lowered his gaze, neither of them wanting to summon memories of the tragedy. He shook his head, as if ridding his mind of dark thoughts. "Sorry. I just get grumpier with age. Seriously, forget what I said about George and Genetive. It's all fine and dandy, I'm sure."

Jenny gave him a half smile and looked at a photo of Dede White again, holding a thumb across the bottom third and a pointer over the left half. "This could work if you crop it."

Ed pushed his glasses higher on his nose and poked a finger at the picture. "I knew we hired you for a reason."

A tinkling bell sounded above the door as Marge walked in, carrying a box of kolaches and a carafe of coffee.

"Welcome, welcome," Marge squealed, plopping down the goodies and hugging Jenny tight around the neck. "I told your momma you'd work here one day, but she bet me twenty bucks you'd never be back. Guess whose money I used to buy these treats?"

Jenny laughed at Marge, her mom's oldest friend. "You two would bet on a three-legged horse race."

Marge noticed the photo of the mayor Jenny was holding. "It's your first ten minutes, and Ed's already putting you to work?"

"She offered." Ed crossed his arms. "But now that you mention it, we do have a full week ahead of us, and you need to show her the ropes. I'm gonna take a coffee to my office and read letters to the editor before I start thinking about this week's editorial."

The two of them watched him walk away before Marge leaned close. "He'll play solitaire for a half hour and then read the two emails that've come in since Sunday's paper."

"I heard you," Ed called back from the other side of his office door.

"Yeah, yeah," Marge yelled, waving a hand. "Now, young lady, have a seat. First thing we'll do is divide up who'll cover what. Thank the Lord we'll have another actual writer. Shonda tries, God love her, but half the time it's basically a press release from the Hoffmans."

"I haven't written much in the past few years," Jenny said, head tilted downward as if she didn't want to admit this.

"As soon as you start typing, it'll all come back to you. Me and your mother talked all about it." She patted Jenny's arm reassuringly. "You'll be fine."

Marge put up a hand and started counting off newspaper duties on her fingers. "Now, Ed writes editorial, advice, wedding announcements, obits, that kind of thing. He also does most of the layout and design. We both write news stories, and Shonda's been handling features—very badly, like I said. I do local sports, and we all take photos, depending on who is where and when." Marge grabbed a pen and a blank sheet of paper and started jotting notes. "We'll add you to the news section and give you all of the features, so Shonda can focus solely on sales and advertising. You'll also approve all photos. That sound doable?"

"News? What does that entail? I was thinking I could do profiles, local fluff, that kind of thing."

"Let's see…" Marge tapped a finger against her chin. "I heard that Dr. Hoffman pushed for the school board to fund a new position this year. A curriculum something-or-other. Apparently, they'll monitor content, get rid of any troublesome books in the library, stuff like that. Probably good with all the crazy stuff teachers are trying to spoon-feed students these days."

Jenny shut her mouth tight. She knew Marge meant well, and she loved the woman like a second mother. She'd also known that moving back home meant she would need to approach politics with a posture of stoicism. That would start today.

Marge eyed her and pursed her lips, misreading Jenny's hesitation. "I know you're gun-shy, honey, after what happened, but this is a good place to dip your toe back in the water. Besides, it's easy enough. Maybe two to three hard-hitting pieces a week. You know, things like, 'Who missed church?' and 'What in heavens did Mrs. Hoffman do to her hair?'"

Jenny laughed.

Marge clapped her hands. "That's settled, then. We'll let Ed finish his solitaire and then we can divvy up this week's stories."

The phone rang and Marge shoved the last bite into her mouth as she answered.

WATCH IT BURN   31

"The *Gazette*." Marge paused, listening for a few seconds. "Uh-huh, okay. I'll send someone right away." She wrote a couple of notes, hung up, and took a swig of coffee. "Seems like you'll be starting at a full sprint. That was the county detective's office." Marge handed Jenny a thin reporter's notebook with blue writing on the front. "There's a body down at the river near the old mill."

"A body?" Jenny swallowed. "This town doesn't do... I mean, it doesn't have...bodies."

Neither of them reminded the other of the truth: that once upon a time, it did have bodies, fifteen small bodies just growing into themselves.

"Who... Who is it?" Jenny asked, racking her brain for ways to get out of this. The last time she'd investigated something, her career had plunged into the depths.

"Deputy says they're waiting for the coroner to arrive before they touch the crime scene—if that's what it is. Didn't give me the whos or whats or whens, but said it looked to be an elderly woman. Probably somebody who wandered away from the old folks' home over in New Braunfels. It's a shame, a downright shame," Marge clucked before raising her eyebrows. "Okay, kid, it's at Fifth and Mill Street, not too far from Nichole's place. Best get goin'."

Jenny glanced at the clock and dried the palms of her hands on her skirt. "I can be there in ten."

"Nice to have somebody who can hustle around here," Marge said, smiling.

In reality, Jenny was a forty-year-old washed-up journalist, so she supposed she should relish being called *kid* again.

She grabbed her purse, a camera, and a notebook, pep-talking herself as she walked to her car. She could do this. She could write about the dead woman in the river.

BEVERLY

ONE WEEK POSTMORTEM
THE NIGHT OF THE FIRE

I'm dead. Otherwise, I'm fine. Good as gold.

I almost like it better this way, seeing things from this vantage point. The town I helped build now hotter than hell, my friends and foes running like ants straining to put out those flames. Kind of poetic, that this fire's gonna bring everything to a halt, especially since the last time destruction visited this town, it was by water.

Look, there's the sweet little turn-of-the-century cottage at the end of Main Street going up in smoke. I once begged George to buy it for me, but he said we needed something bigger for all those young'uns we were gonna have.

That's his way, though. I ask for a two-bedroom bungalow, and he eventually buys up the town. No matter now, I suppose. That cottage is like every other building downtown—singed, charred, smoldering.

Reminds me of when I first saw that ghoulish painting, Gauguin's *Fire Dance*, the oranges and purples and grays melting to black while the couple in the middle keeps on dancing, no idea what's about to hit 'em. A few years ago George took me to the Holy Land. He insisted we go on every tour known to man while we were in Israel, but I found a few hours to sneak away to the museum in Jerusalem.

Seeing it in person made me realize something that no amount of enlarging the image online could do: the couple dancing in the middle, the lady bending her knee to the black-robed man, is complicit. As I studied the painting for a good half hour, the truth resonated in my soul: they started the fire in the first place.

I suddenly know why I liked—and detested—the painting so much—the faceless lady, the one squatting while all hell breaks loose, that was me, bowing to George's every whim while our life burned around us. They say that where there's smoke, there's fire, but I didn't notice the flames until far too late.

Forgive my dark nostalgia. Death has a way of doing that, of making the past the only thing you have to think about. Well, that, and whatever is going on down below.

While peeking in on a few therapy sessions this past week, as I've been wont to do when I get bored up here, I've learned the term *trauma bond*. It took me a couple of appointments to piece together what exactly Dr. Franklin meant—how risk and intensity can meld two people together, how a tragedy can allow one person to control another. I wish my genius psychologist husband had thought to tell me about that one while I was still alive.

It's been one week since I expired. *Expired*. Makes me sound like a piece of meat gone bad or a bottle of pills that don't do a lick o' good.

I prefer to be called plain "dead," but it was all kinds of fascinating hearing the phrases people used at my funeral to avoid that specific word. At the ceremony, I'd "gone home," "breathed my last," and "crossed over to Jordan." But in the cars on the way to the graveside, I'd "given up the ghost," "kicked the bucket," and "checked out." Whichever way you slice it, here I am, waiting above the tree canopy for something or someone to toss me out of this limbo.

I wouldn't know how much time has passed except for the townsfolk lining the banks of the Guadalupe, preparing for the Paddle Parade held every year when the water levels are high enough.

My husband adores this annual tradition, which is fitting since it dates all the way back to when the Hoffmans—my husband's family—emigrated from Germany and founded Edenberg one hundred and seventy-five years ago. This town was where nobleman William von Hoffman and his followers hoped to blissfully start over, free of the political tyranny of their home country.

These immigrants also brought something unique to the hill country: their Catholic faith. While most German immigrants were Lutheran, good ol' Will v Hoffman just had to be different. That's where my husband gets it from.

All that to say, the Paddle Parade lets me know this is my one-week anniversary. One week since the end, the finish, the wrap-up. It hasn't been so bad perching above the bald cypress trees, watching and observing and saying things no one will hear.

Except for you. Thank you. Seriously, you don't know how refreshing it is to be heard, so I really appreciate you tuning in to whatever frequency this is. Unfortunately, my time up here is a lot like the nothing I did down there, nodding along with everything George said and did, so someone listening means more than I can say.

Oh, my husband. I went along with everything.

Appointing himself to city superintendent? *Certainly.*

Taking over the school system? *Go for it!*

Buying back every square inch of available real estate in and around Edenberg? *Why not?*

Luring in the rich and powerful with promises of more and more…and even more? *Great idea.*

If I could go to my weekly confessional one last time, I know exactly what I'd say: *Father, forgive me, for I have committed the sin of silence.* I should've spoken up when I had the chance. I should've left. I should've set the town ablaze myself. Then, maybe I wouldn't be stuck here, watching the literal firestorm below with no way to stop it.

Nothing to it at this point, but there is one thing I can do: now that I'm dead, I can tell you the truth, the godawful truth of it all.

To that end, I do hereby solemnly swear to tell you the truth, the raw truth, the juicy truth, the whole truth.

I won't trick you.

I won't lie to you.

I won't put on my Sunday-morning face and tell you everything's fine.

Nope. I'll tell you like it is, something I was too damn afraid to do when I was still prancing around down there like I knew what came next.

5

JENNY

Jenny's heartbeat was in her throat, so she was relieved that the first person to step into her vision when she arrived at the river was her oldest friend.

As soon as Nichole saw her, she burst into tears, wiping the base of her palm against her eyes.

"Oh, God." Jenny's eyes grew wide with concern. "You didn't—" She stopped and peered around, realizing why Nichole was here. "You found the body?"

"I tried calling you… I mean, after I got back to the house and called 911."

"I'm so sorry. I turned my phone on silent so Curt wouldn't…" Jenny's sentence trailed off. "I thought you'd be at school already."

"I called in…to find…to find a sub." Nichole was stumbling over her words, which wasn't like her.

For a fleeting moment, Jenny saw Emmy arriving to class, anticipating *Aunt Nikki* seated behind the teacher's desk, and her face crumpling when she realized Nichole wasn't there.

Jenny couldn't think about such things now, so instead, she pulled Nichole into her chest and rubbed circles into her friend's back. She couldn't imagine stumbling across a body. Covering death for a story was one thing, sure, but happening upon a dead person was something else. You weren't mentally prepared for the trauma you were about to encounter.

"That's awful," Jenny eventually said, knowing her words were too simplistic as she filled the silence between them. Nichole cried into her shoulder for a full minute until Deputy Alan Harris stepped in front of them. His black cowboy hat tilted over bushy eyebrows, but he managed to take in Jenny from head to toe like he'd done in high school when he'd been sweet on her.

"She's on the job, Alan." Nichole tried to collect herself as she crossed her arms. "Jenny isn't here to see you."

He ignored the comment.

"What happened?" Jenny asked, pulling out her notebook.

"Looks like a slip-and-fall," the deputy said, turning his body toward the tarp-covered mound in the middle of the river. He hitched up his belt buckle. "But we're waiting to release the name of the deceased until the detective gets a good look and the family identifies the victim…er, the person."

"So which is it?" Jenny narrowed her eyes at Alan, her journalist senses tingling. "A victim? Or just…a person?"

He didn't answer.

"It's Beverly Hoffman," Nichole said, her tone flat.

The deputy frowned and then let forth a little whine. "Now, why would you go and tell a reporter that information?"

"Because this is Jenny. You used to make moon eyes at her every day in algebra." Nichole turned back to her friend. "Not that you aren't also a real reporter."

Jenny scribbled down the name of the woman in the river, though she was unlikely to forget. Beverly was a fixture in Edenberg, wife of Dr. George Hoffman and mother-in-law to one of Jenny's childhood friends. She was not the kind of woman who died alone in the middle of the Guadalupe.

"And what kind of injuries did she sustain?" Jenny asked, looking at Alan.

"That's privileged information."

Jenny tried to keep herself from rolling her eyes. Just then the detective on the case called for Alan, and the deputy tipped his hat and moved away from the women. "Duty calls, ladies."

"That man is a bumbling idiot," Nichole mumbled when he was out of earshot.

Jenny shrugged off the deputy's behavior. "What can you tell me?"

"Not much. Beverly was dead when I found her," Nichole said, staring back at the water. "I was about to head home from my run, and at first I thought it was a pile of clothes, like some camper lost a backpack or something. But when I got closer... there was this bruising on her arm, and she was pale but... I don't know...swollen? Her lips...they were...blue." Nichole moved her hands in front of her own face as she tried to describe what she'd seen. "I think she drowned, but the water is so low."

"Did she smell like anything? Alcohol maybe?"

"No."

"And she was fully clothed?" Jenny hated that she had to ask the question.

Nichole nodded.

Jenny stepped to the edge of the river and watched as a team carefully removed the tarp. The gloved hands of the detective were delicate, almost affectionate, as they lifted the arm of the deceased. Even from here Jenny could see the bruising, which from her experience looked like evidence of a previous injury, perhaps even an altercation.

Jenny remembered the camera in her bag, reached inside, and pulled it out. As she lifted the lens and zoomed in on the medics, unbidden images of the bodies she'd seen while investigating the City of Angels Predator crowded at the edges of her mind. Her palms began to sweat, and her mouth went dry. She reminded herself that this was different.

After twenty or so clicks of the camera, Jenny panned to the detective, who was hunched forward and holding a Ziploc bag containing a round object. When she zoomed in, she saw a large locket almost the size of her palm. The jewelry was splayed open, but through the lens she couldn't quite make out what was inside. She clicked a few more photos and then looked around for Deputy Alan.

She spotted him a few yards away and gave Nichole a quick wave before making her way to his side.

"What's the detective holding? In the bag?"

Alan took a long look at Jenny. "Is this off the record?"

"Sure."

"It's a locket the deceased was wearing around her neck."

"What's inside?"

Alan raised his eyebrows. "You just want to know all the secrets, don't you?"

"If this is a slip-and-fall, I figure it's an innocuous enough question."

Before he could answer, a Land Rover ground to a halt a few yards from them. A woman emerged from the backseat. She was wearing a soft pink three-quarter-length-sleeve godet dress, and her hair was pulled back into a bun. Despite her trim figure and polished nails, her hands flailed and mascara rimmed her eyes.

Robin. Jenny startled at the sight of this girl-turned-woman who'd once been best friends with Nichole's big sister.

Robin and Christina—their friendship and lives paralleled Jenny and Nichole from a distance of five years, and by default, the four of them had become close. In the summer, the two older girls would take the younger for snow cones during the hottest part of the day. They'd spend late afternoons at Robin's house, bumping into one another on her backyard trampoline, syrup from the cherry cones running down their arms, turning them sticky and sweet. Afterward, they'd jump into the pool, playing sharks and minnows.

Seeing her now, beautiful but a bit undone, Jenny remembered how she'd wanted nothing less than to become Robin.

Dr. George Hoffman exited the passenger side of Robin's car, and Jenny remembered with a force akin to a slap that Robin was a Hoffman now. Years ago, she'd married into the most prominent family in town, and now she was bringing her father-in-law to see his wife's body. This was a family affair.

George stood stoically, his hands gripped behind his back. His hair—salt-and-pepper—was short and parted, and he was clean-shaven. He wore a pin-striped suit, and if Jenny hadn't known better, she would've thought he was preparing for a presentation rather than waiting to see his dead wife's body.

Robin turned so she and Jenny were facing one another, only a few yards apart. An eyelash extension was hanging by a thread, and Robin's lipstick had been smeared as if she'd run a backhand across her face.

George turned toward the detective. "May I see my wife?"

"Of course." The detective handed off the Ziploc bag to Deputy Alan before leading Dr. Hoffman away.

Robin watched her father-in-law, her hands clenched at her sides and a crease etched into her brow. Then, she threw her keys at the car and stomped in the opposite direction of the river, back toward downtown.

Jenny raised her eyebrows. Gone was the girl who had it all together, and the part of Jenny that would always be a journalist needed to know why.

With each passing moment, she sensed that this was more than a slip-and-fall. A dead woman in the center of the river was a tableau too considered, too calculated, too intentional.

Though she didn't know the details yet, Jenny felt the realization down to her bones, almost as if the dead woman herself was whispering in her ear.

6

NICHOLE

When Jenny called out to her at the river, relief had washed over Nichole. That was the voice that had whispered about boys during middle-school sleepovers, the voice that had debated a pro/con list about continuing her elementary ed major in college, the voice that had soothed her after Christina's death.

Jenny was the only one (besides Emmy and Austen) allowed to call her "Nikki." She was also the only person remaining who knew her actual name: Nichole Ji-Ho Miller.

Nichole had been born in Korea and adopted at six weeks old into a white family with two parents and a blue-eyed sister five years older: Christina. The couple had never been able to have children, and after hearing horror stories on the nightly news of birth parents swooping in to claim their biological offspring, they'd decided to look farther afield for daughter number two.

When she was eight, Nichole had whispered her middle name in Jenny's ear, swearing her to secrecy. She didn't want a *different* kind of name or a *different* shape of eyes or a *different* backstory than other children in town. It wasn't until college at UT that Nichole finally began to embrace her real self. Recently, though, she'd begun to wonder if the town of Edenberg felt the same.

As she walked back to the house after a terrible morning, Nichole used the 5 percent charge on her phone's battery to check her work email. Inside were two messages from the new curriculum coordinator, who was also filling in as her last-minute sub.

Dear Attendance Desk,
All students present and accounted for.
Sincerely,
Dr. Lydia Pound

Nichole supposed she should appreciate the woman's willingness to step into her class on the first day of school, but she couldn't get past the cold tone. The second email was as formal, but the content more concerning.

Dear Ms. Miller,
During recess this morning I took the liberty to review your classroom library and weeded out a few titles based on the recent standards set forth by the board. We want to ensure that the dominant and traditional culture of Edenberg is sufficiently celebrated. Once we've documented changes to our curriculum, we plan to submit our recommendations to the Texas Education Commission. Thank you for helping make history.
Sincerely,
Dr. Lydia Pound

If Nichole hadn't been exhausted, the message would've rankled more, but as things now stood, a Jeep belonging to the man from her bed was still parked outside her house. Good Lord, could this day get worse?

When she opened the front door, she found the man sitting on the floor, his back against her couch as he read her ex's old copy of *Out of the Silent Planet*. He looked at her. "I walked to the end of the street to check on you a couple of times, but you were talking to someone, so I didn't want to interrupt."

Any pretense of manners had worn thin with the events of the day, and Nichole couldn't help but ask the direct question. "Why are you still here?"

"What do you mean?" The corners of his mouth lifted. "I was hoping I could take you to lunch since it doesn't seem like you're going to work."

She rubbed at one eye, feeling the smudge of makeup from the night before. "I met you last night, got drunk enough that I couldn't even remember your name this morning, and then ran in here after finding a dead body down the street from my house." She said each word slowly this time. "So I have to ask: Why are you still here?"

The man chuckled. "You don't remember my name?"

"That's your takeaway?" Nichole cleared her throat and began again, this time trying her teacher voice. "Look. We met last night and know very little about one another, so I think it's totally understandable if you…"

"Yeah, we just met, but I actually know a lot about you," the man interrupted. His gaze unsettled her. Not for the first time this summer did she wonder about her recent life choices.

He began to list things he knew about her on his fingers. "Your middle name, *Ji-Ho*, means wisdom. You like to come home after the first day of school and watch *Pretty Woman* because you and your sister did that every year since you were in kindergarten. Your mother was a lawyer and your father was a doctor, and both of them worked long hours but were still involved. They died in a car crash a few years ago. Your sister—Christina—was your best friend. Besides…Jenny, I think?"

A chill ran up Nichole's spine. Was this man a stalker? Had she brought an actual stalker into her home and offered herself up like a pig on a spit? This is how Jenny's investigative stories always began. An innocent woman invites a total nut job into her life, and a few minutes, days, or weeks later, she's dead. Bam. Just like that.

"How do you… How do you know all of that?" Nichole edged herself onto the arm of the couch. "How do you know about my—" she swallowed hard "—my sister?" She did not talk about her sister. No one talked about her sister, not even Jenny.

He didn't come closer and instead put up both hands to show he wouldn't try to touch her. "You told me last night," he said. "Willingly, I swear." The man stared at her for a moment too long and pursed his lips. "You really don't remember?"

Nichole squinted, trying to envision last night. The River Walk in San Antonio lit with strands of colorful lights: blues and greens and reds crisscrossing one another in a glorious haze. The open-air bar with its high metal tables and pulsating overhead fans. The mariachi band strolling, pausing in front of their table as a boat full of tourists floated past. The heat, the hops, the cars on the streets above them. "I know you bought me a drink and I remember…" Very little.

The man raised one eyebrow. "I swear I had no idea you were that…" *Naive? Promiscuous? Drunk?* "No idea you were that far gone. I would never have come home with you." He gave the Scout's honor sign. "But if it makes you feel better, nothing happened."

"I wasn't wearing clothes this morning—and you were in my bed." She punctuated the last three words.

"You undressed and said I was welcome to join you. I went to the bathroom, and when I came back, you were snoring." He bent his head, a bit sheepish. "I didn't want to leave things like that—I didn't have your number—so I stayed, but like I said, nothing happened. I swear."

Nichole stared at him, trying to read a practical stranger.

He rubbed a finger along his jaw, seeming to consider how to best convince her. "You still had on your…underthings when you woke up, right?"

That was true, but not a foolproof sign. Also, could he not say *bra* and *panties*? Was he blushing? Had she somehow found the only fortysomething-year-old man in Texas who would be embarrassed by those words? It would be endearing if it was believable.

The man rubbed his hands together. "So here's the thing: I really thought we had a connection last night. We talked about how my mom is a second-grade teacher—like you—and how I grew up hearing about kids whose parents were too involved—or not involved enough. We both have...*had* a sister who...passed. I love reading sci-fi, and you confessed that you love reading smutty romance over a strong cup of coffee. It's not much maybe, but I thought..." He left the sentence unfinished. "Let me take you to lunch. Please. We can start over, and if you think I'm a creep by the time the check comes, then I swear I'll drive back to San Antonio and never call you again."

Nichole glanced at the clock. It was nearing noon, and her stomach was rumbling. "What if we have the exact same conversation as last night?"

"Then, I'll think of it as my warm-up and hope to impress you enough today that you'll actually remember my name." He inched closer and put out a hand. "I'm Wes Stewart, graduate of OU Technical College, one-half Creek Indian, and plumber extraordinaire. I like hiking, strong coffee, and IPAs."

She rolled her eyes but felt a smile starting.

"Nichole," she said as she took his hand. There wasn't quite a spark, but his grip was firm and his hand soft. "UT graduate, Korean, elementary school teacher. We'll see how things go before I tell you my last name."

"Too late, Ms. Miller," he said, holding her hand a moment longer.

7

JENNY

Five years ago, Jenny had been covering a string of crimes against women between the ages of twenty-two and twenty-eight. All were single, brown-haired, brown-eyed, middle-class career gals. They'd been doing daily tasks—bringing in groceries, getting back from a run, taking out the trash—when they found a perpetrator in their home.

Two teachers, one paralegal, three dental hygienists, two nurses, and one librarian. When Jenny started investigating the string of assaults, nine young women had already been attacked, and four of them had been strangled to death. The others had been tied up and heavily sedated, but they'd been left alive.

After pursuing the case for ten months, covering every single attack—two more happened while she was reporting—in the Glendora suburb of LA, she was sure she was on the killer's trail. Even after the birth of her second child, Austen, she'd only taken two weeks of maternity leave before going back into the field. She was close; she could feel it.

She wasn't wrong. In fact, she'd gotten so close that unbeknownst to her, the perpetrator was watching. One evening after she left the newspaper and stopped by the store to grab formula and diapers (and Aleve for the lack-of-sleep-induced migraine), she got into her front seat and started the car as a cold knife pressed against the back of her neck. In her exhaustion, she'd forgotten to lock the car.

Drive, a masked man said.

The next thirty minutes were the most terrifying of her life as the man explained that he was the one she'd been investigating. He gave firsthand accounts of three of his victims, describing in gruesome detail what he'd done to them. When he was finished with his monologue, he instructed her to drive to her house. He didn't speak again until they were in her driveway, the dark night sky closing around them as streetlights flickered on. She silently pleaded for Curt to poke his head out the door and check on her.

No one came. As they sat beneath the dusky sky, the man with the knife told her exactly what he expected from her: *you'll tell no one about this. You'll stop the investigation. I know where you live, and I'll come back and kill you and your entire family if you tell anyone, if you don't leave me alone. You understand?*

She did.

At one time in her career, before her children, her moxie might've driven her to find this man and put him behind bars. But she had two kids to consider. She resigned from the *Times* the next day and never said a word to anyone—except for Nikki, whom she'd called in tears—about the real reason why.

In the days leading up to Austen's birth, Curt had suggested she might want to take an extended leave. She let him believe that she'd finally listened to him, and though he'd been surprised by her abrupt departure from the *Times*, Jenny insisted that nothing had happened at the paper to force her out. Technically, that was true. It had happened in their driveway, and he hadn't come.

She'd assumed she would never be a reporter again. At least, not a reporter who mattered. But this morning Beverly Hoffman had been found dead, drowned in two inches of the Guadalupe River, and the old spark for a good story flickered to life.

Marge and Ed were out of the office when she returned, so she took a few moments to orient herself and find a usable desk.

Each investigation was like a jigsaw puzzle without a picture to follow, so Jenny considered what she should do first. She decided to examine the photos of Beverly she'd taken at the river. She flipped on the computer nearest her, grateful to find the login info handwritten on a Post-it and the SIM card reader already connected.

After a full minute of starting up the old tech, she sat in front of the monitor and began enlarging photos, specifically of the bag containing the large brass locket the detective had taken from around Beverly Hoffman's neck. She zoomed in, but whatever was in the locket remained blurry.

Jenny cursed under her breath. She would have to contact her husband for help.

She thought about texting him. On her phone, Jenny still had a mile-long text chain stretching back over the years when they'd shared tidbits from their day.

Simple things like, *Client never showed.*

Sexy things like, *I keep thinking about what you did with your tongue last night.*

Stupid things like, *This sandwich is as big as my face.*

She couldn't remember the last time she'd texted him about anything more than grocery items or the kids' pickup info. She decided it was best to call since she needed to explain what was happening.

He answered on the first ring as if he'd been waiting for her. "Hey, how's your day going?"

The words almost sounded like they used to. She considered answering with a monotone *Fine*, but she'd told him—and more importantly, herself—that she would try.

"I'm covering a big story—I mean, for around here. There

was an older woman found in the river just outside of town. It
was Beverly Hoffman."

"Wow." She listened to him sigh and take a beat. "George
was supposed to meet me so we could go over some of the footage we shot last week, but he never showed. I didn't realize…"
He cleared his throat. "What happened?"

"They're calling it a slip-and-fall, but something doesn't feel
right about that." Jenny couldn't pinpoint what exactly. Maybe
it was Robin's reaction or the bruises up and down Beverly's
arm. Maybe it was Deputy Alan's body language or his cryptic answers to her questions. Putting the details together made
her stomach churn like it always did when she sensed a lead.

"Are you okay? Reporting on something like that?"

"Yeah, why wouldn't I be?" Jenny's voice was sharp.

Curt inhaled. "Right. I'm glad you're getting back to what
you love doing."

"I was calling because… Do you have software that can make
a grainy photograph clearer? I have some pictures of the inside
of a locket Beverly Hoffman was wearing, but there's writing
that I can't make out."

"I'm sure I have something that will work. Send it to me
and give me a sec."

Jenny sent a few images to him and stayed on the phone.

"That's strange," Curt said. She could almost see his brow
knitting in concentration.

"What is?"

"Looks like Bible verses. A list. You got a pen?"

"Yeah."

"Exodus 21:24–25, Deuteronomy 32:35, Esther 7:10."

"Thanks." Jenny scribbled down the verses. "This has been…
helpful." She tried to give him credit where she could.

"The Hoffmans are Catholic, but George doesn't often mention the Bible in his videos." Curt obviously wanted the conversation to continue. "When he does, it's more about lessons

we can learn from the mythology. You think this is some kind of…I don't know…clue as to why she died?"

"Could be."

Curt cleared his throat. "When do you think you'll be home?"

Jenny bit her lip to keep from reacting. How many times had this man called to tell her he would be late again?

"I'm asking because I was thinking about having the kids help me make a fancy dinner—you know, to celebrate their first day of school, your first day at the paper. I was hoping you'd be home."

This was new, but in the past two months Curt had been coming home with a lot of new ideas from Genetive. Like the day he told her he would remain silent for a twenty-four-hour period in order *to introspect* and develop his *life vision statement*. Or the request he'd made to *soul gaze* into her eyes for a half hour. She had yet to consent to that one. Still, some of the practices did seem to be making him more considerate, more thoughtful with the kids.

"I should be home shortly after five," Jenny answered, pushing aside the thoughts of her new and improved husband. "I just need to look into these photos a bit more."

"Okay, take your time."

She hung up, opened Google, and searched the King James Bible translations, writing the full text on a piece of paper at her elbow.

Exodus 21:24–25: eye for eye, tooth for tooth, hand for hand, foot for foot, burning for burning, wound for wound, stripe for stripe.

Deuteronomy 32:35: to me belongeth vengeance and recompence. She'd heard the phrase in everyday conversation, though often a different rendering—*Vengeance is mine.*

One more. *Esther 7:10.* She typed the final reference into Google. *So they hanged Haman on the gallows that he had prepared for Mordecai. Then was the king's wrath pacified.*

As Jenny wrote down the words, the images made the skin on the back of her neck crawl. Eyes and teeth and burnings. Hangings and vengeance and wrath. Beverly's list of Bible verses weren't those of a simpering Southern woman of a certain age, and they definitely had a theme. Beverly Hoffman had literally been carrying revenge around her neck.

Jenny leaned back in her chair and rubbed her thumb and forefinger across her eyes. After the tragedy with the fifteen children years ago, she imagined that many must have wanted revenge on the Hoffman family, but why would Beverly Hoffman want revenge? And against whom?

"Seventeen Dead after Torrential Rains" By Ed Zimmerman
Edenberg Gazette *Special Edition, August 24, 1996*

Seventeen people—fifteen children and two adults—are dead after a bus carrying mostly elementary students washed away in a flash flood at Camp Hoffman in the early hours of yesterday morning. According to officials at the scene, the campers had been instructed to board the bus in order to make it off the campgrounds before the waters rose.

"Camp administration loaded the bus with forty-two six- to twelve-year-olds around 4 a.m.," said Officer Mark Haus at a press conference later in the day after rescue attempts ceased. "The children were part of the Muscogee tribe, visiting from out of state. Within thirty minutes, fifteen children and two adults drowned in the floodwaters."

First responders arrived on the scene within minutes. They found that more than half of those on the bus had already made it to shore. They were able to rescue four additional children from the water. The rest of the day was spent recovering bodies of the deceased.

Camp Founder and Director Dr. George Hoffman expressed his condolences to families at the press conference and vowed to set up a scholarship fund for siblings of the victims, but declined to comment for this article.

An investigation into the timeline of events remains ongoing.

8

NICHOLE

After a quick shower—that she took alone—Nichole and Wes drove the couple of miles to the town's only diner. A year ago, at Dr. Hoffman's recommendation as city superintendent, the business bureau had begun consolidating downtown for better efficiency, closing redundant locales and offering low-interest loans to new endeavors.

Gone were three of the four antique stores, two of the three clothing boutiques, one of the two coffee shops, and the Pentecostal congregation that had been a bit too noisy and ostentatious during their annual revival week. In their place had opened a bookshop, a stationery store, a specialty toy cottage, a wine-tasting room, and a white-steepled Methodist church—all funded by the Hoffmans. There had been a handful of protesters, but as far as Nichole could tell, they'd all been silenced by now.

The diner smelled of hash browns and pancakes from the morning rush, and before they sat, several townsfolk stopped Nichole to ask about what she'd seen that morning, all the while sneaking glances at the man beside her. The last person to approach was Marge, who worked at the *Gazette* and was, Nichole supposed, Jenny's new boss.

Marge gave her a big hug. "You doin' all right, hon?"

She nodded into the woman's plump shoulder. "It was a shock."

"I know. Poor Beverly. And they're calling it a slip-and-fall, but of course they would. No scandal can touch the Hoffman name." Marge whispered the last sentence, glancing around to make sure no one had overheard. Then, she smiled at Wes as if he were the latest menu item. "And who do we have here?"

"This is Wes. He's a…" Nichole trailed off, not wanting to admit how they'd met.

"A friend," Wes finished for her.

Marge tilted her head and studied him. "Haven't I seen you around town?"

"No, but I'm thinking about opening a branch nearby, so Nichole offered to give me a tour."

"Good luck getting a lease these days. Lots of hoops to jump through," Marge said knowingly. "Well, young man, this lady right here and her best friend were terrors growing up. Did she tell you how they disappeared one night? Their families thought the boogeyman had stolen them away."

"We'd gone camping. We left a note," Nichole said dryly.

"And yet, somehow no one ever found that note. Anyhoo, the town went on lockdown, every able-bodied person wandering the streets and riverbanks. Robin and Christina finally found them in a makeshift tent under the old bridge at Mill Road. The four of them thought it was hilarious."

"It wasn't a big deal."

"Like heck it wasn't." Marge offered a bemused smile. "I swear when y'all was growing up, we were on our toes… You remember when you painted smiley faces on all the cop car windshields? Or that time you papered the Baptist preacher's parsonage, except instead of doing it the old-fashioned way, you also Saran-wrapped his front and back doors?"

"Wasn't me," Nichole said as she'd always sworn to do. She'd also never mention that her sister and Robin had driven them to the store and paid for the supplies.

"Well, it was certainly nice to meet you," Wes said, bowing ever so slightly and signaling to Marge that her time with them was coming to a close.

"Oh, I best be getting back," Marge tittered. "I came out to see if anybody knew anything about poor Beverly, but I know Jenny will need help finding info in the archives. The Hoffmans cleared out half of it a while back. You two enjoy yourselves, but not too much." She wiggled her eyebrows at Nichole and looked at Wes. "I swear you look familiar."

Wes lifted his eyebrows. "Maybe you met my doppelgänger."

She smiled at him and playfully pinched his arm. "Wouldn't it be delightful if there was another person who looked just like you?"

After Marge exited the diner, Nichole thanked Wes for intervening. "She's a bit of a talker."

"Now I know who to go to for stories about you as a kid. It sounds like you had a flair for adventure." Wes glanced over the giant menu. "Now you owe me, though."

Nichole laughed with him for the first time. "Owe you? For what?"

"For politely sending her on her way. Look, I'll buy you lunch this time, but in the future I plan on a meal *and* an invitation to watch *Pretty Woman*. Although I guess it depends on how the next half hour goes, so I hope you came ready to impress."

Nichole shook her head and smiled behind the pictures of silver dollar pancakes and double-stacked burgers on the menu. After Brian left, she'd sworn off a real relationship for at least the next year.

But she actually liked Wes. A lot.

This was terrible.

BEVERLY

ONE WEEK POSTMORTEM
THE NIGHT OF THE FIRE

A couple of days before I died, I made it to the post office to drop off a final batch of mail. As I handed over the short stack of postcards to Edenberg's postmistress, she asked after the family. I gave vague replies, focusing my comments on how proud I was of my grandson, all the while watching to make sure she didn't rifle through the postcards before she plopped them in the mail carrier. After I was content that my mail was in safe hands, I could rest.

Practically the next minute, there I was, hovering over my own bag of bones as "How Great Thou Art" howled through the organ pipes at my funeral.

Dust we are and to dust we shall return, but it's typically our souls that can't get a minute of peace and quiet. No matter. Now I live in my memories when I'm not spying on the goings-on beneath me.

The recollection I catch a glimpse of most often is me at eighteen. It was the summer before I, Beverly Fischer, became Mrs. Hoffman, and I wasn't anywhere near dead.

My legs dangled over the troubled waters of the Guadalupe from my perch on the red-and-white bridge, the back of my calves cooling against the iron frame suspending me above the water. I had straight, dirty-blond hair halved down the middle, the strands hanging about my shoulders and midback like a parted curtain. On the sides of my face, I curled two perfect locks that drew attention to my high cheekbones and golden eyes.

Being a farm girl, I had a small wardrobe, but I made the best of my handful of miniskirts, bell-bottoms, and peasant blouses. In our yearbook I'd been declared The Prettiest Gal in Town.

I woke up at 1 p.m. the day after my high school graduation to a summer afternoon speckled with wispy clouds and a sun so bright I had to blink against the sky outside the bedroom I shared with two of my sisters. Momma and Daddy had let me sleep in, something I'd only had the privilege of doing once before when I had a severe bout of pneumonia. The smell of biscuits and gravy and bacon fat lingered in the house.

After I woke, my first thought was not of how much my parents had sacrificed so I could become the first in our family to graduate high school and enroll in college. Instead, I was thinking about sitting atop the bridge the night before, conversing with George. Two words in particular stuck in my mind like taffy.

Marry me. He'd stared at me for so long, I wondered if he was having one of those episodes we didn't speak of.

Even though I shouldn't have been surprised after going steady with him for the past two years, the words had still caught me off guard. George Hoffman, the most promising (and, let's just say it: wealthiest) young man in town, wanted to marry me!

He wore forest green polyester pants and a nylon twill shirt with loud purple shapes angling their way across his chest. His hair hung loose around his ears. With his chiseled jaw, slim nose, and piercing brown eyes, he looked like a young Mark Hamill, and I was dazzled by his attentions.

He'd already given me a silver promise ring with a row of diamond specks last Christmas break when he'd been home from UT. He was in his second year as a psychology major, something his parents weren't thrilled about—they preferred degrees that led directly to clear-cut jobs: lawyer, doctor, banker.

I believed in him wholeheartedly. Who wouldn't? He was gorgeous and able to convince people around him to get on board with whatever ideas he was spouting. In his high school tenure, George had written a petition that ran off the principal, pushed administration to curtail the daily school schedule—for mental health reasons, before mental health was a *thing*—and written to the manager of The Ramones, convincing them to play at prom.

George was a powerhouse, and he made you not even care that half of what he said didn't make a lick of sense. That was how good he was even back then.

Two years into college now, he was enamored with his studies, always talking about thinkers long gone. For example, he disagreed with Sigmund Freud's ideas on psychosexual stages but adhered to Weber's views on the id. He liked Erikson's and Skinner's writings, but couldn't stand most of the gibberish Harlow spouted.

The fact that I can remember this after literally dying should indicate how good he was at convincing people to listen to him.

You don't have to agree with everything, he would say. *Just think. Consider. What if there was a better way?*

I was content to sit and stare into his eyes, hearing whatever he wanted to say to me and occasionally thinking about other things while he spoke. Things like the fact that two other girls from my class were already married, and at least four others engaged. As young women we knew our job: to fill the church nursery with babies who would eventually graduate from Edenberg High and continue the cycle. We were small-town Southern women. Sugar and spice and all things nice. At least until we needed to take care of business.

I wanted marriage, but I also wanted the elusive thing that no one else in my family had ever gotten their hands on—a college degree. The idea of walking across the stage with that paper in hand filled me with a kind of longing I couldn't put into words.

"Beverly? Did you hear what I said?" George's voice was edged with expectancy and something I couldn't pinpoint. Desire? Passion? Ownership?

"Of course I heard you," I said, teasing him. "You want me to marry you, isn't that right?" I looked at him with a matter-of-fact expression that seemed to take him aback.

"So. What do you say?"

Not exactly the most romantic declaration, but it would do.

"What about college?" I asked.

"We'll live here, rent a little place on Main Street, one of those bungalows. You can enroll at UT with me, and we can drive in together. I know it's a couple years earlier than we planned, but I…I can't wait any longer. I need you."

I knew what he meant without him having to spell it out. We'd spent plenty of time in the backseat of his car, but I was only willing to let him take things so far (I'd seen what happened to Mildred Peele when she'd given in to a moment of passion). I'd kept him at bay, but sensed he wasn't the kind to wait much longer. If I was to remain a good girl while keeping his interest, I'd better say yes.

George's face softened. "You can go to school, study music or art. I just want you with me." He leaned closer and whispered in my ear. He knew what I liked, what would send shivers up my spine. "When we started going steady two years ago, I already knew how this would end. Together. It's me and you, Bev."

I smiled. I was living every girl's dream.

"George, I will marry you, but on one condition, understand?" I made sure he met me eye to eye before continuing. "No babies until after I graduate."

"Done." George took my hand and tugged gently at my going-steady ring, trading it for a marquise-cut diamond he pulled from his shirt pocket.

"My grandmother's ring," he breathed as he began to kiss me with renewed fervor. I would soon be all his. I felt the ring slide over my finger and kissed him back, letting his hands wander more than usual.

Eight weeks later, it was done. George and Beverly Hoffman, for better or worse, man and wife. Till death did us part.

The following month I started as an art major at UT. There's a picture from my first day of class, my hip pressed against the porch railing of the promised bungalow in Edenberg that George rented for us until he could buy the biggest house in town. In it, I'm wearing a summer dress with slim vertical rainbow-colored stripes. I have a wide smile and a giant burnt-orange bag, filled with art history books, slung over my shoulder.

I had no idea that I was already pregnant.

Excerpt from "Top Ten Thinkers Influencing Industry"
in Business Trends

Dr. George Hoffman

In his second book, Dr. Hoffman writes about his early years as a professor. When his master's-level students arrived on the first day of his seminar, he would assign them seats, designated by simple yellow Post-it notes.

Hoffman was a popular professor at UT, so this meant an auditorium with a sea of yellow squares at each desk. He'd given his TAs the unenviable task of researching his student roster to the best of their ability—looking specifically for race and gender, but he even asked them to find photos to determine height, weight, and general attractiveness. The TAs would place certain students at the front of the classroom and then the hierarchy would "descend" from there.

For the second class, Hoffman took away the Post-its, and he asked his students to sit where they were most comfortable. To his profound wonder, many of the students selected the same exact location in the room.

Hoffman believed that his students were illustrating a key function of any closed society: at their core, humans want to fall in line. We want someone on top and someone on bottom. The hierarchy exists for a reason.

Though his ideas have been controversial among some naysayers, the impact of his work has been far-reaching, capturing the minds of CEOs, politicians, actors, and even priests. Hoffman has been studying and teaching such principles for decades.

9

TUESDAY

NICHOLE

Six months had passed since her sister's death last February.

The first few weeks after she'd gotten the call, Ambien had helped cradle Nichole to sleep each night, but when the prescription ran out, alcohol seemed to be the only sedative that worked. Now, though, after a couple glasses of wine combined with seeing Beverly Hoffman face down in the river, the dark dreams had resurfaced with even more vibrant colors and new details.

In her slumber, everything underwater was tinged royal blue, even Christina's skin. Her sister's eyes were open and her hand outstretched, fingers forever reaching. Behind Christina were more than a dozen children, calling her to join them, and as her sister shifted her gaze to them, the water's current pulled her farther and farther away. When Nichole tried to swim after her sister, Christina changed form, aging and morphing into Beverly Hoffman, the woman with the tired eyes and kind smile.

As the alarm went off on her phone and her eyes opened on a new day—her actual first day of school—Nichole gasped as if she was coming up for air. Sticky with sweat, she shook away the frightful dream and pulled the sheet off her skin. Her tongue was fuzzy, and she craved a mimosa.

She flipped on her bedside lamp and shifted herself over the side of her bed, sinking to her knees to peer at the box she'd stashed under there after Christina's death.

Open me, the box called to her. *I dare you.*

She touched the coarse edges of the tape, ran her fingertips across the top of the smooth cardboard.

Jenny had flown in as soon as Nichole called her, took a red-eye so she arrived less than twenty-four hours after hearing the news. When they'd driven to Galveston to pick up her sister's things, Nichole asked Jenny to pull over, to stop along the Seawall where Christina's vehicle had careened over the edge, landing on the car's roof before the water came rushing in. The sheriff in Galveston—Sheriff Whiteside—later told Nichole that the impact likely broke Christina's neck before the water drowned her, but Nichole figured he was probably trying to give her peace of mind. It hadn't worked.

The crematorium had required that she identify the body of her sister before proceeding. Jenny placed an arm around her as Nichole buried her head in her hands, whispering that she couldn't do it, she couldn't see her sister like that. But when Jenny asked the man if she could give a positive identification instead, he'd shaken his head even as his mouth turned down in pity. *Has to be next of kin*, the man said apologetically.

When Jenny finally nudged Nichole off her shoulder, she closed her eyes against what she was about to see. The man removed the sheet, and as Jenny kept a hand on the middle of her back, Nichole finally forced herself to look. Her mind had never really stopped looking.

Christina had been gray and bruised, but the set of her mouth was strangely serene, like she was waiting for Nichole to wake her from a nap.

Jenny rented a hotel room for the two of them since Nichole hadn't been able to step foot in her sister's condo. While Jenny had organized and cleaned out Christina's place, condensing four and a half decades of life into one box, Nichole lay in the hotel room bed, curled into a fetal position, not even able to cry. As she'd lain on that unfamiliar bed, she'd considered: Did other siblings feel this kind of devastation when the other passed? Or did she and Christina have an unusually close bond because they'd both been adopted? They both knew the early grief of losing a family and the eventual joy of being brought together. Maybe that reality had tightened the string connecting their hearts.

Nichole wasn't sure, but this she knew: she and Christina were a unit. One did not forge a river without inviting the other to tag along; one did not cry without telling the other all the reasons why; one did not say goodbye without a long and enveloping hug. But now her sister was gone, and Nichole was only one half of what had been a whole. Even Jenny couldn't fill that void.

I thought you might like to have a few things, Jenny had said when she'd returned. Nichole hadn't flinched, hadn't even looked at the box until she moved it from the trunk of Jenny's car to the storage space under her bed. She hadn't opened it—still couldn't open it—because all of the emotions might come pouring out. Then, who would be left to pick up the pieces?

Her parents were dead.

Her sister was dead.

Brian was gone.

Now, Jenny was back in town for good, but Lord knew she had two kids and enough marriage problems for a lifetime.

As Nichole's fingers stretched along the top of the box, she suddenly pulled back as if the contents were hot to the touch. She wouldn't open it yet. She couldn't. Reaching for it was progress enough.

10

JENNY

Mrs. Beverly Hoffman was the wife of thinker, writer, and speaker Dr. George Hoffman.

Jenny had arrived at the office early, knowing it might take her the entire day to write the obituary for Beverly Hoffman, something she'd volunteered to do since she was already diving headfirst into research about the woman. Frustratingly, everything she typed led back to Beverly's husband—the thinker, the writer, the speaker. Even in death, she was swallowed whole by that man.

God, the familiarity of that idea terrified Jenny. After she'd suddenly quit her job at the *Times*, that destiny had loomed before her, sometimes waking her in the night, taunting her with the purposelessness of it all. Not that women couldn't stay at home and tend to children and find meaning. But Jenny wasn't wired that way. She would die for Emmy and Austen, but she did not want to give every second of her life to them.

Once again, she was glad she'd insisted on the move back to her hometown, so she could start fresh in her career. This morning she'd spent time researching the Hoffmans and the town they'd founded more than a century ago.

Edenberg was known for very little, but every kid who attended elementary school learned how German Catholic immigrants settled here in the mid-1800s after arriving through the Galveston port. She'd only just learned that those early settlers were part of the *Adelsverein*, a word meaning "Society for the Protection of German Immigrants." The German culture mixed with the influence of the Mexican people and the Lipan Apache tribe in this newly formed Texas state, and Edenberg was born.

Yesterday Marge had helped her dig through newspaper archives, the same ones that Beverly Hoffman had filtered when her husband purchased a majority share in the newspaper last year. Before Jenny left work last night, she'd texted Nichole about something she'd discovered in the remaining research.

J: Did you know that the Hoffmans own the public schools??

N: Yeah—they bought them last year...remodeled all of the buildings

J: You're okay with this?

Nichole had responded with a shrugging emoji.

Then at dinner last night, Emmy had said something disconcerting out of the blue.

That poor misguided woman. Emmy sighed heavily, like a much older version of herself, as she spooned gourmet mac and cheese into her mouth.

Wait, where did you hear that? Jenny asked her daughter with narrowed eyes.

At school.

From a friend? Curt asked, joining in the conversation.

Emmy shook her head and chewed for a few bites.

Then who? Jenny tried to keep the forcefulness out of her tone. *Who said that?*

Aunt Nikki wasn't at school, so we had a sub. Dr. Pound, like pound cake. Emmy had grinned momentarily. "She said it's very sad that an important old lady died in the river this morning." Emmy blinked back at her mother with a knitted brow before repeating, *That poor misguided woman.*

Jenny had to take a long drink of water to wash down the pasta threatening to stick in the back of her throat. *What else did Dr. Pound say?*

Emmy had twirled her fork on her plate. *Dr. Pound is there to make sure we learn the right things.*

Such as? Jenny wasn't sure why she'd expected her daughter to know the answer to this question.

The right things, Emmy stated.

Then, Austen had spilled his milk—again—and the moment passed.

Jenny pushed her daughter's statement to the back of her mind for the time being. Instead, she wondered why George, a man who owned a self-help company, would purchase the land and the building of a public school? And how? Didn't public schools belong to the city government? But of course, that was her answer. Dr. Hoffman's influence knew no bounds.

The more Jenny searched the archives, the more she was troubled by the Hoffmans' fingerprints. They owned every church building except for the one they attended, Sacred Heart, which belonged to the Catholic diocese. They rented out all of Main Street to local vendors, and one of them sat on the boards of the hospital, the business bureau, and a nonprofit. None of this was a secret, and all of the Hoffmans' encroaching involvement seemed welcome because it came with money, lots of money.

Jenny pictured George leaning over his wife's lifeless body yesterday as the medic gently pulled back the blanket. Robin had stormed off by then, and as George peered into Beverly's face, he hadn't so much as flinched. She knew from years of reporting that family members reacted differently to the death of loved ones, particularly tragic deaths. Some shed dignified tears; others had to excuse themselves to wail into a pillow. Still, she didn't like Dr. Hoffman's stoicism.

She tried to keep herself from thinking about how Curt might react to seeing her lifeless body. Would he feel relieved? Would he move on by moving backward, reconnecting with the woman who had toppled their marriage almost a year ago?

Jenny shook away the questions. This was not about her. This was about Beverly, a woman she didn't really know but whom she assumed deserved the dignity of a decent obituary.

She deleted the sentence and tried again.

Mrs. Beverly Hoffman, wife of George Hoffman—the man who caused the death of fifteen children and two adults—was also a beloved town member, mother, wife...

She set her left elbow against the desk and placed her cheek in her hand, studying the descriptors, weighing the words in the balance of this woman's life before pressing Delete and staring again at the blinking line against the empty white page.

She could write what Beverly's younger sister had told her on the phone that morning: that when they were kids at recess in the schoolyard, Beverly would lean against the tangled roots of the pecan tree with *Little Women* splayed open on her knees. Or Jenny could record what a fellow churchgoer had said about the woman: how Beverly liked to be behind the scenes, contributing to bake sales and donating items for raffles.

Jenny could even write what all the world could find online with a few clicks: Beverly Hoffman's unwavering smile as she stood at her husband's side on the front porch of their colonial home in the center of town, white pillars framing them. The photo was from a couple of years ago, but even though they were in their sixties, the two of them had a Richard Burton and Elizabeth Taylor look about them. George with his deep-set eyes and strong jaw, and Beverly with her curvy figure and direct gaze.

From skimming through decades of photos, Jenny could tell that Beverly's upswept hair received regular highlights until the past year or so, and her eyes were a deep blue, nearly violet in some light. In one moment frozen in time, Beverly wore sensible black heels, a knee-length skirt with a matching jacket, and a small gold pin with ruby-red gems encircling a diamond. The brooch was so small that someone might miss it if they weren't looking closely, but Jenny was looking.

Jenny breathed deeply and pushed away trite phrases that sprang to mind as she tried to encapsulate this woman:

Behind every good man is a Beverly.

A good Beverly is hard to find.

Boys rule and Beverlies drool.

She sighed and used her middle finger to scroll through the archived videos on Genetive's YouTube channel. Curt had been setting up a recording studio for them on-site, which was a good thing because this footage would never meet her husband's high standards.

You know, the ideas they have aren't so bad, Curt had said a couple of weeks after starting his contract gig there at the beginning of the summer. *Some are old-fashioned, but most of it's about empowerment and being a family man. They have a curriculum designed for couples, too. Maybe we should try one of their classes together?*

Jenny had lifted a shoulder noncommittally and gone into the other room to fold laundry. But now she wanted to know what ideas Genetive was touting. Even though the quality of the videos was bad, the content was...enlightening, for lack of a better word.

"The Meaning of Manhood" had half a million views, but

"A Woman's Place" had twice as many. Beverly appeared in most of them but strangely never uttered a word.

Beverlies should be seen and not heard, Jenny had the urge to type.

The air-conditioning kicked on above her, rattling the square-framed ceiling tiles of the newspaper office. It was after seven o'clock in early September, but the heat index still clocked in at nearly a hundred degrees.

Beverly, Beverly, Beverly. Who were you?

The silent woman stared back at her from the computer screen, and Jenny wished she could reach through the glass and ask her all the questions that had been running through her mind since the woman's death.

Why had Beverly been in the middle of the river?

Why was her body already bruised?

And, perhaps most importantly, where had her husband been?

BEVERLY

ONE WEEK POSTMORTEM
THE NIGHT OF THE FIRE

What was I thinking as I lay there face down in the water? Lord knows.

I've come to believe that during our time on earth, the less thinking a woman does, the happier she'll be.

I'm not saying that's how it should be, but I am saying a girl has to find peace of mind however she can. In my experience, standing up to a man never did much good and could very well leave you bruised and broken—or dead.

Take me as Exhibit A.

The only time I ever really found my voice was when I was giving birth to my first baby, but that was only because the screams wouldn't stay contained. With my second child, Max, a couple of years later, the doctor kindly knocked me out and cut me open like a sliced ham, which was fine by me. But memories of that first labor would still make my palms sweat if I had hands.

I can't do it—that had been my main thought. The sharp achiness came in waves only seconds apart. It was almost too much for my nineteen-year-old body to bear.

"I can't. I can't. I can't," I screamed. I was on the edge of motherhood and wanted to run away rather than plunge head-first into the pain. But there was George. He wasn't like some men, the kind who wanted to stay in the waiting room until the difficult part was finished. No, George was there every step of the way.

He reached out one hand and placed it on my sweaty fore-head, his fingertips cooling my skin. I closed my eyes in an effort to block out the lights and the nurses and the demands of my body, and in the blankness I saw the paintings I'd chosen to study in my first semester of art history.

Andrea Schiavone's *Birth of Jupiter* came to mind, the image of a young woman in red-hued ribbons serenely blessing the midwife who removed the baby from her parted legs. A man's version of birth, no doubt.

My husband leaned inches from my face, his chiseled jaw—I'd always liked his strong jaw, especially when he went a day or two without shaving—moving as he whispered, "You can do this."

I knew he meant it. That was part of what he loved about me—my unwavering physical strength. He couldn't boast the same, and we both knew it. At any moment, he was liable to leave me for minutes or hours at a time, to go into himself like a turtle into its shell, only emerging after his episode had passed.

I held on to those words as if they were a buoy keeping me afloat in the storm called childbirth. I wanted to believe him, I really did, but instead, I turned my head and vomited for the third time into the tiny tray a nurse held to my chin. Precious, I know.

"We're almost there, Mrs. Hoffman," the doctor told me, only half looking at the mess that was my nether regions. Gathering every remaining ounce of adrenaline, I spent the next few minutes forcing new life into this bright, strange world.

"It's a girl," a nurse shouted.

"Nurse," the doctor said, motioning to the child. "Call a NICU team."

The rest of the room went eerily silent. Relief had washed over me when the pain ended, but now that feeling was being inched out by the not-knowing.

A hive of people swarmed at my feet. Gone was the doctor's commanding voice. Now he spoke in hushed tones to medical personnel streaming in and out of the room.

"What's wrong?" I craned my head around my legs in the stirrups. I could see George's silhouette, his back straight and his profile pinched as he listened to the doctor who finally said something I could make out.

Arrange for transport to the neonatal unit in San Antonio.

"What's wrong?" Fear clawed at my throat, trying to shut me up, but I wouldn't let it. "Wait. Where's my baby?"

I hadn't even set eyes on her, wouldn't even know it was a girl except that the nurse had let the news slip before everyone realized something was terribly wrong.

"Please, let me see her. Please, I need to see my daughter." I was begging by then, yelling even. I was sure of it. Knowing I'd gotten loud was the only thing that gave me comfort later. At least I had tried to make them give her to me.

No one was listening, not even George, who had become lost in the flurry of people. It was almost as if I'd done my part. Now the child belonged to all of them. An afterpain rolled across my belly, and I shut my eyes, a wave of emotion washing over me. I began to cry.

George was back at my side, one hand on me. "Bev. Hey, Beverly. You need to stay calm." His tone held something I'd never heard before: fear.

The doctor came back and began working between my legs, yanking on my body and stitching up parts of me that I would've rather never seen again. He explained as he worked. "The baby has significant bruising around her forehead, and she's largely unresponsive. You may have noticed that she didn't cry?"

I struggled to sit upright, but the doctor put his knuckle against my inner thigh.

"But she's alive?" I asked.

The moment between my question and his answer stopped time.

"She is," he answered. "For now."

The sob that had threatened to escape lurched out in a loud convulsion. I reached for George's hand and held tight.

"The baby's APGAR score was low, which is concerning."

I looked from my husband to the doctor, gauging whether or not this term—APGAR—was one I was expected to know.

"What does that mean?" George asked, his voice tense. It took a lot for that man to admit he didn't know something. I loved him even more in that moment.

"It's a way for us to check the baby's well-being within the first few minutes of life." The doctor stood, removed his gloves, and washed his hands too slowly for the urgency of the situation. He came to stand at the railing of my bed. "The letters stand for Appearance, Pulse, Grimace, Activity, and Respiration. We score the baby in each of these categories, and when we add them up, nine is the highest."

George cleared his throat. "What does this mean for our... for the baby?"

The OB addressed his words to my husband as if I'd left the room.

"Your baby scored a four. The team will take the child to the neonatal intensive care center in San Antonio. It's a facility dedicated entirely to premature infants and newborns in distress." The doctor looked down at his hands. "You saw the bruising I mentioned, and the baby's pulse was slow. But the most concerning part of the diagnostic assessment was reflex and muscle tone. The infant's left side was floppy, unresponsive." He looked straight at me for the first time. "If the baby survives, I believe your child will suffer from paralysis, most certainly on the left side."

The infant. The baby. The child. No *she.* No *her.* Nothing to personalize my baby girl.

"For how long?" It was all I could think to ask.

"Her entire life," he said blankly. "However long that may be."

There was a wall of knowledge between us, one that I couldn't climb or dismantle. I knew there was something—many some-things—he wasn't saying, but I couldn't find the questions to ask. My whole life I'd been taught to be pretty and quiet, and even though the pretty was long gone, the quiet stayed put.

You've got to understand that this was 1978. Five years ear-lier, the Rehabilitation Act had made it possible for children with special needs to go to public school, but most parents still didn't send them. Teachers weren't equipped—most school buildings didn't have wheelchair ramps much less aides to push them around the halls. But even knowing all that, I didn't care. I would make it work. I would not send my child away to a special home, like so many families before us had done.

I attempted to pull my feet from the stirrups and stand. I wanted my baby. I wanted to take her in my arms and will her back to health. My child had been fine—fine!—only hours ago, burrowed inside my womb. The pain rushed over me again, pushing me back onto the bed.

George settled me and then pulled the doctor to the window for a more private conversation. I closed my eyes again and tried not to wail.

During my pregnancy, I'd lived in denial, ignoring the con-gratulations and steering conversations away from types of for-mula and the merits of cloth diapers. I hadn't wanted this baby. Not yet. Now I wondered if I'd somehow caused my baby to be born this way.

I began muttering the prayer I'd learned during Confirmation classes, changing the words to fit my situation. *Our Father, who is in this hospital…hallowed be thy name… May your kingdom come to my baby…*

That's as far as I got before the sobs took over and I opened my eyes and called for my husband. "George, make them bring her to me."

But George and the doctor were gone. I was alone in the room, the sun shining through the window as if the day had no idea what had happened.

Without realizing what I was doing, I began pulling at cords and screaming for a nurse. She came running, saw the state of me, and shook her head in pity.

"Please, I need to see my baby."

The nurse moved quickly to hang a new IV bag while she spoke kindly to me. "Of course, darling," she said, her East Texas accent thick. "Let's just have you calm down for a little rest."

Seconds later my world went under, the room spinning until gravity forced my eyes closed.

When I woke hours later, George sat beside me, holding my hand and rubbing his thumb across my lifeline. His eyes were red and puffy.

"Hi, sweetheart," he whispered. Before I could respond, he spoke again. "She didn't make it. She's gone." The words caught in his throat, the last two coming out like a hiccup before he cried into the back of my hand, his tears running over my fingers. I'd never seen my husband weep. "I'm so sorry. I'm so sorry."

He would say those words over and over to me in the coming months, but of course, it wouldn't make anything easier. Or better. Nothing could.

For me, this loss was only the beginning.

11

JENNY

On her way back home after finally sending the obit to Marge for editing, Jenny phoned her mother, who had frustratingly moved one town over right after Jenny decided she was bringing her kids back home to live.

"Hey, baby girl," her mother said as soon as she picked up the phone.

Jenny's body relaxed with those three words. Her mother—who had lived among these people her entire life, who had sung in the choir with Beverly Hoffman, who had dealt with all of Edenberg's politics—would know whether or not Mrs. Hoffman's death was actually suspicious.

"How's your first day back on the job?"

Where to begin? "Yesterday Nichole found a body in the river."

"Oh, God. I heard about Beverly, but I had no idea Nichole found her. That girl can't catch a break this year." She let out a slow breath. "Marge and I are playing bridge with the girls tonight, so I figured she'd fill me in."

"Right now the police are calling it an accident, but that feels...*off* for some reason." Jenny could hear her mother shuffling around, probably in the tiny kitchen in her retirement village where she liked to bake dozens of goodies to pass out to the other residents. "What do you think?"

Her mom sighed. "I have no idea, hon, but I'll tell you two things."

Jenny had already reached home, but she turned off the ignition and sat in the car, waiting for the wisdom she needed right now.

"First, trust your gut. I know you're nervous about getting back into the newspaper world, but you have good instincts. Go with them." Her mother cleared her throat, and Jenny could almost see her pulling a hot pan of brownies from the oven. "Second, I told you that something strange was going on in Edenberg. It's why I left. The Hoffmans have always had their hands in things, but after George's books went…what do you call it? Viral?"

Jenny smiled. "Yeah, that's kind of the right word."

"Well, after he got a big name, he started getting a big head: buying up the town, getting himself elected to the school board, running for city superintendent, even speaking in pulpits some Sunday mornings. Things started to feel different, like him and his little business were taking over."

Jenny loved that her mother called the Hoffmans' multimillion-dollar organization a *little business*.

"It wasn't all bad getting the buildings a fresh coat of paint, but Marge says they can't even publish a story now without George's say-so. She called it…previous…or, no…prior *something*."

"Prior restraint?" As a journalist, Jenny knew this term well, and she also knew it shouldn't be allowed. It gave the government or another institution censorship power. Neither Ed nor Marge had explicitly mentioned such a thing, but that didn't mean her mother was wrong.

"That's it. Prior restraint. I think George is trying to build his own little world." Her mother cleared her throat. "I guess what

I'm saying is that I'm not sad I left. Suits me better." She paused, and Jenny heard the sound of a mixer in the background. "But you stay put and figure out what the devil is happening with poor Beverly, you understand? I know if that man has done something untoward, you'll figure out a way to make it right."

"I appreciate your confidence." Jenny said goodbye and hung up, but before she went inside the house, she grabbed her purse and checked the mailbox for the first time in days.

There were a couple of bills, one piece of junk mail, and a postcard. On the front was a woman in white- and gold-toned Renaissance garb holding a sword with a gold hilt. She was using the blade of the sword to slice into the neck of a man lying on a bed of pillows; he was already beginning to bleed out. The woman's face was pinched, and a maid watched from behind, ready to clean up the moment the deed was done. Quite a piece of mail.

Jenny turned it over to find a scribbled message: *Stop him.*

She considered possible senders, but couldn't think of anyone who would write her such a cryptic message. No name but there was an address: *79 Main Street, Edenberg.* Like most things in town, that was only a couple of minutes from here.

The sky above was growing dark. Jenny contemplated as she fanned herself with the postcard, studying the murderous image again. Thunder rolled in the distance, causing her to hesitate for only a moment before she made sure she had an umbrella and got back in her car to see if this was a residence or a business since Main Street featured both.

A few minutes later she stood outside a narrow storefront under her umbrella, postcard in hand. There was faint lettering on the window that had once read *The Hoffman Gallery.* Except *Gallery* had been scraped away as if the name was being changed.

She'd driven by this place on her way to work, assuming it was some sort of nonprofit art collective. Now she opened the door to see paintings hung on every inch of the wall space. Impressive.

"Welcome to The Hoffman Cultural Center," she heard a voice say. "I do need to let you know that we're about to close, but may I help you with something in particular?"

Jenny's eyes landed on a woman with gray hair and a wrinkled face standing behind a raised desk. On her shoulder she wore a pin with two gems in the center, and around her neck, a charm in the form of a slanted letter G. Jenny couldn't recall her name, but she recognized her as the library assistant who would hush her and Nichole as they giggled over the covers in the romance section when they were kids.

"Oh, hello. I, um…" Jenny held up the postcard and left her half-open umbrella at the door. "I received this in the mail from this address. Do you know this painting? Or…do you have any idea who might've sent it?"

The woman took it from Jenny, whom she obviously didn't recognize. "We don't have this painting on-site, of course. But we do have the postcard in our gift shop. It's a Caravaggio."

The older woman led her past the framed art, most of them depictions of southwestern landscapes: rolling plains, fields of bluebonnets, small windmills. "Ms. Hoffman only sources… Well, only *sourced* from local artists to sell, but she always kept a wide collection of reprints and cards featuring well-known artists across time. She prided herself on having seen many of these works in person."

Jenny followed the woman to turning displays in the back of the store before finding the row from which her card had come. "Are all of these by Caravaggio?"

The woman tried not to laugh at Jenny's lack of knowledge. "Not quite. The one on your postcard is a Caravaggio from the end of the sixteenth century. But this one…" The woman picked up another card, an image of a woman in a gold dress. "This is by Gustav Klimt from the early twentieth century."

Jenny pointed to a man's severed head in the bottom right corner of the Klimt image. "They have a similar theme."

"That's because they're based on the same story: Judith beheading Holofernes. Do you know it?"

Jenny ran her eyes across four more 3x5 reprints, each of them depicting a beautiful woman and a man's severed head. "I've never heard that story."

"It comes from the Book of Judith in the Apocrypha," the woman said as if a docent at a real museum rather than a lady standing in what amounted to a small-town art gift shop. "Holofernes was an Assyrian general oppressing the Israelites, so a beautiful widow went into his tent and feasted with him for days, distracting him until he finally passed out drunk. Then, she cut off his head and saved her people."

"That's one way to get things done." Jenny raised her eyebrows. "Do you have any idea who would've sent these to me? Or why?"

"I could swear that's Beverly's handwriting." The woman tilted her head, eyeing the writing on the back. "Perhaps Mrs. Hoffman is sending you postcards from the grave."

A shiver went up Jenny's spine as if a cold wind had entered the shop. She glanced at the other images on the turnstiles mostly filled with women in various acts of violence, perhaps even acts of revenge. Just like the Bible verses Beverly had been carrying in the locket around her neck on the day she died.

The woman considered. "Your name doesn't happen to be Judith, does it?" She laughed lightly. "Perhaps Beverly wants you to slay a monster."

A cough caught in the back of Jenny's throat. Judith. That was actually Jenny's real name, the one she'd used when she was a reporter in LA, another lifetime ago. But in her personal life, only a handful of people knew the name on her birth certificate. Those people included her mother, her husband, Nichole, Christina, and… Robin.

Jenny swallowed back an answer.

"Poor dear. Beverly's death has been hard on all of us," the woman said kindly, mistaking Jenny's fear for a sign of grief. "Well, except for her son, perhaps."

Jenny perked up, and the woman looked around the gallery to make sure no one had wandered in while they'd been conversing.

"Do you know I haven't seen him shed a tear? Not around town, not when he came by to check the financials. Stoic. Like a rock, that man."

Like father, like son.

Jenny remained quiet, having learned as a longtime journalist that this was often the best tactic to keep the source talking.

"I don't know how she did it for all those years." The woman wrinkled her nose. "A few weeks ago I was letting myself into the gallery, and I heard Beverly and Max—that's her son—arguing in the back. I tried to make a lot of noise to let them know someone was here, and everything went quiet. Then, less than a minute later he was hightailing it out of here without a word. I heard crying and went to check on Beverly. She was on the ground. She'd fallen, she said. She admitted that she and Max had been arguing, but she swore he hadn't touched her. I never could bring myself to believe her."

Jenny couldn't keep the shock off her face. The bruises— could Max Hoffman have caused them? She thought of the little she knew about Robin's husband. He'd been a quiet child, not nearly as charismatic or energetic as his father. He never ran for class president. He didn't play sports. He wasn't top of his class.

"What do you think about George?"

"Dr. Hoffman," the woman corrected, fingering the pin at her shoulder. "He's done a lot for Edenberg: brought in tourists, fixed our school system, ensured us locals have steady jobs. He even helped my niece get into her top university pick: Princeton! Can you imagine?" The woman sighed dreamily. "And I, for one, wouldn't have this job at my age except for the good work Genetive is doing."

"He strikes me as a bit...overbearing," Jenny said, pushing back carefully.

The woman attempted to straighten her curved back. "I know you're not from around here, so I feel I can speak freely."

Jenny didn't correct her.

"Dr. Hoffman and Genetive are the best things to ever happen to Edenberg. Ask anyone here, and they'll tell you the same." The words were spoken with such force that Jenny didn't think it wise to tread any further. "His family built this town on traditional family values, and he's reclaiming those for our community."

"Well, thank you for your time," Jenny said before leaving the gallery and driving home to ponder the woman's words throughout the evening. She couldn't help but think that this estimation of George was wrong, primarily because she felt a single truth deep inside: one way or another, that man was the death of Beverly Hoffman.

BEVERLY

ONE WEEK POSTMORTEM
THE NIGHT OF THE FIRE

The story goes that Our Lady of the Guadalupe appeared to a Chichimecan young man named Juan Diego in sixteenth-century Mexico. The Spanish Catholics had been attempting to convert reluctant natives for years, but they were unsuccessful until a dark-skinned Mary with black hair appeared to recently converted Juan.

Our Lady looked like she could've been his own mother, his aunt, his sister. So when she told him to gather flowers at the hill of Tepeyac in Mexico City in the middle of winter, he obeyed. He reached the top, which should've been covered in frost, and was astounded to find flowers of every color in full bloom. Juan gathered the spectacle, made a coat, and took it to the bishop, convincing the man to build a church on that very hill in honor of the Virgin of the Guadalupe.

I love that story. A holy figure among us broken mortals.

There was a time when I saw George that way, not as the Virgin—I knew better than that—but as the figure of Juan Diego, bringing a message of hope, of potential, of a better way. Now I know better, and it may be too late.

From my perch up here, I like to skip over the couple of years between my first daughter and the birth of Max because, really, who does like to dwell on sad things all the time?

But if you must know what it was like for me, imagine being held underwater for as long as you can stand, then being yanked into the air at the last possible millisecond only to find you would've rather stayed under.

I didn't leave bed for weeks.

I sipped soup broth that someone brought me.

I took whatever pills were on the bedside table.

I stared at the fluttering curtains.

I waited to die.

Today nurses have training; they offer to bring the child to the mother for her to hold as a sort of closure, but in the late '70s, there was no offer to see my infant. The best I got was a tiny marker on the columbarium. When I finally got out of bed, I visited her there every day until I came home sobbing too many times and George begged me to stop.

He had no idea what to do with me, but I like to think he did his best. For those first few weeks after we lost our girl, he stayed with me every moment he wasn't at school. He pushed my mother and sisters to visit even though they'd never been terribly chatty or affectionate. He didn't have a single episode during those months, almost as if his own mind knew he couldn't afford to leave me alone. I might fall through the cracks and disappear.

After about two months he hired a maid to clean the house and prepare dinner every night. Sally was the motherly sort, the kind of housekeeper who pushes you out of bed in the morning because she claims she needs to wash and iron the sheets—oh, and while you're up, why don't you dress and visit the beauty parlor?

Sally and George conspired together to make me reenter the world. My husband really could be a good man. He pulled me out of the darkness. Maybe that was why I felt so forged to him; maybe that was why I never doubted him. Maybe that was why I trusted him, almost to the very end.

When I started to get out and about again, I began to regularly visit the San Antonio Museum of Art. Consolation came as I walked those gallery halls and stared into the faces of subjects long dead.

For reasons I couldn't explain, even paintings of children were a balm to my soul. I sat for hours in front of Correggio's *Madonna and Child with the Young Saint John*, soaking myself in the olive greens and blues, imagining my child in the Virgin's loving arms, her eyes sweeping over my baby girl with a smile on her face.

As I sat in these mostly empty galleries, art began breathing me back to life, and when Max was born, I finally stepped out of my solitary tomb and met the world again.

12

WEDNESDAY

JENNY

For her first few years at the *Los Angeles Times*, Jenny's main beat had been the Marine Safety Division, not a bad gig as things go but certainly not hard-hitting journalism. She'd met Curt while covering a story on a new pier being built near his studio apartment, and they'd married two years later.

Write-ups about the history of lifeguarding, an occasional beached whale, and the importance of water safety had been her mainstay until a skull washed ashore the summer after she and Curt married. Jenny investigated the hell out of that story, and after she wrote a three-part series about a new mother who'd gone out for a run half a decade earlier and wasn't declared dead until a lifeguard stumbled across her mandible, the *Times* finally took note and promoted her to the investigative team.

Reporter Judith Howell, as she was known then, loved the work. She made a niche for herself by earning the confidence of assault survivors and telling the stories of their trauma with empathy and precision. But a decade and a half into her career, she became more than a reporter: she became a survivor, a silent survivor.

She thought about this fact as she sat in couple's therapy with her husband.

"In my time studying under Dr. Hoffman, I've learned an important tool that has helped thousands of couples. It's called ultimate transparency," the only therapist in town said as he sat across from them. Jenny recoiled at the mention of George but kept quiet. "Have either of you heard of this practice?"

"I just recorded a video for Genetive on the topic," Curt answered, leaning forward with his elbows on his knees. The therapist smiled, obviously pleased at Curt's knowledge. He looked to Jenny, who merely shrugged.

"Ultimate transparency is a simple but profound concept that demands the answer to one question: Do you have any secrets you've kept from one another?"

"No," Curt answered immediately.

"But only because I found out you cheated on me," Jenny huffed. "Until that day, you had a secret—a big one."

Curt swallowed hard and looked from Jenny to the therapist. "I've been learning a lot about the importance of integrity in all parts of my life."

The therapist nodded approvingly. "Dr. Hoffman says that a real man makes real mistakes and real confessions."

Jenny rolled her eyes at the trite phrase.

The therapist didn't flinch as he turned to her. "Jenny, would you mind answering the question: Do you have any secrets?"

She squirmed before answering with a firm "No." At this point, why should she have to relive trauma for Curt's benefit? It wouldn't change that he'd killed their marriage by cheating on her.

When the session ended, the tension in her shoulders finally eased. She gave Curt a quick nod and got in her car to head back to work. Once there, she left messages with the detective on Beverly's case, wondering if she was wasting her time.

At the end of the day, she was already irritable when she

opened the back door of their bungalow and spotted Emmy and Austen lying prone on the couch, each staring at their own iPad as *Bluey* blared from the television in front of them. Double screens. Joy. A cardboard pizza box had been flayed open, and Curt was nowhere in sight. She dropped her things on the kitchen table and kissed the kids on the tops of their heads, noticing the red sauce that lined both of their bottom lips.

Jenny stood between them and the television and pulled the iPads from their greasy hands. "Where's your daddy?"

Austen shrugged and Emmy pointed to the back of the house.

"Anything amazing happen at school? Did you learn brain surgery?"

Emmy giggled at her mom's joke, and Austen stood to jump on the couch, chanting, "I like to obey. It's the best way."

Jenny grabbed him around the waist and pulled him into a hug. "Where'd you learn that, bud?"

"Dr. Pound falls upside down."

"They had emotion circle today," Emmy explained.

"Good boys don't cry. On them you must rely," Austen continued rhyming.

Jenny bristled at the strange phrases, but she couldn't deal with this problem right now. "Five more minutes of *Bluey*, okay?"

The kids grunted something that sounded vaguely like agreement, and she dropped their devices on the kitchen counter before plodding to Curt's office in the back of the house.

Years ago he'd been so proud and grateful when he'd arrived home after a weeklong shoot to find that she'd done what she could with a small corner of their apartment, painting an accent wall, framing and hanging two of his favorite movie posters—*Full Metal Jacket* and *Attack of the 50 Ft. Woman*—and restoring a spindled office chair she'd found at a garage sale.

By comparison, his office now was more spacious and less cluttered, but it was dull, with a built-in wooden desk and shiplap walls lined with boxes he hadn't unpacked and pictures he hadn't hung. Pushed to the side was a deflated air mattress with one flat pillow and an unmade *Disney Princess* comforter that Emmy had already declared she'd outgrown.

Jenny didn't care. She wasn't fixing things for him this time.

"Pizza?" she asked, raising her voice enough so he would hear her through his noise-canceling headphones.

"Oh, hey," he said, pausing the video he'd been editing. "Yeah, there's some left. I ordered a cheese for the kids and ham and pineapple for us."

Those were her favorite toppings, but she didn't want pizza. She wanted him to cook dinner like she'd done for most of their marriage.

"How was the kids' day at school?" she asked, trying to keep her tone lighter than she felt.

"Fine." His gaze drifted back to the video he was working on.

When she realized he wasn't going to give her any more, she rolled her eyes and turned to leave the room. Her leaving must've signaled his mistake because he popped out of his chair and stepped toward her, touching her arm.

She pulled away. "Why did the kids eat in front of the TV? I thought we said no electronics after five o'clock."

He ran a hand up and down the back of his head. "Did we?"

"We said that when the new school year started, we would…"

"I think *you* said that," he interjected, cutting her off. "Not that I don't agree…"

It was like that these days, this jarring conversational dance, full of jerks and starts, flailing and failing to communicate with her husband.

"I was trying to see if I could work with some of the Hoffmans' existing footage. This job is bigger than I thought, and time goes fast between drop-off and pickup."

Jenny laughed out loud. She shouldn't mock her husband. She really shouldn't, but come on. "Sorry, I just…"

Curt looked at his feet before lifting his eyes to face her. "I know you did all of this for years, mostly on your own."

Yes, she'd done this for years on her own, first while holding down a prestigious full-time job, one most journalists would kill for, and later as a reluctant full-time mom. But that was not the fight she wanted to have right now. She pursed her lips and began backing out of the room.

"Wait," he said, his eyes pleading with her in a way his words rarely did.

She paused midstride. She'd waited half her lifetime for him, letting him start his film company when they were first married, supporting him until it was finally profitable, raising his kids while he worked twelve-hour days six days a week. She'd been a good wife until he—and life—had broken her.

"I'll do better," Curt said, his eyes eager.

He needed to do better fast. He had a deadline for improvement: one year in Edenberg. That was all she was giving him.

Not that she'd told him.

13

THURSDAY

NICHOLE

Nichole rushed into the back door of Sacred Heart two minutes after Beverly Hoffman's funeral service had officially begun. She squeezed into the back row beside Jenny, and she couldn't help but smile as Emmy grabbed her hand and Austen passed her a picture he'd drawn of the two of them. He'd written *Ant Nike* across the top.

Josh Groban's "You Raise Me Up" played over the speakers, and as she settled into the pew, Nichole's eyes drifted to the mound of white lilies draped across the closed casket.

The scene was too familiar: a congregation filled with mourners, a priest at the front, a giant photo of the deceased. Though her sister's funeral had been a blur, the memories of the smells and sounds from the day unexpectedly assaulted her. Perfume and lilies, the organ and whispers, the casket and the drowned body.

Nichole tried to slough off the sensations as she noticed a camera with a blinking red light in her periphery. She turned and saw another. This service was being recorded…or, no. Was it being broadcast?

She removed her arm from Emmy's grasp momentarily and

searched "Beverly Hoffman Funeral" on her phone while Austen tried to take the device out of her hands. Headlines about Beverly's death appeared, mostly on conservative news outlets. A link to the livestream of the service was available as well, and when she opened Facebook, there were 6,742 viewers tuning in. Wow. That was more than the population of their entire town. Nichole refreshed and a hundred or so more people appeared in the feed.

The instrumental music faded out, and the service proceeded as one might expect: a eulogy given by Max, a reading by Robin, the placement of a single rose atop her casket by Beverly's ten-year-old grandson, Lance. George did nothing, but wasn't that to be expected of the grieving widower?

Nichole eyed Lance as he sat back down. The boy's face had the same heart shape as Robin's, and Nichole remembered his green eyes, also the exact same shade as his mother's. He wore headphones today, something Nichole had suggested when he was her student in order to reduce overstimulation. She was glad they'd finally agreed to have him tested, but she regretted losing almost all contact with Robin after suggesting that her son might be different in some way.

Nichole ignored the thought. She was here to honor Beverly and to remind Robin that she still cared—but mostly she was here because Jenny had asked her to come. Jenny was stuck on the idea that Beverly's death wasn't an accident.

After the pianist finished the final stanza of "How Firm a Foundation," Nichole followed Jenny and the kids to the front where the family waited to greet mourners. Curt moved to the back to speak to one of the camera operators.

As she watched people gaze adoringly at George—many of them wearing tiny pins she'd begun to see around town—Nichole considered stepping out of line. This wasn't her scene. These weren't her people. Not that she really had people anymore, except Jenny. But getting out of the queue of well-wishers would raise more attention than she wanted, so instead, when her turn came, she took George's firm hand in hers.

"So sorry for your loss," Nichole murmured.

The look he returned was filled with warmth, but his tone somehow still seemed authoritative. "Yes, thank you for coming."

Nichole took Max's hand next, offering condolences again. Max received them with a swift nod of acknowledgment. His stoicism made a cold shiver run up her spine.

Lastly, she arrived at Robin, who stood with her son in front of her. The boy, who was showing signs of the Hoffmans' prominent jaw, gave Nichole a nod as if he recognized her from kindergarten.

She offered him a faint smile before addressing his mother. "How are you?"

Robin's mouth was set in a thin line, but her eyes were wet and absent of makeup. "I told Jenny…the three of us…we need to catch up," Robin said quietly, glancing at her father-in-law to ensure he couldn't hear. Keeping her arm around her son, she pitched forward. "Maybe tonight? At the wine bar?"

There was something plaintive in her tone, and Nichole knew that despite her own fatigue in the midst of a long week, she couldn't deny her. "Wine sounds perfect."

"Nine p.m.?"

Nichole nodded and took her hand. She hadn't talked to Robin—not really—in years, but her eyes were pleading. Maybe it was time to reconnect. Maybe Robin knew something that she could only say to people who'd known her for a lifetime.

Excerpt from the Foreword to Sphere of Influence
by Dr. George Hoffman
Copyright 2009

Last year I accompanied my son, Maxwell, to purchase his first
iPhone, and as I watched the people with itchy fingers waiting
at a Best Buy in Austin, I was struck by humanity's longing
to hold something in their hands, a tangible thing with which
to occupy their minds. I stepped out of line and demanded he
drive me back home that instant. I did not want either of us to
become one of the dead-brained masses.

Our society is moving into an era in which attention will
become the primary commodity, and those who control where
their minds wander will be the fittest to survive. Having a
sphere to influence requires mastery over one's thoughts, and
the people most able to obtain this mastery will be the leaders
in tomorrow's brave new world.

Making it my aim to study society, starting with time among
children and college students, has provided me with numerous
benefits throughout the years, one being the ability to wait pa-

tiently for an outcome. As I studied the dynamics of the children at the Hoffman Family Camp, I learned to be still and wait for the insights my subjects would reveal over time. What these children taught me—and what the students in my classes daily teach me—make up the contents of this book, one that I hope will challenge you to take back your own mind in order to lead other people to greatness.

For all of the men reading this, we need you to guide society and—if not yet, then someday—a family that embodies traditional values. For all of the women reading this, we need you to nurture us, to be the angels at our hearths, to be the conscience we can rely upon. For any children or students who happen to pick up this tome of knowledge, listen to your parents. If they are reading this book, then they are on the right track.

BEVERLY

ONE WEEK POSTMORTEM
THE NIGHT OF THE FIRE

Two years after I lost my baby girl, Maxwell Hoffman arrived, as healthy and whole as his sister hadn't been. George, showing him off for our visitors, held him more than I did those first couple of days in the hospital, and I was content to let him be a proud father.

I would never tell anyone, but I was disappointed to have a son. Even then I sensed that George would get his talons in a boy. Oh, I know. Gender doesn't matter for the first few years. I could diaper and feed with the best of them.

Before he started school, Max and I visited art shows, galleries, or museums once a week. On the other days, he would help me run errands to the grocery store, the bank, the doctor. Sometimes we would chat with one of his grandmothers for an hour or two, us women sipping iced tea and gossiping while he drew pictures of flowers at our feet. Every Thursday afternoon we would bake sugar cookies together: Max could crack an egg without any shells getting in the bowl by the time he was three.

All that to say, my son may have been a bit of a momma's boy, but George didn't have time to notice until he caught Max putting on rouge one afternoon. I thought my four-year-old was adorable with those pink circles on his cheeks and my pearls thrown around his neck, but George pitched a fit like I'd never seen, calling our son all sorts of names I won't repeat here. Max changed that day and has tried to live up to his father's expectations ever since. I changed too, though imperceptibly. Still, I knew my son now belonged to my husband in all the ways that mattered.

Years later, when Max told me he was marrying Robin, I was ecstatic. I'd missed feeling connected to my child, and the promise of Robin as part of our family allowed me once again to hope I might have someone to call my own.

After they married, I noticed that Max—despite his best intentions to be a good husband—was doing Robin just like George had once done me: keeping her busy with his needs, keeping her by his side at every business event, keeping her home every evening. That was why I later suggested she start her businesses downtown and why I started taking her with me on my art-collecting trips.

After Lance was born and his differences became more and more apparent, Robin was practically confined to home or driving him to-and-fro to doctor's offices and therapists. Perhaps that was why joining Genetive was such a relief for her. We provided for her, as we did for so many, a place to connect with other like-minded people. At least that was how I saw it.

I came to realize that George saw our organization as so much more: as a way to reclaim American hearts and minds to mold them into followers who respected his power and authority. They would submit, obey. That was the kind of language he began to use. He even talked about running for office in coming years. Mayor was beneath him and senator was too tedious. But governor…or even president? That sounded just right.

I know. Perhaps it seems unbelievable that I wouldn't have sooner understood my husband's agenda, but to be honest, I never read his books. (Don't tell anyone.) Remember, too, that I lived with *and* for George the man, not Dr. Hoffman the genius.

I'd come of age with George the man. I'd had children with him. I'd washed his clothes and bought his medicine and cooked his favorite meals. His ideas were, at times, interesting, but I could tune them out at will.

Now that I'm dead, I can no longer distract myself from the truth, and the truth is that this town and the fire raging below are no longer about George and me.

It's about Robin and those two women down there beside her. It felt good to see her talking with friends, even if it did happen to be in the receiving line at my funeral because here's the thing: I need Nichole and Jenny to help her redeem Edenberg. A hot enough fire can make dross rise to the surface. It can purify. It can cleanse. And after George and Genetive's effects on this town, that's exactly what Edenberg needs.

I couldn't have told you this a year ago. Back then I was still living in blissful ignorance, burying my head in the sand so I didn't have to do anything about the problem.

But now, as I reach my end, there are two things I know: one, I'm dead, and two, it wasn't an accident. Drowning in two inches of the Guadalupe? Please. I was in that water from the time I could crawl to the edge. Daddy found me asleep on the banks of the river too many times to count, and Momma called me "sunfish" because she said I lit up when I got around the water.

Robin, Jenny, and Nichole know these truths. They know what happened and who's to blame. That's why one of them started this fire in the first place.

14

NICHOLE

Nichole was exhausted on this Thursday evening. It was nearing the end of the first week of school, which meant that weeknights were for going to bed early and Saturday mornings were for sleeping in late. People who didn't teach children for a living didn't understand the rhythm of the school year, how for 187 days, your time, energy, and focus were poured into people whose brains and hearts needed more than you had to give.

She knew this would happen, that after a summer of drinking and sleeping around, her body would reset and want to crawl into bed by 9 p.m. each night, but when Robin and Jenny both asked her to meet this evening, Nichole couldn't say no, so she'd rallied and was now stepping into the Tributary Tasting Room, the wine bar Robin had opened a couple of years ago with Hoffman money.

The wine dive was low lit, bringing out the dark hues of the redwood, and each table was set atop an aged barrel. The high chairs were sleek and black, lit by Edison bulbs suspended from the ceiling.

Behind the bar, Robin nodded at her when she arrived, and Nichole tried to keep her head from drooping onto the table as she waited for the last few people to leave.

A few minutes later Jenny entered and sank into the chair across from Nichole. Without a *hello* or *thanks for meeting us instead of your bed*, she pushed a 3x5 card across the table.

"Check it out," Jenny said, her hands tapping the table in a nervous rhythm.

"Interesting." Nichole studied the image. "I had something like this in my mailbox today."

Jenny sat up. "What?"

"It was a different painting."

"Was there any kind of message on the back?"

"No. Just a blank postcard. Not even a return address."

Jenny narrowed her eyes and stared at her hands, almost speaking to herself. "But she knew you would tell me."

"Who knew? I would tell you what?" As Nichole asked the questions, the last pair of customers in the corner signed their bill, stood up from a nearby table, and made their way out the door and into the still-warm night.

"Beverly. Yesterday I stopped by her gallery, and the gift shop was full of these."

Nichole's mouth turned down at the corners. "A dead woman is sending us postcards?"

"Yeah. And mine is about the story of a woman named Judith."

Realization dawned on Nichole. "Judith. Like your real name."

"I can only assume." Jenny lifted her chin to Nichole. "What was on the front of yours?"

Nichole shrugged. "A picture of a lady in a white dress. I don't know. I thought it was an ad for an art exhibit. I threw it away."

Jenny took out her phone. "Describe what you remember. Besides the white dress."

"Um...it looked like something that the lady with the eyebrow might've painted."

"Frida Kahlo?"

"Yeah, her." Nichole thought for a few beats. "The lady in the painting had short black hair and the background was really plain. Like a whitewashed wall…maybe a plant in the corner?"

Jenny typed key words into her phone a few times before holding up an image. "Is this it?"

Nichole raised her eyebrows. "You're good." She took Jenny's phone and held it closer, reading the caption.

"Portrait of…" Nichole swallowed.

"Portrait of what? Frida?"

Nichole coughed and cleared her throat, trying to say the words aloud. *"Portrait of Cristina My Sister."* The name was spelled differently, but still…

Jenny's eyes widened. "Oh, my God, Nikki. I didn't realize…"

Nichole dropped the phone onto the table.

Jenny picked it up. "Look, that's a terrible thing to send you, but I do think it's a message of some kind." Jenny flipped over her own postcard, reading out loud the two words: *"Stop him."*

"Stop who? George?" Nichole made a face. "Good luck with that."

Robin joined them, bringing three glasses and a couple of bottles of chardonnay to the table with her. She slung a work bag over the back of the chair, filled the glasses, and sat.

Nichole took a long sip of her wine, trying to piece together the information. Someone—likely Beverly Hoffman—had sent her a postcard, the titular painting referencing the name of her own sister. Was this a bereavement card? Was this some kind of cruel joke? Was this actually a message as Jenny was suggesting?

Jenny looked to Robin. "Hey, how are you after the funeral?"

Robin swirled her glass before taking a sip. "I've been better."

"I'm sure."

The conversation, though brief, was stilted and awkward as if too much time and sorrow had passed for the three of them—

missing the fourth—to converse as they had in their carefree adolescence.

Jenny hesitated only a moment before pushing the postcard in front of Robin. "Do you know this painting?"

Robin froze, her knuckles white as she clutched the stem of the wineglass. With her other hand, she brushed a finger lightly against the image before flipping it over and reading the back.

Robin's lip curled into a half grin. "That woman and her art."

"Beverly?" Jenny asked.

"Yeah, it's definitely from her." Robin reached into the bag she'd hung on the back of her chair to pull out a postcard of her own: a portrait of a brunette with short hair and semi-exposed breasts surrounded by gold filagree. She pushed it to the center of the table.

It took Nichole a few seconds to notice that in the bottom corner, the subject—a woman sweet, seductive, and deadly—was holding a bearded man's head in her left hand. Her heart sped a bit faster even though she wasn't quite sure why. Jenny met her eye, and she could sense that she was feeling the same apprehension.

"I think this story matches yours," Robin told Jenny.

Jenny studied the paintings side by side. "What do you mean?"

"It's another depiction of Judith beheading Holofernes, but mine is blank on the back. She knew I would understand the meaning."

Jenny's eyebrows knit in confusion. "Which is?"

Nichole finished off her glass and refilled it, grateful for the warmth spreading across her chest and down her throat.

"Beverly was an aficionado of all types of art." Robin ran a hand across her forehead as if she had a headache. "She dragged me to a bunch of museums and art shows, and for as long as I've been married, she would give me postcards featuring works of art that went with whatever was happening in my life. The first one was on our wedding day. She gave me *Starry Night*. Before I went into labor, she handed me *The Scream*, and on my son's first birthday, she gave me one I'd never seen before: Abbott Handerson Thayer's *Sleep*. She was a serious art collector, though most of her stuff is out at their headquarters or in specialized storage facilities."

"So she sent you postcards as a kind of code?"

"Not so much a code." Robin rested a hand on her chin. "More to mark momentous occasions."

"Like a death?" Nichole asked, her mind beginning to mellow as she finished off her second glass.

"Not till now," Robin mused. "The cards were sweet, sometimes funny, a thing just between the two of us. As the years went on, the art references became more obscure, more like…" She considered. "More like a puzzle I had to solve, like a game. That's why I'm certain these postcards are from her."

"But why would your…Beverly…send anything to me?" Jenny asked.

"And me," Nichole said, leaning in to the conversation. "I got a—" she considered how to explain what she'd received "—a condolence card."

"I talked about you two—and Christina." Robin looked almost shy as she admitted that she still thought of them. "About how you were a great writer—" she gestured to Jenny and then Nichole "—and how you were so good with kids."

"Hello?" Nichole laughed loosely as she opened another bottle. "You've basically ignored us since you married into the Hoffman family, and the year after I taught Lance, you…you cut me off entirely." She didn't add that Christina never heard from Robin unless she was the one to reach out first. Some friend. "Lest you forget, I was here the whole time Jenny was living it up in California and—" she swallowed, trying hard to say the

name and then giving up "—and my sister was in Galveston. You were best friends, and I thought the four of us—"

When Nichole couldn't finish the statement, Jenny cut in. "You and Christina were always the people we wanted to become, and we thought that, in some way, all four of us were close."

"We were." Robin covered her face with her hands. "There's no excuse except that…the Hoffmans are…insulated, for lack of a better word, and I became…protected, especially after I had Lance. Max and I relied on Beverly and George for…for pretty much everything. Max has worked with his father for years, learning the ropes so he can someday take over at Genetive, and until recently I'd been right beside him."

Robin fidgeted with the gold cross she'd always worn around her neck, even as a child, and Nichole noticed something on the inside of her wrist.

Nichole took Robin's hand and pulled it to her, examining the black letter monogrammed into her skin: G. "What's this? A tattoo?"

"It's just…something Genetive does. It's part of the program when you…when you reach a certain level." Robin snatched her hand back. "This is why I wanted to see you two…at least part of the reason." She took a practiced deep breath in through her nose, holding for four counts and then releasing. "Listen, I believe in the work George—and Beverly—have done with Genetive. Years ago I might've laughed at self-help stuff, but after spending time learning the principles, I see how the ideas actually help make people's lives better. It gives them… It gives me purpose, meaning. Or, at least it has until now. I have a feeling that with Beverly's death, with George having his way, all that may change."

"Is that why you wanted to talk to us?" Jenny asked.

Nichole took another long sip. "You want us to sign up or something?"

"No," Robin cut in. "Months ago Beverly stopped attending events, started becoming something of a recluse. It wasn't like her. She'd always been quiet, shy around visitors, but she was always there, a friendly face to greet newcomers or another pair of hands to make preparations for events. A couple weeks ago when she wouldn't respond to my calls or texts, I drove over to check on her. She couldn't—or wouldn't—give me a real answer. Kept saying she wasn't sure if she trusted her own mind anymore. She seemed paranoid, said George had changed, that she knew the real him, that he wasn't what everyone thought. It was strange, but I honestly thought she'd bounce back to her usual self. I brushed aside my concerns, but then…"

Jenny and Nichole waited for Robin to figure out how to best continue.

"Then I was out at headquarters last weekend, dropping off wine for an event when I overheard Max and George talking about 'the best treatment facility.' I was sure they were talking about Beverly, but when I inserted myself into the conversation, they both grew quiet." She took a steadying breath and bit the inside of her cheek. "Do you know why Lance attends private school?"

"Because he has special needs?" Nichole asked matter-of-factly.

"No. I mean, yes, but it's because George doesn't want him in an Edenberg school. I would've been fine keeping him here, getting him extra support. But George told Max it wasn't an option, that kids like that should be 'with their own kind.'" She put air quotes around the last phrase.

"God," Nichole breathed. "What an asshole."

"Max finally admitted that they weren't talking about his mother—they were talking about Lance. The private school isn't good enough for George. He wants to send Lance away to a boarding school for kids with autism for most of the year." Robin began to tear up. "That broke me. I was so angry. I couldn't even stay and argue. I had to move, to scream, to hit something."

Robin's voice began to tremble. "I rushed to Beverly, told her what George was planning, but she wasn't herself, couldn't help me. She'd been to the post office and had arrived back home exhausted from trying to appear...I don't know...normal? When she didn't even flinch as I told her about George's plans for Lance, I should've known something was very wrong. She loves...loved...her grandson more than life itself. If she'd been in her right mind, she would've been irate. She might've even stood up to her husband." Robin wiped at her eyes. "I should've taken her to a neurologist, a specialist, someone besides George, who always said she was fine. He wouldn't let any of us—not me, not her, not Max, not Lance—be anything less than fine." Robin stretched out her hands on the table, considering where to go from here. "By Monday morning, she was dead."

Robin swallowed hard. "Her coroner's report already came in. They're calling her death an accident, the cause of death hypoxia."

"Hypoxia," Jenny repeated. "So...death by drowning?"

"In two inches of water," Nichole added, remembering the water levels and how the town had been concerned they would need to cancel this year's Paddle Parade. "That can't be right."

"Yesterday I went and spoke to her doctor," Robin added.

"Isn't HIPAA a thing?" Jenny asked.

"You've been gone too long, my friend," Nichole said, one side of her lip lifted as if she already knew the answer.

"Not in Edenberg and not if you're a Hoffman," Robin answered. "The doctor said Beverly was having headaches and fatigue—*that* I already knew. The only thing the doctor added was that she'd started having slight tremors, and she'd..." Robin trailed off, seeming unsure about whether or not to say more. "I don't know if this is at all relevant."

"Everything is relevant right now," Jenny told her.

"In recent weeks Beverly had started...seeing things." Robin exhaled. "She would wake up at night and think someone was standing at the foot of her bed."

"It was probably her creepy-ass husband," Nichole suggested. "His whole demeanor gives off bad vibes. The patriotic suit and that radio announcer voice he uses. I don't like it." Nichole's neck tensed and she rubbed at it with an open palm as she considered the possibility. "Do you think George was actually standing at the end of Beverly's bed, watching her sleep?"

"Maybe. Except he wasn't there much all summer, not even to stay the night. Max was gone a lot, too, overseeing the building of a project out at headquarters." Robin closed her eyes and inhaled. "There were other things, the doctor said. Beverly came in frantic one day about a week before she died. She was nauseated and her heartbeat was rapid. They assumed it was a panic attack, but then Beverly told the doctor that she knew there was more to it, that her plants were dying, that the paintings in her home...that they'd started moving."

Nope, nope, nope. Nichole shook her head. She was not a fan of ghosts, especially having grown up with the memories and stories of those children who'd died. "The paintings were... moving?"

"She told the doctor that the eyes of the portraits were following her, the trees in the landscapes swaying. I had no idea it had gotten so bad... I should've seen the signs before it was too late, but I was so busy with the stores and Lance and Genetive. I should've gotten her help."

"What about Max? Where was he?" Jenny asked pointedly.

"Max lives for his father's approval." Robin sighed. "I saw some of that when we married, but it's gotten worse since George founded Genetive. Now Max is like his father's disciple, not just his son. It's caused...problems between us...but I've tried really hard to be a good wife."

Nichole bristled at the last few words.

Jenny ignored the sentiment. "So this…figure at the end of her bed and the…moving pictures… Did the doctor have any read on that? I mean, I assume he diagnosed them as hallucinations?"

"Well, yeah, but he didn't tell her that. Beverly would've freaked out if he'd used any kind of word signaling psychosis. That was not acceptable—and now I'm realizing why. Her husband would've had her committed in a heartbeat." Robin's jaw clenched. "And except for…these things, which I know is a lot…she seemed pretty pulled together. Or, at least, she could fake it. She could get out of bed, put on makeup, smile at all the right times."

As Robin's voice trailed, Nichole finished her third glass, once again grateful for the swimmy feeling the liquid provided. Alcohol made everything—even this—more bearable.

Reviews of Genetive Inc.

"Dr. George Hoffman and his program changed my life. His innovative treatments taught me to look inside myself for the answer, and his lectures reminded me that I am in charge for a reason. Before I took my first class at Genetive, I had no idea of my full potential, much less how to reach beyond my limits."
—Mark Pryor, CEO of APEX, a Fortune 500 company

"Run, don't walk, to sign up for your personalized course today. Dr. Hoffman's insights and guidance will transform you and your work."
—Presley Raymond, Golden Globe Nominee

"Everyone needs and deserves access to the amazing resources this organization provides." —Theresa Upton, Life Coach

"Edenberg continues to thrive under Dr. Hoffman's benevolent hand. Some say a prophet will never be accepted in his hometown, but we'll keep George with us for as long as he'll remain."
—Lindsey Nolan, owner of The Edenberg Eatery

15

JENNY

"There's something I want to show you," Robin said as they finished off a bottle. "Come with me."

Jenny and Nichole followed Robin to a dark loft above the wine bar. As they crept up the stairs, Jenny couldn't help but think of books she'd read as a child—Nancy Drew and the Hardy boys, poking into dark corners—but when they arrived at the landing and Robin flipped on the light, she saw that the scene wasn't as ominous as she'd expected. It seemed to be storage space for basic supplies like napkins and cleaning agents, as well as rows of wine bottles. A desk in the corner held a few scattered papers.

Robin took a key from her pocket and went to the opposite end of the room where a large cabinet stood, tall and wide. She opened the top drawer and pulled out a stack of files.

"These are the archives George asked Beverly to comb through at the *Gazette* a year ago after he decided to buy the newspaper. She agreed to go through the material personally and throw out anything *problematic*, but she didn't get rid of anything. She gave it all to me. She must've sensed something was wrong. She told me it was *just in case*."

"In case of what?" Jenny asked.

Robin stared hard at her. "That's what I want to know. I can only imagine something in here could be useful if you think her—" she swallowed against the word before making herself say it "—if Beverly's death wasn't an accident."

"You think there's something suspicious about Genetive hidden in these documents?"

"I have no idea, but nothing is adding up anymore. I was at headquarters for the ribbon-cutting ceremony a few years ago, and we were all so proud to be a part of something that was not only financially successful, but also helpful to people in their everyday lives."

"How? How is it helpful?" Jenny asked as Nichole opened and closed folders, not really looking at their contents.

"They teach about reaching one's full potential. There are so many testimonials online from actors and politicians and executives, saying that better understanding themselves and their flaws and strengths has allowed them to achieve their goals. People are inviting friends to join all the time."

"It sounds like any other pyramid scheme," Nichole slurred. "Or any other health and wealth philosophy."

Robin bit her lip, seeming to try to figure out the best way to explain. "I know, but Genetive is different. Even now, despite how I feel about George, I still think the principles are fundamentally true. I would keep Genetive and get rid of George any day. Maybe if Max was running things…"

Jenny thought of what the woman at the gallery had told her about Robin's husband arguing with Beverly shortly before she died. "Do you know if Beverly and Max were on good terms? Before she…"

Robin's eyes narrowed. "Why do you ask?"

"It's just…the woman who works at the gallery heard him… raising his voice."

"That doesn't sound like Max. Perhaps she was mistaken." The words were frustratingly dismissive. "Although…"

"Yes?"

Robin lifted her chin and arched her shoulders. "I suppose he could've been speaking with her about Lance and his schooling. I know Beverly would've fought him and George on something like that. Just like me. Or, they could've disagreed about Genetive's next steps."

Jenny listened as she began opening folders. The contents had been organized neatly, and the first was filled with articles about the death of seventeen people at the Hoffman Family Camp in 1996. It wasn't new information, but it contained details that George obviously didn't want to be part of the archives at the newspaper he now owned.

The next folder was filled with information about George's first book, the one that won him so much acclaim: *Sphere of Influence*. The book sold four million copies worldwide and, from what she could tell, was mostly a how-to-win-at-life guide for rich white dudes who were already doing just that.

She'd downloaded it a few nights ago, but she was finding it difficult to stomach the drivel. George occasionally quoted psychologists and questionable research to support the main premise of the book: *order is necessary to any functioning society or individual. If you order your mind in the proper way, then you will experience success and happiness. You'll also be equipped to teach others the proper way to live.*

Perhaps a harmless enough idea to some, except that many of his assertions subverted these very ideas. Woven through his rather innocuous statements were troubling conclusions.

Take, for instance, the passage she'd highlighted in the middle of a chapter on the importance of self-confidence: *as a man, you must claim your rightful place of power in your family, your church, and your workplace. Only then can you do more than influence those around you. You can change them. You will control the narrative that others believe.*

The ideas were darker than self-confidence. They reeked of manipulation, coercion, and control.

"What did Beverly think about George's ideas?" Jenny asked as Robin and Nichole peered over her shoulder.

"As far as I know, she mostly agreed with him," Robin answered.

But then she'd died. Suddenly and mysteriously. Jenny's journalistic senses were tingling. She was more convinced than ever that Beverly's "accident" couldn't have been an accident. She was also beginning to wonder if George's business wasn't just a business, but a movement, a faction, a belief system. It was all too...*cultish*, for lack of a better word.

Something was wrong with Dr. Hoffman and Genetive Inc., and Jenny knew that the best way to find the fly in the ointment was to dive into the filmy liquid.

Jenny bit her lip as she thought. "When can I take one of Genetive's classes? Are they online?"

Nichole sat against the desk and crossed her arms. "You would hate that."

"There's a retreat this weekend. It's for couples and it's an unpublicized event, invite only," Robin answered. "Max said they'd thought about canceling it, but so many people have already paid thousands of dollars and arranged travel."

"Can we go?" Jenny asked.

"You'd have to come with someone and I'd need to vouch for you, but we could probably make it work."

"Curt will go. He's been wanting something like this." Jenny looked at Nichole. "Could you bring someone?"

"Maybe...but...a couples' retreat?" Nichole frowned. "I just met Wes. I'll sound crazy."

"Tell him you got free tickets," Robin said. "The food is good, and the accommodations are great...except..."

"Except what?"

Robin's eyebrows knit. "They might give you separate rooms."

Nichole laughed before realizing she was serious.

"Family values are important," Robin added, almost defensively. "I know I don't like George, but the curriculum can be life-changing." Robin's eyes lit up as she answered, and Jenny wondered again about how her old friend had come to be involved in such an organization. "The therapists there are top-notch, and they'll meet with you—and your partner, this weekend—to unpack the root of any issues in your relationship. It helped Max and me years ago, although lately…"

Robin waved away the thought. "George's talks are mostly inspirational, about how you were created for a specific purpose, about how to set goals, about how to motivate others. But I especially love the time with the other women. The networking is phenomenal, and the wisdom is reason enough to be there." Robin caught herself expounding upon the organization she was supposedly coming to doubt. "Like I said, it's great information. George is the real problem. If we could get rid of him…"

"How much is a weekend retreat?" Jenny asked, cutting her off.

"Ten thousand dollars," Robin said without flinching.

"Good Lord." Nichole coughed. "There's no way I can afford that."

"Like I said, free tickets. I'll get you approved." Robin turned to Jenny. "I'm not sure I can convince Max to give me two scholarships. Can you cover it?"

Curt's business had sold well, and they had a stockpile invested for years to come. "Sign us up."

"Okay, good. Just be aware: it's technically a couples' retreat, but there's a lot of work on the individual as well." Robin pointed at Jenny. "I can tell Max that you're specifically interested in Genetive's program for businesswomen, that you want to know more about how to join."

"Not a bad idea. It'll give me a deep dive into the organization."

Robin turned to Nichole and closed one eye. "For you, I'll say you're interested in working on the school's curriculum in more depth."

"Fine." Nichole brushed her hair off her face, pulling it into a thick ponytail. "Do we need to act a certain way?"

"Just be yourself," Robin reassured them. "Seriously, a lot of the teachings are solid. It's George that's the issue."

Jenny wasn't so sure about that view, but she wasn't going to argue. Instead, she was going inside.

If the devil is in the details, then Jenny was planning to dig through the minutiae of Genetive until she found the devil and dragged him out, pitchfork and all.

PART TWO

"To love is to burn,
to be on fire!"

—*Sense & Sensibility,*
Jane Austen

The idea for Genetive Inc. was birthed in the late '90s as the entire world watched the Clinton trials unfold and the very nature of the family attacked on news screens in every culture and language. The idea that a leader of a country as fine as America, one founded on the values of faith and family and loyalty, might so flagrantly violate his role as a father and husband was abhorrent, not to mention the behavior of the tawdry young woman who seduced him. Although Genetive Inc. was birthed from this ruinous moment in history, it would be years before the vision for our organization became reality.

Shortly before Clinton's impeachment, Dr. George Hoffman was running a successful children's camp during the summer, thanks to generous donations, and teaching psychology at the University of Texas while managing a boutique private practice. Hoffman took his research on the hierarchy of power in society and turned it into a series of lectures entitled, "Taking Back Family Values in the Free World." With the advent of YouTube in 2005, these lectures slowly became available to the public, and in the past two decades, these lectures and all of the free Genetive content have received more than seven million views.

In 2009, after the election of Barack Obama, Dr. Hoffman published his first mainstream book outside of academia. *Sphere of Influence* argued that the foundational elements of the country were being eroded by leftist ideology day by day. This critique of America's waning belief system hit the *New York Times* bestseller list for more than forty weeks.

While Dr. Hoffman continued teaching, he also served as adviser to a multitude of conservative politicians across Texas. It was this experience of reconnecting with like minds that prodded him to purchase and develop the land that became Genetive Inc., an oasis in Edenberg, Texas, that encourages free thinking and a return to core family values.

In 2016, Genetive opened its headquarters for the first time, welcoming families to week-long bonding camps, men to weekend wellness workshops, and couples to parenting, marriage, and premarital classes.

Now run by a team of more than a dozen coaches, an extensive groundskeeping and catering staff, and a business department, Genetive Inc. seeks to provide training so families will have the tools they need in order to take back the values that this country was once founded upon.

BEVERLY

ONE WEEK POSTMORTEM
THE NIGHT OF THE FIRE

Art became a language between Robin and me. The images allowed us to communicate without having to bare our souls, which was much preferable to me.

Soon after she and Max married, I dragged her to every museum and show I could find in Texas—from the Dallas Museum of Art to Houston's Museum of Fine Arts to Abilene's Grace Museum. I could wander those halls for days, gazing into Parmigianino's straitlaced ladies or Alice Neel's topless, wiry wonders. My favorite has always been the impressionists, those tiny strokes making the light dance across the canvas, the subtle colors erupting into a vibrant image.

After George and I founded our camp in the early '90s, I taught classes to children. The kids and I would study a painting—in actuality, with our lean budget in those days, a poster of a painting—of, say, Manet's *Young Woman in the Garden*. The children would move closer and farther away to discern the subtleties as well as the entire composite. (They didn't realize this was what they were doing as I moved them around the room, but I certainly did.) Then, they would try their little hands at their version, throwing splotches of color onto inexpensive canvases. I loved every moment.

George was good at running the camp, just like he was good at academia. Anything he touched, it seemed, turned to gold.

He'd earned his doctorate in psychology and taught classes while he acquired his own patients, whom he would convince to try new treatments, new therapies, new studies. He loved research and focused primarily on the interaction between the upper echelons of society, writing articles about the 1 percent and what made them the 1 percent. He argued that their perceived success went far beyond savvy business decisions or generational wealth. Something about them made people pay attention, and he wanted to find that intangible something.

"Someday we'll have our own organization. We'll help people of every class reach their potential," he said on more than one occasion after I'd put Max to bed for the night.

He would talk about his hopes and dreams, endearing himself to me by rubbing my feet while Bob Ross spoke in a gentle cadence about brushstrokes in the background. I would half listen to both of them and nod along as I mentally made my grocery list for the next day.

George wasn't one to start small, so I shouldn't have been surprised when he told me he'd bought some land on the edge of town. (To be more precise, his parents had bought the land and deeded it over to him.) He wanted to establish a summer camp, a place where kids could grow and play, a place where he could study society, where he could learn how to make us all… better. Because of his interest in behavioral psychology among socioeconomic classes, he vowed that eventually half of all of our campers would be on scholarships. He would watch how they engaged with one another, how their financial situation affected the dynamics between them. Of course, this meant that he would need to mix and mingle with those in the upper echelons in order to solicit donations, but that was his cross to bear. He would observe his subjects—aka, the children—in the summers and publish his findings during the school year.

The camp was a gift for Max and me, George said. I would have all the children I could ever want. (Successive attempts at pregnancy had been unsuccessful, and IVF was prohibited by the Catholic church.) Max was in junior high, a bit of a loner at school, and now he would have so many friends descend on his home turf every summer.

A win for everyone!

The next year when we opened, we hosted only a total of seventy campers across socioeconomic spectrums. By our fifth year, the year when the terrible thing happened, we hosted three hundred and nineteen kids—children from all walks of life.

News outlets across the country covered what happened next: the rain, the flash flood, those who died.

After fifteen of our little ones—and two chaperones—drowned, George swore and cursed at the media coverage. *They only see the fifteen! What about the hundreds of lives we've changed?*

I didn't dare say a word.

For so long, I believed in that man. For so long, I bought in to George's vision for this town, for families, for the nation. *Faith, Family, Fidelity*—that was his motto, and it meant something. It meant we could help make the world a better place.

Don't be fooled. I wasn't some mealymouthed wife playing a part. At one time I was actually on his side for better or worse.

But that was well before I died. Now I know for certain where and when it all went wrong.

16

FRIDAY

JENNY

Marriage was an ever-changing story; that was what Jenny had learned. Some days were the fluff pieces, all surface and fun and easy; others, especially after becoming parents, were *just-the-facts-ma'am* news blurbs, in which you only had time for the highlights before putting things to bed for the day. But lately, her marriage was a hard-hitting investigative feature that demanded time and attention.

Curt and Jenny drove in silence to the Hoffman Center, where they'd be attending one of Genetive's unadvertised ten-thousand-dollar relationship retreats. Rain beat against the roof of the car. The forecast projected several inches over the next couple of days, enough for the Guadalupe River levels to rise to hold this year's Paddle Parade. Jenny couldn't wait for her kids to experience the night of lights and music that she'd always loved as a child. She only needed to get through the next two days at the Hoffman property, the site of Edenberg's greatest tragedy nearly three decades ago.

Goosebumps prickled her arms every time she thought of the Hoffman Family Camp and the day she'd heard the news. Much like this weekend, the forecast had projected storms and heavy rain throughout the night. Jenny's mom was a nurse and needed to stay at the hospital, so she'd sent her to sleep over at Nichole's house. As always, Robin and Christina were there, Christina painting Robin's nails royal blue. They were seventeen, almost eighteen, and about to enter their senior year.

Christina and Robin were Jenny and Nichole in five years, a prophecy of what was to come. Together, the two made the perfect girl: one—Christina—sharp and steady; the other—Robin—adventurous and witty. Not only were they cool and smart and beautiful, but the older girls also had full-size boobs that the younger girls both envied and feared finding on their own bodies any day now. It was the summer before Jenny and Nichole's eighth-grade year, and the newness of adolescence had widened their eyes to take in the expanding world. They were setting aside Beanie Babies and Barbie dolls to adopt AOL screen names and CD collections.

The night before the tragedy, thunder in the clouds and rain pelting the roof had soothed them to sleep, but Jenny awoke with Nikki's feet in her face. In the early morning the sound of crying echoed from the front of the house, so Jenny shook off the blanket, crawled out of bed, and tiptoed down the hall to find Robin bent over the counter, her head nestled in her forearms. Christina leaned her head against her friend's shoulder. Nichole's mom, dressed for work, slipped off her heels as she held the phone against her ear, speaking in a hushed tone.

"What's wrong?" Jenny whispered, her voice crackly from lack of sleep.

"It's the camp," Christina answered in a soft voice. "There was an accident..." She trailed off as Robin began sobbing again.

The older girls worked at the Hoffman Family Camp, helping out in the kitchen part-time.

"All those kids," Robin said over and over. Those words stuck in Jenny's mind.

All. Those. Kids.

Later, Christina explained that she and Robin had forgotten to set the alarm clock for their shift at the camp, and they'd woken up an hour later than they should've. *Robin thinks that if we'd gotten up in time, we would've seen the rising water, that we could've called and warned them before the campers were loaded onto the bus.*

Even at a young age, Jenny knew such logic was flawed. Shouldn't it be the Hoffmans who checked the rising waters and kept the bus from leaving? Shouldn't they bear the blame?

A form of survivor's guilt, some might call it, but whatever it was, Christina and Robin—and the entire town—changed from that day on.

Now Jenny was on her way to the very place where the worst had happened.

When Jenny had arrived home after the meetup at the wine bar and told her husband about the retreat, his face had lit up like the Guadalupe on the day of the Paddle Parade. She hadn't had the heart to tell him the real reason she wanted to go: to put to bed once and for all what had happened to Beverly Hoffman—and what was happening to Edenberg. Jenny's mom had agreed to stay at their place for a few days to watch the kids.

As he drove to the retreat, Curt gripped the steering wheel with one hand and held out the other to Jenny. She took it for a full minute before pulling away with the pretense of flipping through the instructions for the weekend.

They were basic.

How to get there: *the location is not on Google or Apple Maps.*

An overview of the goals: *to enable you and your significant other to explore yourselves individually and as a purposeful couple.*

Clothes to pack: *three types of outfits: one for outdoors, one business casual, and one formal.*

"After checking in, we drop off our bags and then head to a mixer. There will be thirty couples total," she informed him.

"Who's Nichole bringing again?" Curt asked, checking the rearview mirror even though this far out of town, no one was on the road with them.

"His name is Wes." Jenny looked out the window at the hackberry trees and the giant rows of pecans; on the other side of the road was a cornfield recently harvested.

"And your other friend—Robin—she'll be there with Max?" Curt was trying to make conversation about something other than the kids or the state of their marriage, which was...nice? She reminded herself that normal couples, the thing they'd once been, talked about their friends. It had been so long since they'd been normal. Not for a full year. Not since she'd found those texts that another woman had been sending her husband.

She'd been trying to make a DoorDash order. Her phone had logged her out, so she jumped on the laptop he'd left open in his office. The message box said that he had three unread texts.

Up until that day, she hadn't been the kind of wife to pry. Even though they were open with one another—and perhaps because of it—she didn't feel the need to look through his pockets, check his passwords, or track his phone. They trusted each other. But that red *3* propped like a footnote above the green message icon called to her. Just a quick peek. It was probably work related anyway.

She clicked the app. The sender at the very top was *Tracy* and the first line read, Hey. Are you coming over to...

Wait. Who was Tracy? She couldn't see the rest of the message unless she clicked.

At that moment she had two choices: she could close the app, assume it was an innocent text chain. Or...she could look.

She really did waver, so much so that she almost missed evidence of her husband's infidelity.

As she scrolled, the world she'd so carefully pieced together after her car had been hijacked and she'd resigned from her job…all of that shattered. And she hadn't been able to find the pieces—much less put things back together—ever since.

Now Curt's hands glided along the leather of the steering wheel, driving her to a place he hoped could repair what he'd broken. After another ten minutes, he turned at a gate that had no actual signage.

Jenny sat forward and gazed down the lane at the few yards she could see ahead of her in the gathering darkness. "It looks like we're driving into the middle of nowhere."

"It'll clear up soon. Dr. Hoffman says he likes how we're tucked away back here."

She couldn't help but notice the use of *we*, and she didn't like it.

They made their way through a dense thicket of trees for another three-quarters of a mile, but then the landscape opened to a road lined with solar-panel lights that led to a sprawling estate.

"Here we are," Curt said, pulling in to a parking spot labeled with his name.

Jenny frowned. "You're a contract worker. How do you have your own parking space?"

Curt lifted a shoulder. "I'm here a lot."

They emerged from the car, and in front of them stood a cream stucco fortress with red Spanish-tiled roof. Texas ash and cedar elm trees hedged the stucco. A coyote howled in the distance, and a white flash passed a few yards from their feet as an opossum tried to make its way into thick underbrush.

Jenny shuddered and then looked back to the house, turning her head from side to side. "Doesn't that look like…"

"It's shaped like the Alamo. Apparently, that's how Beverly Hoffman wanted it built. George agreed, says it 'reminds him of the weight of history.'"

Great. Now her husband was quoting this man.

Jenny felt of two minds about Curt's job here: on one hand, it had provided her the opportunity to get more of an inside scoop on the teachings; on the other hand, her husband might seriously be brainwashed by now.

"Strange," Jenny said as if she wasn't concerned. "But I'm actually getting less Alamo vibes. More like Mediterranean meets the Wild West."

Curt opened the trunk and pulled out the rolling bag and the carry-ons they'd packed for the weekend.

As Jenny climbed the steps to the threshold, she considered what she needed to accomplish in two days' time: get close to Dr. Hoffman and find proof that his wife's death wasn't an accident. A simple agenda with complex implications.

Jenny gazed at the massive house. She knew that uncovering the truth would make for a killer story, but more than that, she was beginning to crave justice for all the Beverlies of the world.

17

NICHOLE

As she drove up I-35 to pick up Wes for their bespoke weekend—instead of the "Wild Nights" curriculum, the unmarrieds were subjected to a "Waiting Works Wonders" handout—Nichole's mind went to Brian, as it often did despite wishing she could exorcise all thoughts of him, especially with this new chance at some semblance of happiness with Wes.

Four years ago she'd first spotted Brian across the playground's blacktop at the elementary school carnival as he stepped from number to number at the Cake Walk Booth. The carnival was an annual tradition for residents, and it was especially popular that year since the Hoffmans' sponsorship had brought in a Ferris wheel and bumper cars.

Christina drove up from Galveston, where she worked, to support the school and relive the nostalgia of her childhood. The sisters had attended every Blacktop Carnival since Christina started school, and since she was five, Nichole had dressed as the Stay Puft Marshmallow Man from *Ghostbusters*. Christina acted as her bodyguard, clearing the way for Nichole's wide, white costume. She would upgrade her size every year, so she could stuff filched candy into the inflatable arms and legs. By the end of the night, her calves were nearly overflowing with melted KitKat bars, rolls of pastel-colored Smarties, and pink Starbursts.

The look on Brian's face when his number was called to come forward and select his cake was so delighted that you would've thought he'd won a much better prize than a lemon confection baked by one of the PTA moms.

"That's the guy I brought with me," Christina said, walking up to her and pulling her into a hug. Nichole had been so busy with her assigned duty that she hadn't gotten to say hello. "He's a huge nerd," Christina added. "You'd like him."

Nichole knew that being a nerd was a high compliment from Christina, who had won every geography bee, quiz bowl, and trivia game she'd ever attempted. "He's studying virology at UTMB. Twenty-eight and supposedly some kind of wunderkind. His name is Brian."

"So you two are...?" Nichole prodded.

"Friends. Colleagues," Christina answered. "He's new to Texas, never been to the hill country, so I told him he could tag along. He's renting a room at the bed-and-breakfast."

Brian walked over, holding his Saran-wrapped prize for them to see. "I cannot believe I won an entire cake. I never win anything."

His asymmetrical smile was charming, his lips curling in a way that reminded her of Elvis. He had a sweep of black hair and wore thick-rimmed white glasses.

"Brian, this is my sister, Nichole. She's a saint for teaching all of these hooligans running around." Christina motioned to the ghouls and superheroes and princesses strung out on sugar. "Nichole, this is my newest lab partner, Brian."

"That's a nice way of saying she's actually my boss. I hold the vials, and she mixes the potions." Brian stretched out a hand to Nichole. "What grade do you teach?"

"I taught kinder for a few years, but last year I moved to second grade and love it."

Christina lifted a shoulder and said with a smile, "We can't all live on an island and get a thrill out of working with Ebola."

Nichole liked Brian immediately. Living in a small town, she didn't meet many men, except for the ones who were passing through as tourists—and most of them were taken. Earlier that year Genetive had conducted their first workshop for single men—a prospect that had intrigued her until she happened to run into one of the attendees at the bookstore, a handsome guy who asked her to coffee only to talk about how important it was for men to protect and provide for women in these changing times. She'd run as fast as she could.

After the carnival the three of them went out for enchiladas and margaritas at El Vaquero, Christina's favorite, and the next day Brian asked for Nichole's number. Within a few weeks, they were doing the long-distance thing, and she was falling hard.

Nichole loved that every few weekends when she drove down to Galveston, she saw not only Brian but her sister, the person she adored most in this world. The three of them would take ghost tours on the Strand and visit the historical society's homes on Broadway. They ate at the Mosquito Cafe, drank coffee at MOD's, and watched movies at the only theater on the island, out west where the Seawall ended. After a full day Nichole and Brian would drop Christina off at her condo before heading to his apartment, where they would hole up until they saw her sister the next morning for brunch. It was a good life.

After Nichole and Brian dated for a year, he transferred to a job in San Antonio and moved in with her. Nichole begged Christina to apply at labs in San Antonio and Austin, to get all three of them in the same place, but her sister refused, content to stay on the island in the same job she'd had for years.

On Nichole's way to work on a chilly day this past February, her sister hadn't answered her phone when Nichole called like she did every morning. She figured Christina was sleeping in. She'd earned a morning off after being awarded a big grant the day before. She'd probably stayed out late celebrating.

Around 10 a.m. though, while Nichole was in the middle of teaching a math lesson on congruent shapes and symmetrical lines, the assistant principal had walked in and taken over the class so Nichole could step into the hallway where Brian was waiting to tell her the news. His face was swollen and his nose runny as he pulled her into his arms.

Christina had been in a terrible accident. Something about her car and the Seawall. Words Nichole's mind couldn't form into complete thoughts. One of his former colleagues had seen it on the local news and called Brian immediately.

Christina had been enjoying a lovely evening with four co-workers. She'd had two glasses of wine over several hours. It was February and the island fog had rolled in a few hours after the sun set, a hazy web that could entangle even locals. Her car careened over the edge of the Seawall near Sixty-First Street at high tide, landing upside down.

Nichole and Brian had been discussing the possibility of marriage, but after Christina's accident, it didn't seem right to talk about a future that her sister would never see. Why get married? Why have kids? What was the point of it all?

Nichole knew her nihilistic questions hadn't helped their relationship find a way forward, but she still wasn't quite sure of the exact reason why Brian eventually left. She knew she told him to, but even she couldn't exactly pinpoint when. Maybe she'd had one too many, a pattern that had only worsened.

Nichole missed Brian, but not as much as she missed her sister. If she could will one of them back, she wouldn't need a single second to consider whom she would summon.

Nichole thought about all of this as she drove toward San Antonio, toward a new man and all the new possibilities that came with him. Part of her wanted to turn the car around and head for the hills, but another part of her was hoping that she might start to feel alive again.

18

JENNY

Curt followed Jenny up the steps, and one of the giant stained wooden double doors swung open before they could knock. The foyer was a light marble with swirls of the faintest tint of red that matched the stucco roof. It was Max Hoffman, Robin's husband and heir apparent.

"Welcome," Max said, his smile not quite reaching his eyes. He wore a dark blue fitted suit with a maroon tie, a bit too patriotic for Jenny's tastes, but she probably didn't like the look because he was the spitting image of a young George Hoffman in the photos she'd been examining this week.

"Max, good to see you again," Curt said, extending a hand.

"You, too." Max's face stretched into an actual smile at seeing Curt. "Glad you two could make it."

It sounded like they were here for a party rather than a transformative experience.

"Are we late?" Curt inquired politely, an apologetic tone lacing his words.

"You're fine." Max stepped back to usher them inside. "If you'll place your keys and your phones here…" He opened a safety-deposit box lined with small plastic inserts.

Curt didn't hesitate, but Jenny demurred. "I left mine at home."

Curt shot her a look. He'd seen her hide her phone inside a rolled-up T-shirt, but he wasn't about to call her out, and she was not about to hand over their only way out of this place. Curt could obey as if he didn't have a choice, but Jenny knew better. You always have a choice.

As they stepped farther into the estate, Jenny took in the series of giant photographs lining the stairway, all of them hill country landscapes.

Max caught her gaze. "Those are in and around Enchanted Rock. My mother loved to support local artists as well as collect the expensive stuff."

That rang true with what Jenny had seen at the Hoffman Gallery. As Jenny stood staring up at the flowering cacti, the flat stone, and the sunset printed on canvas in the marbled foyer, a young man appeared from nowhere to take their bags. He was dressed in all black and appeared to be a college student.

"One of our interns," Max informed them before turning to the young man. "They're in the *Sam Houston Suite*."

Just then George strode in wearing a bolo tie with a turquoise pendant. "Mr. Martin, good to see you and your lovely bride." Dr. Hoffman turned to Jenny and wrapped both of his hands around hers. His grip was like a damp cave. "Jenny, thanks for letting us borrow your husband. He's been doing wonderful things for our team. Fits right in." That last phrase made her cringe, but she composed herself as George turned to his son. "Welcome reception's set for a half hour from now?"

Max nodded diminutively.

"I'll be in my study till then." Dr. Hoffman checked his Rolex. "You two are going to love this weekend. So glad your mom could watch the kids, Jenny."

She startled at the mention of her children and darted a glance at her husband, who didn't seem to think it alarming that George knew things about their lives. Did Curt have actual conversations with this man? Did he…open up? Her stomach turned at the idea of them confiding in one another…although, that could be useful.

"We keep the schedule pretty tight around here," Max told them after his father gave a broad smile and left. "If you'll follow Lewis up the stairs, he'll make sure you're settled in. As the instructions say, you'll want to change into something more—" he looked at both of them in their jeans and T-shirts "—refined for the reception."

At the top of the stairs, Lewis turned right and led them past six other closed doors, all of which Jenny assumed must be ac-commodations with en-suite bathrooms.

Despite their suite being named after the statesman, general, and third president of the Republic of Texas, Sam Houston, the room was painted a pale lavender with lilacs and forget-me-nots stenciled in diamond patterns along the wall. The king-size bed was overshadowed by a cream canopy and faced a window over-looking the back of the house. Jenny peered out to see a stone patio, a full-length pool, and greenery that extended until it ran into forested overgrowth. The stars would soon be visible this far out of the city, and the fading sun illuminated a kitchen garden that wound around the side of the house.

"This suite was Mrs. Hoffman's favorite," Lewis said as he set down the bag. "She stayed here when she was teaching or participating in the workshops or retreats."

"Is that right?" Jenny's interest piqued at the opportunity for inside information. "How long have you been working here?"

Curt gently shook his head, but it wasn't like he didn't know why she was here. Okay, she hadn't exactly told him her *real* reasons for coming this weekend, and he might be under the mistaken impression that she'd moved on from her suspicions about Beverly Hoffman's death. But he should know her bet-ter after fifteen years.

Curt moved to hand Lewis a five-dollar bill for bringing their bags to the room, but the kid waved away the money. "I don't accept tips, but thank you," Lewis said before turning back to Jenny. "I started here my senior year of high school, but I'm a junior at UT now, so this is my fourth year at Genetive. I'm hoping to get a full-time position after graduation."

Jenny noticed that he wore a circular pin, similar to the ones she'd seen on Beverly and George in pictures, except this one was silver and instead of jewels, there were two black letters— *RF*—in the center.

Jenny pointed at his shoulder. "I thought Max called you Lewis? Why does your pin say *RF*?"

He glanced at the pin and smiled. "Oh, those aren't my initials. It stands for *Respice finem*, Latin for..."

Curt cut in, proud to know the answer. *"Consider the end."*

Jenny's eyes cut to her husband and then back to the young man. "Why attach a reminder to *consider the end* to your shoulder?"

Lewis's head oscillated to her. "Before participants at Genetive are twenty-five years old, we're enrolled in the Apprentice Program. We cannot attend most of the seminars and workshops, but we can listen in if we're working at them."

"You work for free?" Jenny was taken aback upon realizing anew why the college student hadn't been able to take a five-dollar tip—he wasn't allowed. "But you're in school."

"Knowledge is our currency," Lewis answered evenly. "That's what Dr. Hoffman says."

Oh, Lord. Jenny could easily believe George would spout that kind of nonsense.

"Did you know Mrs. Hoffman? Did you ever hear her speak at one of the events? Did Dr. Hoffman stay here with her, in this room?"

Curt raised an eyebrow, signaling for her to stop with all the questions.

The student shook his head and smiled as he moved toward the door. "Mrs. Hoffman liked to be on-site whenever Dr. Hoffman was conducting his workshops and retreats, but she only ever taught or counseled the women, and in the last few months, she wasn't doing much of that. As for Dr. Hoffman, he's usually in his office or out at the cottages."

The cottages? Jenny was about to ask, but Curt stepped closer to the door.

"Thanks for helping us get settled." Curt motioned for Lewis to leave.

Lewis gave a faint smile and a quick bow. "Of course, sir. May you have a productive evening."

Curt smiled back and closed the door behind him. As he shut it, Jenny caught sight of the painting—one in line with Beverly's taste—that had been hidden when they entered. The image was of a dark-haired woman upending a uniformed man into a water well.

Curt followed Jenny's eyes to the artwork. "That's disconcerting."

Jenny took the suitcase, placed it on the bed, and reached for the T-shirt that held her phone. She took it out, grateful to see that she still had service out here, before studying the painting for a signature.

No signed name, but etched into the bottom of the stone well was the information she was looking for: *Elizab Sirani, 1659.*

She googled a few details along with the artist's name to find that this painting was *Timoclea Killing Her Rapist* by the Baroque artist Elisabetta Sirani, a painter and teacher of female artists. It was one of her most well-known works and detailed the story of Timoclea from Plutarch's biography of Alexander the Great. After the destruction of Timoclea's city, a captain had raped her and then asked if she knew where any money had been hidden. She told him yes, walked him to the well, pushed him in, and then piled stones on him until he died. Revenge at its finest.

Curt took Jenny's phone and tucked it inside a drawer on the end table. "Can we at least try to follow the rules this weekend?"

"I can't help it. I'm curious," Jenny prevaricated. "George and Beverly, they became this power couple, and they...changed so many lives. Don't you wonder how he...how they...built this?"

Curt narrowed his gaze as Jenny reached into the suitcase to unpack the three days' worth of clothes they'd brought. "Are you just here for a story?"

She didn't answer. He knew her well.

"That's what I suspected when you said you wanted to come this weekend, especially with those questions you were asking about Beverly's death." He sat on the end of the bed and studied Jenny before sighing ever so slightly. "Look, I've worked with George for the past couple of months, and some of his views are old-fashioned, but...I don't know...have you thought about what this weekend—what taking time for ourselves—could do for our marriage?"

"Yeah," Jenny answered too quickly. "I mean, of course."

"*Yeah?* That's the answer you give when I ask if you want spaghetti for dinner, not for a question about *us.*"

Jenny sat next to him, their legs a few inches apart. It wasn't that she didn't want to forgive him. She still remembered the way they would morph into a single organism on the couch while watching a movie, arms and legs draped over one another, a popcorn bowl between them. She missed nuzzling into him each night before bed and sharing a shower before they ran out of hot water in their first tiny apartment. She even missed arguing over who would get up with the kids in the middle of the night, shoving one another and mumbling *your turn* until one of them, usually her, gave in.

She supposed that she could tell Curt what had happened years ago in their driveway when a serial killer had wedged a knife between her shoulder blades, but what was the point now? He would feel sorry for her, and she would feel ashamed that she hadn't dared to tell him earlier—and that she'd let this one moment determine her career.

Jenny understood that couples could move past secrets and infidelity. She read "Modern Love" and listened to Esther Perel. That was how Jenny knew that other issues were at play, namely that she wasn't sure she wanted to do the work required to trust him again. She wasn't sure she wanted to sift through the rubble and rebuild what they'd broken.

Marriage required vulnerability and sacrifice, two things that had waned ever since she quit her job, stayed home with the kids, and experienced the tedium of mothering and housekeeping. Yes, the affair had been the nail in the coffin, the last straw, the tipping point, but she'd shut her mouth and her heart long before.

She met his eyes even though she knew it wasn't her job to bridge this gap between them.

"You know I'm trying, right?" Curt put a hand over hers. "I need you to at least meet me a quarter of the way here. I'm happy to do the other seventy-five percent. Shoot, I'll take ten percent if that's all you've got, but I need you to try. At least a little."

Jenny didn't say what she was really thinking: that this week she'd awakened in the middle of the night from a dream in which she was the one face down in the Guadalupe, that sometimes when she was home with the kids—even before she found out he was talking to another woman—she'd felt like she was drowning in only a few inches of water.

Giving up her career, though it had felt necessary at the time, had also been like a punch to her gut. Maybe that was why Jenny felt a kinship with Beverly that went even further than her desire to see justice. She imagined Beverly might've felt the same: that she could do, could be, could have…more.

Curt stared at the ceiling for a few seconds. "Okay, so I'm aware that some of what George says is over the top, but this is a weekend to ourselves, and I figure it can be what we make of it. At least we'll have time alone to talk without Emmy and Austen running circles around us. We can even fight in more than two-minute increments if you want."

When he reached for her hand again, she let him hold it. That was all she could do for him, but he seemed satisfied.

Jenny smiled faintly. "I guess I can fight uninterrupted with you this weekend if that's what you really want."

For a few seconds, they felt normal again.

"It is," he said, surprising Jenny by leaning in for a quick kiss, the first they'd shared in nearly a year.

She closed her eyes and let him.

Seven-Point Mission Statement of Genetive Inc.*

If you feel like your life is divided and chaotic and without purpose, we are here to help. If you feel like your family system is breaking down, we are here to help. If you feel like your work is disordered and meaningless, we are here to help. Read below to find out more about the key principles guiding our organization.

I. At Genetive Inc. we believe that a natural order exists in the world. The individual must learn his or her place in this hierarchical society and adhere to the dictates set forth by the natural order. Genetics, race, gender, and ability determine one's place, but that said, we also believe that, with help, each individual can reach his or her own potential within the established hierarchy.

II. Genetive Inc. strives to make a more perfect society. No culture, time period, or people have been or ever will be without fault; however, it is essential for us to take the best from each social system to create a better world. Founder Dr. George Hoffman has studied a variety of cultures and social systems; he uses this wealth of knowledge to help individuals neurologically remap their brains so they can become their best selves.

III. Genetive Inc. acknowledges power of all kinds: physical, spiritual, mental, and emotional. We also attempt to increase the power of those most worthy while stripping away power from the undeserving. The powerful should use their position to guide and direct society into an evolved state of being. Those in this organization have been awarded the honor of power, and they will learn how to use their strengths to guide those around them into a better tomorrow.

IV. At Genetive Inc. we encourage community. Those outside of the Genetive family may not understand the magnitude of the work here. In order to discourage naysayers of the organization's curriculum, discussions, and workshops, content must remain private and confidential. Resources and material may not be shared online or outside the organization.

V. At Genetive Inc. we accept Biblically established gender roles. Men are the heads of the households, and women must remain in submission to the head. To that end, we believe that a woman's place is in the home during the formative years of children's lives. Healthy, well-adjusted children are the product of a blessed union and should be nurtured and celebrated.

VI. At Genetive Inc. we believe in continued research. While our workshops and retreats are not necessarily opportunities for ongoing research, each attendee must sign a consent form in order to participate in events. As in life, any given moment should be a learning opportunity. To that end, we also encourage those who adhere to our program to invest financially in all endeavors that Genetive Inc. undertakes.

VII. At Genetive Inc. we embrace creativity. We encourage cutting-edge therapeutic intervention to lead our members to wholeness and happiness. Together, we can make a new and improved you.

★This is an internal document. Please do not share publicly.

BEVERLY

ONE WEEK POSTMORTEM
THE NIGHT OF THE FIRE

From high above the town we built, I've had time to think, and this is what I've realized: one doesn't make a monster overnight.

As a boy, George was given everything he asked for—trips, bikes, cars—but not the one thing he really needed—discipline. The entitlement and spoiling was a Hoffman family tradition.

I grew up watching George, just like the rest of this town, and when he finally noticed me, I was over the moon. Here I was, a farm girl whose parents birthed four girls and tended failing cotton crops, hob-knobbing with the rich and powerful. All because I was the prettiest girl in our school.

Perhaps that sounds arrogant, but maybe you'll feel differently when you understand that my blond hair, trim figure, ample bosom, and golden eyes were the only currency I had to offer. I knew I had to make the most of them—not only for myself, but for my family. A connection to the Hoffmans meant good things would come the way of everyone connected to me.

It had to be the indulgence of being an only child in a well-to-do family that made George rather...self-absorbed, for lack of a kinder word. It also was the thing that propelled him into his field of study.

Back then, all the hullabaloo in psychology was about animal studies. People raising chimps alongside their own children had become mostly a thing of the past, but it had only been a decade or two since Dr. John Lilly started injecting LSD into sea creatures and Margaret Lovatt tried to teach a dolphin named Peter to speak English. These were wild times.

George found such ideas tedious and unworthy of scientific study—much less the money necessary to fund such ridiculousness. He wanted to study people. He wanted to take the class philosophy of Karl Marx and the historical theories of Michel Foucault and apply them to modern-day contexts. His entire focus became understanding what made a handful of individuals powerful while most of humanity remained weak.

"What do you mean by *weak*?" I'd asked while he was writing his Philosophy of Psychology Essay for his grad school application. "For example, would you call me weak?"

"No, sweetheart. Never weak." He'd looked at me with tenderness. "Wounded, yes, but from this you will grow stronger. You do have me, after all."

At the time I'd smiled, thinking he was teasing. Now I know he was completely serious.

In the 1970s and '80s in our tiny town, psychology was not a well-known field of study. In fact, it was almost an act of rebellion. Between his career ambitions and selecting me as his wife, his parents weren't happy with him for a handful of years, especially since I couldn't even give them a proper grandchild. But then Max came along, and George became a doctor—even if it was in a useless field—and by the time we were nearing thirty, their favor shone on him once again. Besides, they were getting old and would need someone to inherit their wealth.

When he told me that the focus of his doctoral dissertation would be on family systems theory, I was delighted that he'd taken such a keen interest in something that would make us stronger together. Little did I know.

His adviser had actually encouraged him to dive into a newly coined term in *The Diagnostic and Statistical Manual of Mental Disorders*: narcissistic personality disorder. From this vantage point, my guess is that he refused the advice because he saw too much of himself in the diagnostic criteria. Although, maybe narcissists can't see much of anything real in themselves. What do I know?

Instead, he convinced his adviser that a study in family systems theory would allow him to pursue what had interested him for as long as he could remember. He would examine how power and influence—and even affection—were acquired and utilized within the smallest unit of human organization: the family unit. He would not, however, confine his definition of family to a husband and wife and children. He would observe interpersonal relationships within the home, sure, but also classrooms, workplaces, and nonprofits.

For the last two years of his program, George set up a camera in our home. He enlisted five other families to do the same. He sat in his office and scribbled notes. He experimented on his own students. Then, he spent hours a day poring over his findings. When he was finished, his adviser was impressed.

I know what you're wondering: What exactly was in that fabulous dissertation? Wouldn't it be great if I actually knew? But honestly, after having to watch every word and action for two years of being videoed in my own home, I had no desire to read what he'd surmised about me and Max.

From what I gather from everything that Genetive teaches, he learned that (surprise!) men have more power than women and that the rich have more power than the poor. He also learned a lot about how to manipulate people, to tell them enough of what they want to hear (you're worthy, you're smart, you're better than the other guy!) to get them to read his books and give him money and invite him to speak at conferences.

The strange thing is that even when I began to doubt him, I mostly agreed with his teachings in principle. That's how it is with him: a spoonful of truth chased by a speck of a lie still makes the medicine go down. To this day George is seen as a strong man, as a good husband, as a generous father, but that was only because the people in his life—his wife and his child—behaved.

After he'd been teaching and publishing articles for several years, he decided to continue his research by founding our camp. Guardians (his favorite subjects were orphaned) signed consent forms and the kids took a twenty-minute questionnaire before they so much as put their bags on their bunks. Then, off he went to study data while campers attended their first archery class. Throughout the week, he would rearrange things based on their answers.

Maybe they expected a hike, so he would switch that hour to time in the pool instead. Or he'd send half of the kids on the hike and send the other half to the pool and watch how they interacted afterward. Were there more arguments between the children? Fewer arguments? The same as the previous week's test subjects? Which was more preferable—time in nature or splashing around in the chlorine? Which did the children view as more desirous? And most of all, who held the most power throughout it all?

Sometimes I felt like I could tell him his results without all the trouble, but I let him do his thing, and he let me do mine.

I adored the children, their silly antics at mealtime and their sleepy grins at the end of a long day of swimming and kayaking and shooting. George loved them for their wiry brains.

He started many of his sentences with *Let's see how they behave when...*, but most of the things he did were harmless, really. Mixing them into new groups halfway through the week. Leaving one less chair in a discussion session. Allowing only the losers of the game into the ice-cream social.

"When you tip normal on its axis, that's when things get interesting," George would tell me.

To my everlasting shame, I let him tilt away.

Excerpt from Video: "A Man's Place Is In the Home"
featuring George Hoffman
Produced by Genetive Inc.

Script: In the first two centuries after America's founding, the man was expected to act as the breadwinner, a term first recorded only seven years after our founding fathers signed the "Declaration of Independence." From time immemorial, men have been expected to leave the house—or hut or tent or teepee—each morning, to work diligently at their trade or as a huntsman, and to return each evening to provide bountifully for their wives and offspring.

I want to open to you a new concept today, one in which the man's place is actually more inside than outside of the home. I know, I know, hear me out, men. I'm not suggesting that you neglect any of your necessary duties. You should provide and protect, but by necessity, that provision and protection must mean that you spend as much time as possible at home.

Think of Odysseus battling monsters and manipulating goddesses, but all the while, his heart yearns for what? For home.

And it's not only you who should be yearning to have a wife and a family and a respectable place to call home. Your wife and children should be happy to have you near them. They should benefit from your presence and your leadership.

Do not yell at your children unless it is for their good. Do not belittle your wife unless you are teaching her respect. They need your leadership to follow. After all, as Aristotle said in *Politics*, "The male, unless constituted in some respect contrary to nature, is by nature more expert at leading than the female."

Men, do not live contrary to your nature. Go home. Lead your families. They will thank you.

19

NICHOLE

The grand hall was in the center of the estate and had four entrances, labeled with North, South, East, West. The high ceiling did little to alleviate the claustrophobic feeling of the dark gray walls lit by sconces. A black grand piano stood in the corner. No seating was available, as if this room was merely for show, not enjoyment or relaxation.

Nichole wore a floral shift dress and glanced around for Jenny and Robin while Wes went to the bar to get her a drink. She knew none of the couples in their semiformal attire, but she did vaguely recognize one or two of them from somewhere… perhaps they were actors or news anchors or politicians. That was the kind of person she expected to see this weekend.

She was extra-anxious, thinking about Brian and Christina all the way here. Once she'd arrived on property—the site of the once infamous Hoffman Camp—she'd added Beverly and all those children to the swirling vortex of her mind. This place had to be full of ghosts.

Nichole was keenly aware, after watching participants trickle in, that she and Wes were the only people of color in this space. Wes could pass as a tanned white dude, she supposed, so really, that left her. She'd become used to such a thing living in a small Texas town and being raised in a white family, but she'd naively assumed that if visitors were coming from across the US, surely there would be someone else who looked like her. That did not appear to be the case.

Wes handed her a drink with a smile as Jenny approached her from behind and tapped her on the shoulder, startling her.

"Sorry to frighten you," Jenny whispered. She was wearing a floor-length black dress and a blue jewel-toned shrug. "What are you drinking?"

"I don't even know." Nichole held the pink drink in a long-stemmed glass and took a first sip before almost spitting it out. "What the crap? It's a mocktail."

"Didn't you read the brochure? It's a 'dry' weekend," Wes said with a smile.

"How are we supposed to get through *this* without fortification?"

The room filled with men and women in their forties, fifties, and sixties. The sound of chatter and delighted greetings hummed around them, and several laughs echoed across the marble floor.

Nichole opened the purse on her arm and pulled out a flask. "Good thing I brought a bit of my own." She poured a generous portion into her glass and offered some to Jenny, who shook her head and frowned.

"I need to be alert this weekend." Jenny gave her a pointed look. "Are you sure you don't want to take a break? Just for the weekend?"

Nichole grimaced. "Jenny. Seriously? This is not the time to stop drinking."

Jenny pursed her lips as her gaze wandered over the crowd. She did a double take when her eyes landed on a beautiful brunette woman in the corner. She elbowed Nichole. "Is that…?"

Nichole glanced over her friend's shoulder and raised her

eyebrows. The woman was an actress, a supporting character on a show they'd both watched as teenagers.

"It seems that we are among the rich and famous this weekend," Nichole teased, taking a sip of what was now a passable drink.

Silverware pinged against a glass, and George emerged from the crowd into the center of the room with a flute of something bubbly. Max and Robin stood only a few feet behind him.

"Thank you all for coming this weekend. And, more importantly, for taking time to work on you and your relationships," George said. "We began conducting this specific retreat two years ago after Beverly read a piece in *Family Today* about the increase of the divorce rate in America over the past fifty years. She came to me in tears, saying that we had to do something to help marriages thrive again. Because this retreat was her idea and because she was my truest and best partner, I'd like to officially begin this weekend by toasting my beloved wife." He lifted his glass and raised his eyes to the ceiling. "I will miss you every day, Beverly."

Robin's face turned down as the man toasted his wife.

A respectful silence blanketed the room until Max, his features thoughtful and reserved, spoke. "To my mother." He raised his glass and took a sip. Everyone followed suit.

"Thank you, son." George took a deep breath. "As you may have surmised, there are two primary tracks of the retreat this weekend, with several mini-tracks that spur off them. Depending on how many Genetive events you've attended, you'll know that tailoring classes and workshops to your needs is our *modus operandi*. A bespoke experience, if you will.

"With that said, I'd like to introduce two lovely people, Senator Jim Riley and his wife, Mrs. Riley, who've attended more than a dozen workshops and retreats, separately and as a couple, and will be teaching their own seminar for the first time."

Nichole's eyes followed George's hand to the couple standing nearby. They both wore gold pins with emeralds that glimmered in the lights. The crowd applauded their perseverance—or perhaps their ability to pay the exorbitant cost of all the training.

"Within these two primary tracks—one for married couples and one for those considering nuptials—you'll find that schedules vary, depending on the concerns we flagged in the psychological profiles you completed two weeks ago."

Nichole was keenly aware that she'd completed her own profile only last night after arriving home from the wine bar and pouring herself a glass of brandy that hadn't helped her sleep as well as she'd hoped. She could only imagine the nonsense she'd written in the boxes online, asking about her family history and whether or not she had fantasies about ruling the world.

"On your schedules you'll notice that some activities and seminars overlap with small groups of attendees, but others are deliberately individuated in order to cater to your stage of personal development and coupledom."

Nichole nearly snickered at the way George said *coupledom* in a velvety tone. Wes placed his arm across her shoulders, and she wished she could melt into him. He was such a good sport, coming along with her this weekend. She'd texted him the invite, and he hadn't even thought she was nuts for suggesting it. A good man, that one.

"This evening, after you've had time to mingle and eat a few hors d'oeuvres, you'll receive a tablet with an electronic schedule. This schedule may change throughout the weekend based on how you and your partner progress, so please keep it with you at all times and be sure to course-correct as needed. First-timers often end up in the wrong place during the weekend, so checking your schedule at least ten minutes before the next event is essential."

A few chuckles rose, presumably from those who'd been the lost first-timers.

"Our goal for this weekend is not only that you will grow

in your love for one another, but also that you will better understand yourself and your potential," George said, lifting his glass again.

Senator Jim this time offered a *there, there*. "To George Hoffman," he called loudly, and the room erupted in applause and hoots that lasted for a full thirty seconds.

There, there? Why was the senator using such an odd turn of phrase? And why was everyone applauding George? For his scheduling abilities? For helping so many reach their potential? God, all she wanted to do was crawl in bed next to Wes. Then she remembered he had a separate room.

Wes leaned against her, breathing into her ear in a way that sent a shiver up her spine even though the words weren't at all romantic. "This guy's good at controlling a room."

Nichole tilted her head and then looked at him. "Who? The senator?"

"No. George. These people love him."

"He wrote some books," Nichole said vaguely before pulling out her flask again and offering it to him.

Wes let her pour. "Good idea. I'm not sure how far a Shirley Temple will get me this weekend."

"Here's to two more days," she said as she poured a couple thimblefuls more into her own glass.

20

JENNY

George put up both hands as if halting an oncoming bus.

"Thank you, thank you." He took a steadying breath and pushed back his shoulders. "But this weekend is all about you and your needs. To that end, our hosts are bringing around a sealed envelope for each couple."

As soon as he said the words, several workers wearing all black and holding stacks of thick envelopes appeared at the two entryways.

Jenny shifted, running a hand across her collarbone. She was suddenly warm and could use a glass of water. She'd spent so much time anticipating this weekend, imagining the man who'd founded Genetive Inc. But here he was, just a person with flesh and blood and bones.

She hadn't expected George—the man she'd come to see as a potential killer—to be this composed, this sincere. He wasn't the mad scientist or domineering dictator she'd imagined. He was warm, inviting, charming. Maybe that was what made him so dangerous.

After the research she'd conducted this week, Jenny would sum up Genetive and George's basic message this way: some people are born to be at the top of the social hierarchy while others are meant to be in service to them. One seemed able to move up the ranks of Genetive Inc. by attending—and paying for—lessons and workshops and retreats in order to tap into their own power. A straightfoward system.

Last night Jenny had taken home several folders from Robin's wine bar and spent a few hours looking through the contents until she found notes from an interview that the *Gazette* had written about years ago. In it, Beverly openly described the levels at Genetive. Each rank in the program was signified by the number of jewels set into circular pins and worn on the shoulder.

The first level—the simple gold circle without a jewel, the one she could presumably aspire to this weekend—were the Listeners. Their purpose was to listen and regurgitate the information that Genetive poured into them. Next were the Learners. Then the Guides. After them came the Leaders, and at the very top, the Essentials.

Of course, besides Beverly, only white men had risen to the highest level of the organization. Racism and sexism weren't directly woven into the message, but privilege and oppression seethed just beneath the surface, and Jenny was fairly certain that any high-ranking positions were off-limits to almost anyone with extra melanin in their skin or without a penis.

George brought her back to the present. "It's almost nine p.m. now, and you'll notice that there's nothing else on the agenda this evening except for you and your partner to read over your letters, sign them, and place them on the foyer table in a designated receptacle. No one will read the contents of this envelope except for you, your partner, and your assigned counselor, who will discuss the outcomes during your coaching sessions."

He looked around the room, smiling and making eye contact with each person—well, each man. "In the morning please look for the electronic itinerary that I mentioned earlier. It will be placed outside of your door and, remember, it's subject to change, depending on how the retreat progresses for you and yours."

Senator Jim stepped forward as Dr. Hoffman made his exit to another scattering of applause. "Here at the Hoffman Retreat Center, we have a lovely patio with strands of lights, an outdoor firepit in the back, and—of course—your excellent room accommodations. Feel free to spread out, read the contents together, and discuss as long as you need before signing and placing them in the foyer. With that, you are dismissed for the evening." He put his hand on the small of his wife's back to lead her away. "Enjoy, everyone!"

The sound system began playing easy jazz over the speakers, and with that, those who'd attended these retreats previously wandered away.

21

NICHOLE

"I guess we'll need to chat outside," Wes chuckled as he rubbed Nichole's shoulders. "Remember, the two of us aren't allowed in one another's rooms."

"I think they put all of us *unmarrieds* on the third floor in some kind of servants' quarters," Nichole said to Jenny and Curt. "The rooms are tiny."

Curt finished off the last sip of his drink. "We'll see you tomorrow, then," he said too eagerly, and Jenny raised her eyebrows before giving Nichole a hug.

"Send me a screenshot of your envelope," Jenny whispered into her ear, knowing Nichole wouldn't have allowed her phone to be confiscated either.

"Shall we?" Wes offered his arm and escorted Nichole outside to an oversize patio chair.

A wood-beamed portico covered a stone terrace lined in blue and green outdoor carpets, which was a good thing since the rain continued to beat down above them. The chairs sported all-weather cushions and were arranged for intimate conversations. Low yellow light shone from the electric candles, strings of fairy lights, and lanterns lining the walls. Beyond the patio was a firepit and a pool. A handful of couples had also stepped onto the porch with their refilled glasses, but the space was so large and people were speaking so softly as the rain fell around them that there was a sense of privacy in the open space.

"Should we read our letter?" Wes asked after settling into the seat beside her. Both of their first names were calligraphed in gold lettering across the front, and Wes wiggled his eyebrows as if they were about to open some kind of prize.

"Go ahead." Nichole shrugged. "The host handed it to you."

Wes propped the missive in his open palm for a few seconds, almost as if trying to weigh the contents before ripping the top off in one quick gesture and reading in a low voice that only the two of them could hear.

"Dear Wes & Nichole,
Welcome to the Genetive Relationship Retreat. We hope that you find your stay comfortable. You are on the first step of your journey to a better you and a better partnership."

"Ooo...exciting. I didn't know I could be even better," Wes joked.

Nichole lifted her pointer and rotated it in the air to tell him to move along.

"If you find this weekend beneficial, we invite you to attend another such retreat, as no two are alike. We pride ourselves on making each experience unique and unmatchable."

Wes sped up for a few more lines. He obviously wasn't expecting a useless sales pitch, but slowed again as he got to his name.

"Wes,
Based on the responses in your evaluation, we believe that this weekend should be one of rest and reflection. You've been working hard to grow your business. In the past three years, you've

opened three new locations, and based on your credit score, you are financially sound. Well done."

"My credit score?" Wes muttered. "I had no idea they'd be digging that deep."

"You gotta read the fine print," Nichole told him. "I mean, not that I read it—Jenny told me." She leaned her head against the cushion and closed her eyes. "Keep reading."

"During the free time allotted on your schedule, we encourage you to take a guided tour of the grounds, enjoy a long nap, or participate in one of our meditation sessions. You may sign up for these by calling ★4 from your bedroom phone or by stopping by the Great Room in the morning between 7–8 a.m. You will also, of course, participate in all of the scheduled events and activities—a variety of them with your partner—listed on your schedule. If you agree to follow the guidance set forth in this document, please sign and date at the bottom and place in the mailbox in the foyer."

Wes looked up from the letter. "That sounds easy enough. You want to read yours?"

"Not really." Despite her answer, she took it and began skimming the contents.

"Out loud, please," Wes said, sounding like a teacher.

She inhaled. "Fine."

"Nichole,
We are so excited that you are joining us this weekend to work on the most important person in your life: you. Based on the responses to our questions, we believe this weekend should be one of growth and reflection. In the past year, you've suffered two major losses—the death of..."

Nichole trailed off, her eyes suddenly tearing. "I didn't tell them that. How would they…"

Sensing her distress, Wes sat up straighter and rubbed her arm. "Oh, whoa. It's okay." He reached out a hand and placed it on her knee. "You don't have to read it—or I can do it for you. We really just came for the food."

She took a deep breath and wiped at her eyes. Nichole could—and would—get through a damn letter. She had the instinct to reach for her flask, but instead, she gritted her teeth, determined to finish.

"…two major losses—the death of your sister and a breakup. This weekend will allow you time to process. As such, Nichole, during the free time allocated on your schedule, we encourage you to participate in one of our Sharing Circles, enroll in one of our Painting Emotions & Auras sessions, or sign up for one of our Grief Massage appointments. You may sign up by…"

She handed the letter back to Wes and tried to ward off the heat creeping up her neck.

"It looks like the rest is the same as mine," Wes told her as he skimmed. "Hey, it's not that bad." He lifted her chin and looked at her. He did have beautiful brown eyes. "I'll take a nap and you'll get a massage, and after this weekend, we'll never come to one of these ever again."

Nichole closed one eye and pursed her lips. "Except by *massage* you mean *grief massage*, whatever the hell that is."

"Yeah, that part might be a little strange." Wes stood and pulled her to her feet and into his arms, lacing his fingers around her back. "How about I give you a massage?" She let him pull her closer, and his mouth brushed her hair. "It'll make you feel so good you might cry."

Nichole laughed into his shoulder. This was what she liked about him, his easy way of helping her see the world as something amusing rather than scary and sad. With him beside her this weekend, she would get through this. She might even leave better than when she came—but probably not.

Nichole leaned back until her face was a few inches from his. "You want to see my tiny room?"

Wes glanced over her head as if someone might be listening. "We're not allowed."

The corner of Nichole's mouth lifted in a smile. "Don't you think that'll make it even better?"

She wriggled out of his arms and took his hand as she led him back inside and to the third floor.

He didn't protest and no one seemed to be policing them, so she shut the door behind them until morning.

22

SATURDAY

JENNY

"This morning we'll be doing a bit of navel gazing," the yoga instructor intoned with a breathy voice. "But instead of taking a myopic view of your own, you'll be examining your partner's metaphorical navel."

Oh, Lord. It was 6 a.m. and Jenny and Curt had obeyed their schedule and made the trek through the mud and rain to the yoga studio, a small structure set along a path from the Main House.

This was the sort of thing she and her husband would've cackled about early in their relationship, but today he was focused on moving into position, bending forward at the waist and lifting his arms to lean into her whenever she decided to mirror his stance.

Last night their letter had instructed them to block out the world around them and to focus solely on one another this weekend. After he finished reading it, Curt had sat on the bed beside her, looking into her eyes expectantly.

"Do you think you can set aside Beverly's death for forty-eight hours and be here with me?" he asked, echoing their earlier conversation upon arrival.

"I can't set that aside, but I can try to be here with you at the same time," she answered, trying to be honest. "That's as good as I can give you."

He nodded. "Fine. But know that I'm here for one reason: us."

They went to bed soon after, he daring to kiss her once again before he turned out the light. She resisted the urge to put a pillow between them for the rest of the night, but there was no need. He didn't touch her, and he fell asleep within minutes. She'd always hated that about him.

The instructor looked her way with raised brows, and Jenny felt sweat already beginning to bead on the back of her neck. "If this is too difficult…"

Jenny ignored the lithe twentysomething woman, huffed out a frustrated breath, and joined her husband, leaning forward and gripping his lifted hands until they were face-to-face, staring into one another's eyes.

"Good," the instructor breathed as she paced the room, her feet padding against the mats. "As we move into position this morning, your focus should be on seeing your partner. Take them in with your eyes, breathe them in with your nostrils. Look past their physicality and search for what lies beneath."

What Lies Beneath. Wasn't that a horror movie? Jenny was starting to feel like she was in one, the terrifying thing being how normal people were acting in this place. Six other couples were in the room, all rich and white and ready to metaphorically naval gaze.

As the instructor encouraged slow breathing, Jenny thought of the second of George Hoffman's books, this one also a *New York Times* bestseller. The cover of *A Natural Order* was understated with a white font against a black background. Climbing up the cover diagonally were gold stairsteps, hanging in mid-air. The content of the book had been developed from lectures he'd taught in his psychology courses for years, and there was an entire section devoted to the experiments he'd designed and conducted for nearly a decade with his unwitting students.

Jenny glanced to the corners of the room to see if there were cameras watching her now. She didn't see any, but that didn't mean they weren't somewhere.

"Stare into your partner's eyes and notice the color. What sort of pigmentations do you see? Are there any crypts or furrows?"

Jenny wrinkled her nose. What was this woman—a walking eye exam?

"Are there any imperfections? Anything you'd rather not see?"

Curt gave her his full attention and she noticed the creases around his eyes, the ones that had appeared in the past year. They were forty now, yes, but she was certain these lines were mostly from stress. She darted her gaze, but Curt tilted his head and frowned at her, bringing her back.

"Close your eyes and see how many details you can recall of what you've seen," the instructor droned.

Jenny obeyed but when she tried to count the number of details, she didn't see her husband's eyes. Instead, she saw the image of the woman her husband had been messaging a year ago.

It was autumn, but in southern California that meant a breezy high of eighty. Austen had started preschool and after the drive to and from school, she'd had a whole six hours to herself every day five days a week. She knew she should be productive, but most of the time she watched reality TV, her preference being for shows with a bungling couple trying to buy a too-expensive house.

Curt asked her if she'd thought about freelancing, to get her name back in the writing world. She'd thought about—and promptly dismissed—the idea. She'd already been too cowardly to finish the investigative series for those young women years earlier, and the guy who'd taken over her research had worked her angles and her leads until he helped identify the perpetrator—a retired middle manager at a local sales company. The man who'd threatened her at knifepoint in her driveway, and subsequently robbed her of her career, was seemingly one of the most normal of normal men alive.

She should've been grateful for justice served, but when the reporter had been nominated for a Pulitzer for the series of stories, all she felt was regret. And anger. Not an ideal combination.

The same week that she'd heard about her former colleague's Pulitzer nomination, she'd also found the messages between Curt and Tracy, a woman living in Pismo Beach four hours north.

Jenny was livid. There were no words for the things she could picture herself doing to her husband, but most of these flashes of anger involved a very sharp knife.

Instead of confronting him, Jenny texted him: Could he pick up Austen and Emmy from school?

He said it would be hard to shift things around, but he could make it work if it was absolutely necessary.

It is. That was all she told him. Then, she went for a long drive up the 101 to Pismo to pay Tracy a visit. Not that Jenny would reveal she was Curt's wife. Instead, she purchased a cheap vase and a half-price bouquet of dying roses from a nearby grocery store.

When she knocked on Tracy's apartment door and delivered the flowers, she was wearing black pants and a white button-down, so no questions would be asked as she watched the woman's reaction.

Jenny's heart pounded as she knocked at the door and called out, "Delivery," like she was in some kind of bad film. The pretty idiot read the card Jenny had scribbled—*Miss you. Love, Curt*—and smiled a stupid grin as she shoved a one-dollar bill at Jenny.

Jenny wanted to throw open the front door and scream out the truth: "You stole my husband, you whore!"

Instead, she forced her feet to carry her back to her car, and the whole drive back she mused on the core issue of this betrayal. This woman and Curt had taken something precious from Jenny that would never return: the naive trust she'd held in her heart that her husband was someone she could count on.

Suffice to say, Jenny was gone for the entire day. Curt texted and called, called and texted. She sent him to voice mail every time, but then, finally, deigned to send a message for the sake of the kids:

J: Will be home later. Don't wait up.

Of course, he waited up. When she confronted him, Curt was pathetic. Crying, remorseful, claiming that he didn't love the other woman. He loved her. Only her. It was an accident. They met on set. She was a temp makeup artist for some pilot that probably wouldn't even air.

As if that mattered.

Tracy—he'd actually said her name—and he had grabbed burgers on dinner break. Then, the next night they'd grabbed Thai food. They'd talked, and when he dropped her off at her hotel, it just...it just happened.

"For how long?"

"How long?"

"For how long did the affair *just happen*?" Jenny asked.

A couple of months. It meant nothing. He was an idiot.

On and on he went, all of his prevarications and protestations only fueling the fire within her. If you're going to cheat, at least have the nerve to tell the truth when you get caught.

"And I suppose your penis just stumbled into her, too?" Jenny had demanded.

He wouldn't look at her.

"How many times?"

"Stop," he begged. "Please, just stop."

"No. How many times?"

Curt hung his head.

He refused to answer, but he did begin his own defense. "You've been different ever since we brought Austen home from the hospital. I thought it would pass, but then you resigned from a job you loved out of the blue. You've been detached for years." He inhaled. "Do you even know how long it's been since you and I...since we had sex?"

Jenny's mouth fell open. "So this is my fault?"

"No, I was the idiot," Curt admitted. "I'm just trying to explain why I even considered...but I haven't seen her in a month. I knew...after that last time— It was like I came out of some kind of fog and I was like, *What am I doing? I love Jenny.*"

Jenny still couldn't explain why that statement hadn't made things any better. Sometimes she wondered why her husband couldn't have just had a one-night stand on location in Canada or Australia with some B-list actress. She could've forgiven that. Maybe. But this was a different kind of iniquity, one in which Curt had to give time and energy and planning to how he could best cheat on her.

Now, at the Genetive Relationship Retreat on this warm morning in a yoga studio with her eyes closed, Jenny tried to recount the details of her husband's face, but all she could see was Tracy's peach-like complexion and her straight blond hair. She'd been thin and more than a decade younger than Jenny.

The only saving grace about her husband's selection for an affair was that she seemed eminently immature. Tracy's messages were written like a middle schooler's.

4ever

how are u

want 2 meet

Tracy rarely used punctuation or said anything of substance, which meant that perhaps even though they'd shared a bed, perhaps he hadn't shared his intellect or his heart. This thought wasn't quite the consolation she sought.

The night after she confronted him, Jenny kicked Curt out. He stayed with a guy who'd come up in the business with him, and he called every day for weeks. When Jenny finally agreed to let him see the kids one afternoon at the park, he'd snuggled them and played with them and then begged her to let him come back home.

"Please. I swear, I'll do anything. Jenny. Please."

And that was when she gave him the opportunity to prove it. She'd had time to think about her demands, and she made them.

Jenny knew what she wanted. "Sell your business, move with us back to my hometown, and let me try to rebuild my career."

She wanted to be close to Nichole and her mother and the life she'd lived when times were simpler, more black-and-white. She was sick of LA and everything that came with it. Now was the time. She and the kids were going with or without him.

He'd taken a couple of days to think about it, and when he met up with her again to talk, Jenny's back was rigid, steeling herself for his refusal. She'd already determined in her own heart that she would accept no compromise. Ifs, ands, and buts were for men who had been better behaved.

"All right, I'll do it. Give me a few months to get everything organized and finalized and sold, and then we'll leave."

And they had. A half-country move to Edenberg, Texas, in the middle of summer, and she still wasn't certain she could ever forgive him.

"Jenny, Jenny, Jenny," Curt whispered into her ear, jarring her from her jaunt into the past. His voice was low and soft like when they used to make love.

"That's right," the yoga instructor said. "Repeat your partner's name like a mantra, like a loving chant."

He continued his endless repetition.

After another moment, the instructor put up a hand and balled it into a fist as if conducting a symphony. "Good, now stop. And...switch."

Curt stared at her expectantly, and Jenny swallowed hard. "Curt," she mouthed but no sound came out. "Curt," she said, louder this time, the word tumbling out like a curse.

He jumped at her tone, and she knew she sounded angry.

The instructor floated across the mats and placed a warm palm on her shoulder. "And how are we?" she asked, glancing from Jenny to Curt.

"Fine," Jenny said and then clenched her jaw, the muscles tightening into place the same way they were every morning when she woke.

"Good, good. Breathe," the woman crooned, most likely for the benefit of the other couples in the room who seemed disturbed by the aggression in Jenny's voice. The woman then lifted a phone from some unseen pocket in her skintight pants and made several swipes and pokes. "Why don't we move up your first counseling session to just before lunch instead of waiting until later in the day?"

Jenny had no idea what a counseling session here might look like, but if the beginning of the weekend had given her any indication, it was probably something she'd rather skip altogether.

Then she glanced at her husband again: Curt, his face open and trusting as a puppy, his head nodding up and down as if he'd do anything to fix the problem that was their marriage.

She sighed, but this time instead of the usual frustration or desperation, the image of that sharp knife came to mind. She didn't even try to stop the fantasy of plunging it into his gut. Good thing there weren't any weapons nearby.

BEVERLY

ONE WEEK POSTMORTEM
THE NIGHT OF THE FIRE

George changed after the flood. I'm more certain of that fact than I am of anything else. But I suppose I should go ahead and admit the truth: so did I.

It was 1996. The night before the flash flood had been a perfect hill country summer evening, which is tough to come by at the end of August. We were in our fourth session of campers, ages six to fourteen.

Every Thursday was a sort of celebration because it was the last night that the kids would be together that summer. It had only been a week, but even the littlest ones could sense the impact of the friendships they'd made, of the confidence they'd built out on the ropes course, of the appreciation of nature that had crept into their souls as they hiked hills and swam laps and rode horses.

As the camp mother, I taught art classes in the day and oversaw evening activities until lights out. I asked the chef to prepare a favorite for dinner—enchiladas verde with Mexican rice and refried beans. Even the kiddos who traveled from different parts of the country and had never eaten Tex-Mex raved about that particular meal.

After dinner the campers had an hour to run around the grounds before making the short hike to our campfire spot and gathering for one last story. By 1996 several of our kids were on financial aid, which was intentional on George's part. Each summer he would write articles and essays about what he observed and send off his findings not only to academic journals but also in his annual letter to philanthropists, who often re-upped their donation for the following year.

George's findings came from every moment of the camp experience. During the morning wake-up call, he watched to see which students were at breakfast first. During the afternoon on the ropes course, he observed how the children selected their team leader. At night he took notes as children received—or didn't receive—a letter from home. I told him that withholding those letters seemed cruel, but he brushed aside my concern in the name of science.

On the last night of camp, I always selected a heartwarming story for our time around the campfire. Sometimes it was the one about the children lost in the woods who, through fortitude and teamwork, found their way back home. Occasionally, I'd go a different direction and detail the legend of the firefly, how they'd been gifted their light by God in order to shine the way to safety for the lost. That one was a bit religious for our camp, where we certainly taught Christian values—our family personally attended Sacred Heart every Sunday—but never explicitly proselytized our faith. George said we had to preserve our "nonsectarian" status to keep some of our donors happy.

That night, as the children sat around the crackling flames, George surprised me by asking if he could tell the story. I gave over one of my favorite events of the week to my husband, consoling myself by sitting amongst the children, who quickly surrounded me, their small bodies pressed against my hips and arms and legs—even one hanging about my neck as we listened to George's deep resonance.

He adapted a Native American myth he'd learned in honor of the children of the Muscogee tribe that we had staying with us that week. In these moments I think he saw himself most akin to his ancestor William, repurposing indigenous material for his own use.

The tale was about a puppy howling to warn his master of the coming flood. I remember thinking that it reminded me of Noah's prophetic voice in Genesis, but with a dog giving the orders. At the time, I was proud of George for stepping out of his comfort zone and learning about a new culture, but as I watched the tribal children frowning at him, I wasn't sure he was telling the story the right way. Observing their down-turned faces in the orange glow of the firelight sparked doubt in my mind about my husband's methods, probably for the first time ever. Unfortunately, it would take decades for this ember of concern to fan into a full-blown flame, and I wouldn't be the one to get to light the match.

Either way, it was almost prescient, the story that he told. A flood was coming; that much was shown to be true.

23

NICHOLE

Wes hadn't woken Nichole for breakfast, and that was one way she knew she was starting to fall in love with him. He balanced a couple of muffins, a cup of coffee, and two tablets, glancing down the hall as he shut the door behind him.

"Thank God we didn't have yoga this morning like Jenny," Nichole said as she took a bite of the lemon poppyseed. It was the best muffin she'd tasted in her life.

"Good, huh? These people may be a little nuts, but their spread was superb. I had eggs Benedict. They didn't have any to-go boxes or I would've brought you one of those." Wes squinted one eye at her. "Wait, how did you know Jenny was at yoga this morning? I thought you weren't supposed to compare schedules—or have your phone."

She shrugged. "Those rules feel more like suggestions. That's why I let you sleep over."

Wes chuckled and reached for the tablet he'd taken from outside her door. "Ooo…looks like you have Sharing Circle at ten a.m."

"Wait, what?" She took the device from him. "Last night the letter said I could do a grief massage."

"Remember their mantra: *schedules are subject to change*." Wes rubbed a hand along his mostly smooth jawline. "Sorry, babe. Time to open up to perfect strangers about things you'd never want to share with anyone."

Nichole rolled her eyes and motioned to the other device. "What're you supposed to do this morning?"

"You don't want to know."

When one corner of his mouth rose, Nichole lifted an eyebrow and crossed her arms, waiting.

"I'm doing one of those floating spa things," he said, almost sheepish.

"I cannot believe—" A couple of days ago they'd been texting and she'd joked that she needed a sensory deprivation tank after a difficult day at school. The lack of noise, light, and touch had sounded glorious, but when she'd looked it up online, the closest place was a forty-five-minute drive. Not exactly the relaxation she was looking for.

"I cannot believe that you are getting to do the one thing I actually need."

Wes smiled that charming grin he had. "I'll put in a good word for you."

"Like hell you will." She shoved him gently and he crawled across the bed, capturing her in a long kiss.

"It'll be fine," he told her when she finally pulled away. "When it's your turn to share, just talk about how grateful you are for the amazing person who recently came into your life."

"Ha ha. And who would that be?"

He kissed her again.

Nichole arrived in the *Ima Hogg Seminar Room* and thought once again how unfortunate it was that the prominent Texas Hogg family had chosen that first name for their daughter. It was 9 a.m., and even though the sun was peeking through the clouds outside, this room was low lit with candles in the center of a round table. It looked like they were preparing for a séance.

George walked into the room, and everyone turned toward him, several people lightly applauding.

He waved two fingers back at them. Not *to* them or *with* them, but definitely *at* them. The room quieted as he wandered past each person, gently touching the circular pins on the shoulders of anyone wearing one.

When George stepped in front of Nichole, he smiled and bowed like some sort of royalty. She cringed. That son of a bitch was guilty of the death of fifteen children—and possibly his wife. But no one else in the room at that moment—except for Robin, who'd just entered and was standing in a dark corner—seemed to share her belief.

After George greeted everyone, he took a seat on a stool in the center of the circle, the candlelight painting shadows across his face. He pulled an item from his pocket and cupped the object in both hands as if holding a baby bird.

"Welcome to the Sharing Circle," George said as he lowered his palms so each person could see what he held.

Nichole peered into his hands at a long strand of black pearls wound like a snake.

"Together, we'll spend the next hour exploring our innermost feelings and processing them with one another." He looked expectantly around the room while Nichole leaned back in her chair and crossed her arms in front of her chest.

Personally, she wanted a sip of bourbon. Just a little taste to help blur the next sixty minutes. George smiled widely and continued speaking slowly in a soft voice.

"I learned the practices we'll be doing today at the knee of my father, Edward Clarence Hoffman. He was the Great Prophet for the Society for Better Natives, the first fraternal organization in the US—even before the Masons." He let everyone take in his storied pedigree. "My father wasn't Native American, as you may have guessed."

There were a few chuckles that Nichole didn't quite understand. This was worse than she'd expected. *The Society for Better Natives?* God, she wanted to go home.

"My ancestors learned about the practices of the Lipan Apache Tribe that once roamed these lands, and my father passed on the best part of that learning to me. So today I want you to think of our time together as a powwow, a campfire where we can wrestle any lingering demons and finally cast them out, here and now. You'll notice that these pearls—which are not an Apache artifact, but instead a very expensive gift for my wife after the birth of our child—are not actually black, despite their nomenclature of 'black pearls.' When held to the light, they reflect deep green and purple hues."

As George continued explaining the minutiae of the strand of pearls and attempting to make some sort of connection to his father's fraternity, Nichole felt herself drifting, her arms unfolding and her shoulders relaxing.

As he spoke, she was reminded of Beverly and all those children who'd lost their lives because of this man. A deep calm settled in her chest as she realized why she'd actually agreed to come this weekend: it was for them.

As George droned on about his pearls, the lights dimmed even more.

Nichole blinked a couple of times and her eyes watered. She rubbed at them, but George was suddenly at her side, touching her shoulder, and commanding her to do…something. To let go. To release. To sleep.

Her eyelids began to flutter until she decided to close them entirely. His words poured over her, smooth and warm as butter. She could no longer decipher each syllable, but she knew she had to trust whomever was guiding her.

Nichole was so far down in her chair now that she could

lean her neck against the back, but this position didn't bother her. She sensed that the lights had been totally extinguished, and there was a feeling of release in the room. Her breathing slowed, and her muscles let go of the tension she'd held ever since she'd learned that her sister was gone.

At the man's suggestion, Nichole could see herself back at the place where the trauma had begun, walking to the edge of Galveston Seawall, peering over the edge of the concrete to where her sister's car had been found. By the time she'd arrived, a team of rescue workers and a cleanup crew had already removed the vehicle, and the tide had erased all signs of the intrusion, leaving the sand unblemished. A couple of joggers passed, one person walked a dog in the lapping surf, and two children in light jackets threw a Frisbee a few yards away. A happy, though chilly, day at the beach. Nothing here to see.

The setting was *so* normal, and that fact had appalled her. How could this be the place of her sister's death less than twenty-four hours ago? It wasn't right. This should be a sacred space, a shrine.

The fog had been dense on that February evening, and Nichole could see how a person might drive off the edge in the dark, especially after a few drinks. But it wasn't like her sister had been out partying. She'd had a couple of glasses of wine, and she'd driven home along a road she'd traveled hundreds, if not thousands, of times.

Those three simple, otherwise innocuous, facts had conspired to forever rob Nichole of her sister, and now in this dimly lit space, Nichole was sinking into the reality that she'd tried to ignore with Ambien and drinking: her sister was gone, and she would never see her again.

24

JENNY

After Couples Yoga, Jenny gladly let Curt go back to the room to shower ahead of her. She wanted to check out the library anyway. Books had become one of her only intellectual activities over the past few years. She wasn't picky either. From romance to thriller to historical, she was here for it. Anything except sci-fi. She wanted to escape, but she didn't want to meet any robots or aliens along the way.

Jenny had noticed a sign for *The Old Three Hundred Library* last night, and now she wandered the halls, looking for the one place she might feel at home in this grand estate.

When she stepped through the tall dark doors, two floors of books wrapped around her. Windows lined one wall, letting in sunlight, and scarlet fabric framed them. Jenny hadn't slept well last night in a new space with her husband snoring beside her, and combined with the early morning, she could almost see herself curling up in one of the oversize reading chairs and napping the day away.

She was surprised to find Robin's husband, Max, perusing the shelves, his finger tracing spines of books as he searched the titles. He heard her footsteps and turned, giving her a quick smile.

"Good morning, Jenny."

"Morning."

"Did you have an insightful yoga session?"

Jenny startled before remembering that Max and his father had access to all her movements this weekend. They were probably dictating them.

"It was great," she answered too enthusiastically. "I mean, it was different, of course, but different is what we need right now."

She plastered on a smile even as she chided herself for babbling. She wanted this man to trust her, to let her bypass whatever layers existed between her and the information she sought.

He took off a pair of reading glasses and pinched them between his fingers. "Is there something I can help you find?"

She looked at the stacks and let her eyes wander to the end of the library. A small alcove contained a collection of objects in glass cases.

"May I?" she asked, gesturing to the display.

"Certainly."

Jenny walked over and took in the contents. On the center wall hung a portrait of Dr. Hoffman that must've been taken a couple of decades ago, years before Genetive was founded. Only a twinkle in his eye. George gazed into the camera, a pin on his tie similar to those that the members of his organization now wore. He peered into the camera with an intensity that suggested he alone held all the answers.

The rest of the collection, or perhaps *shrine* was a better word for it, seemed more haphazard. Perched on the far end of the alcove was a carved wooden African mask, the face devoid of eyes, set in a grimace. A plaque read, *Burial Mask, West Africa, Circa 1805 A.D.* Another pedestal featured a corn-husk doll lying in repose as if awaiting the child who'd dropped it. *Folk Art, Mexico, Circa 1932 A.D.* Next to that was an antique gun of polished silver, the track lights glinting off the hilt. *Civil War, Confederacy, Circa 1863 A.D.*

Jenny jumped as Max approached her from behind.

"My father's collection," he said almost wistfully. "He's like my mother in that way. She scoured the globe for art, and he searched for artifacts and lost treasures, some even from other cultures."

"What's this?" Jenny asked as she approached a handstitched booklet splayed open with a smiling caricature of a Native American in headdress and loincloth, running faster than his own horse. On the opposite page was a letter written by George. *More than five hundred years ago, our forefather, Christopher Columbus, founded this great land we call America, taming the savages and teaching them the ways of civility and generosity.*

Wow. Quite a rewrite, Jenny thought.

"That's from when my father was the head of the entire Society for Better Natives. He was the youngest chief ever elected. Only thirty years old." Max shook his head as if in awe of how much his father had accomplished.

Jenny couldn't dampen the journalist inside her. "Does your father have other booklets like this? Or perhaps an archive of his collection? Anything not on display?"

Max narrowed one eye at her, perhaps sensing her investigative leanings.

"It's just… I've never heard of the Society for…" She couldn't bring herself to actually say the name. "I'd love to see what they accomplished."

Max waved away her interest. "They're all but defunct now—couldn't get enough members to continue past the 1990s. There was a women's branch, too: the Order of Sacagawea. Mother never joined, so after my parents started the camp, my father resigned. But since he took many of the teachings from those organizations and incorporated them into Genetive, being here this weekend should give you a good feel for them."

Perfect. She tried to fix her face into an open and receptive expression, the look of someone ready to learn.

Max must've bought it. "You know, I remember you. From school."

"I remember you, too. You were only a couple years ahead of Nichole and me."

He gave a reminiscent half grin. "I was sandwiched right between the two of you and Robin and Christina. The whole town knew about your friendship, how adventurous the four of you were." He cleared his throat, seeming to consider the best way to continue. Max looked into Jenny's eyes. "When we heard that Christina had died, well, Robin might not show it, but she struggled. For the past few months she hasn't seemed like herself. I'd love for her to have an old friend here, someone who can walk with her as a fellow wife, mother, and professional."

"I'd... I'd like that," Jenny said, trying not to stumble over her words. This was her chance.

"My wife said that you're eager to restart your career, to plug into a group of women who can help you network." Max paused to read her expression.

She lifted her eyebrows in anticipation.

"If you're really interested in getting to know what we're all about, I could ask Robin or one of the other ladies to give you a more...inclusive tour of the grounds and to talk to you about our mission." He studied her for a few more seconds. "You know, we could always use a writer with connections like yours. Didn't Curt say you worked at the *L.A. Times*?"

She nodded, afraid that if she spoke, her tone might somehow give away her desperate desire for exactly this kind of inner-circle experience.

"Well, then. That might be useful to share with one of our leaders." He nodded in a sort of farewell before walking back to the shelf, taking down a book, and tucking it under his arm. Less than a minute later, he exited, leaving her there to study the odds and ends that represented Dr. George Hoffman.

25

NICHOLE

Tears rose to Nichole's eyes. Her throat constricted. Her breathing accelerated. She was tumbling over the edge of the Seawall, falling and flailing forever. But then Robin's voice pulled her back. "You're okay, you're okay. Nichole, you're okay." She felt two hands holding her up.

"It's all right," the man's voice, still low and serene, intervened. "Nichole, you don't need to stay in the sadness. Let's move into the light."

"Stop. This is too much for her," she heard Robin whisper, her voice agitated.

Nichole tried to open her eyes, but they wouldn't budge.

"It's time to start healing," George's dulcet tones suggested. He touched her shoulder again. "Sleep."

Dr. Hoffman told her how to feel, and her brain filled in the rest. She didn't want to think about the place of her sister's death. No. She wanted to think of good things, of happier times. She had dwelt in the sadness long enough.

Yes, that was right.

Here was a chance to start anew. It might be a different reality than she'd expected, but it was a reality that could have goodness in it. If only she would choose the goodness.

The man was saying as much, though she could barely register that it was his voice and not her own.

Her brain fought hard to follow his calming commands, but her sister's death was dark and sticky, like a tar pit she couldn't escape. It was by far the worst thing that had ever happened to her, the thing that made her pour another glass of wine or stop by the liquor store one more time on her way home. She would never recover. She couldn't. It would be a betrayal to her sister's memory.

Christina. She would think about the time when it had been storming outside. She was seven, and she'd crawled into her sister's bed and nuzzled against her back. Christina, at twelve years old, had rolled over and pulled her closer, tucking the blanket underneath the two of them so they were cocooned together. Nichole's fear of the rain and the thunder and the lightning had dissolved, and she'd known that as long as her sister was alive, she would be safe.

"And I will snap my fingers," the man said. She could hear the friction of the pearls as he wound them in his hand. "And when I snap my fingers, you will wake up rested and refreshed and ready to share your journey with those around you."

Nichole heard the click and emerged from a sort of drowsy fog. The lights were on, and she blinked against their intensity. When she looked around, only about eight people remained in the room, including her and Robin and Dr. Hoffman, who sighed contentedly as if he'd had a productive day at the office.

"Good, good," he breathed as he gazed at the remaining people. "Congratulate yourselves, my friends. You are open to the power of suggestion. Each of you is a sensitive, creative, imaginative individual. Because of these qualities, you also have a high propensity for hypnosis, something that only a quarter of the population shares, though here at Genetive, that number is always a bit higher, owing to the sort of people drawn to us. Well done, well done."

A participant on Nichole's right was still emerging from the haze of sleepiness.

"That's all right," Dr. Hoffman said, addressing the awakening woman with a tender voice. "You come as you are and as you are ready."

Nichole blinked and took a deep breath before glancing at her watch. Nearly a half hour had passed while she was in some kind of trance.

"Where is everybody else?" Nichole mouthed to Robin, who now sat beside her, her lips set in a thin line.

Robin started to answer, but Dr. Hoffman spoke first.

"They were moved to another space that can better accommodate their journey—they'll be offered alternative forms of therapy." He inhaled slowly. "I'm remaining with you because I want to tell you my story and then give you time to share anything that arose for you during our...exercise." Nichole caught the pause before he said the final word. He knew that the kind of therapy he was conducting—hypnosis without consent—was unorthodox, possibly unethical. He also didn't seem to care. "Sharing is one of the fastest roads to emotional recovery."

Dr. Hoffman proceeded to detail the story of the loss of his first daughter at birth, something Nichole had never heard. She glanced at Robin, who seemed to know it already. George teared up at one point as he spoke about Beverly's ensuing postpartum depression.

"Over the years Beverly began seeing a hypnotic therapist and found great healing in the experience. That's why we offer this exercise to our guests, especially those who've experienced trauma. I, myself, this morning returned to the moment only days ago when I found out that Beverly..." George paused, collecting himself. "...to the moment when I was asked to identify her body. It is painful, but there is beauty in that pain."

"There, there," several of the listeners said in unison as he finished.

That phrase again. Nichole sensed that this must be the way members showed empathy or support—or even allegiance.

Nichole couldn't deny that Dr. Hoffman's past was sad. As a teacher, she couldn't imagine losing a child at any stage of life, and losing a spouse after a lifetime together had to be heartbreaking. Still, she wasn't brought to tears like several other participants. Robin remained stoic beside her.

"Would anyone else like to share?" George asked.

One woman stood and gave details of a complicated diagnosis and how she used hypnosis to deal with chronic pain. Two others spoke about family tragedies.

George dabbed at the corner of his eye with a tissue, so moved was he by the participants' stories. Then, he settled his gaze on Nichole.

"Nichole, what about you? What brought you to Genetive? We get so few participants like you, so I'd love to hear your story."

Though she still felt dazed, she couldn't help but catch his description of her. She also couldn't keep silent. "What do you mean by a *participant like me*? Korean? A poor teacher?"

George offered a patronizing grin. "I actually meant someone who has recently lost a sibling, but we appreciate you acknowledging your differences. Would you mind sharing?"

She crossed her legs and stared back at him. "I'd rather not."

There was an audible gasp from someone in the room, and when Nichole turned toward the sound, she saw a woman about her age who wore a bronze pin with two jewels.

"One of the first rules of Sharing Circle is that you must come to share," the woman informed her.

Too bad Nichole hadn't actually read the instructions attached to her schedule.

George grinned with a bit of levity and put up a pointer finger. "But that sharing may be anything. A recipe, a joke, a memory." He stared at Nichole for a full thirty seconds. "She is correct, though: everyone shares."

In that moment Nichole wondered how the great Dr. George Hoffman would handle things if she stood and hurled her chair across the room. But then she remembered the ever-changing electronic schedule. She did not want to be subject to anything resembling this experience over the remaining thirty-six hours.

George waited. Robin put a hand on her shoulder in encouragement or solidarity—Nichole wasn't sure which.

Nichole swallowed and tried to come up with something—anything—to say. But there was only one thing in her mind at that moment: "Like you said, I lost my sister."

"And did you return to the scene of her death during our exercise today?" George probed.

Nichole's heart beat a bit faster. She nodded.

"And what did you see?"

Her mouth went dry and her palms began to sweat.

"It's all right. This is a safe space," George breathed.

Her chest began to tighten. Nichole glanced toward the exit and then at Robin.

"It was in Galveston," Robin said on her behalf.

Another gasp. Nichole looked around to see the participants staring at the floor for the first time.

George's eyebrows rose and his lips pinched. "Learner Robin Hoffman, you know the protocol. The individual speaks for him or herself. Please apologize to Nichole and those assembled here."

Robin stared back in defiance. "No."

George sighed. "You also know that we follow strict program parameters. There are three strikes. You've only committed two infractions, speaking for another person and refusing to apologize." He held up two fingers. "I remind you here and now that you still have a chance to redeem yourself by staying silent while Nichole—"

But Robin cut him off. "Nichole's sister's name was Christina. She was my best friend, and she died in a car accident last February. There's not a day that passes that I don't miss her and wish that I'd been a better friend to her."

George's eyes darted to a staff member dressed in black who'd just appeared in the doorway. It was a man who could've been a bouncer at any Austin club. He came to Robin's side and gripped her arm firmly before dragging her away.

"You can put me in the Blue Room. I don't care," Robin called, her volume escalating with each sentence. "You contacted Christina, and she died. Beverly told me, and now she's dead. There's no way that you weren't somehow—" Robin's voice was cut off as the person in black held her with one hand and with the other took a handkerchief from his pocket and placed it across her face.

Robin fell limp in his arms, and silence settled across the room as he carried her out.

Nichole covered her mouth in an effort not to scream.

26

JENNY

Curt stood behind Jenny, guiding her into the office where someone they'd never met would presume to diagnose their marital problems. All within twenty-four hours of arrival.

The counseling rooms were off a long hallway deep in the recesses of the house, and a muscled man wearing all black rushed past them.

A woman in a pale pink button-down shirt, a black pencil-line skirt, and shiny pumps ushered them into a spacious office with a desk facing a love seat. She wore a gold pin with three jewels. Leader level. Impressive.

Jenny also noticed a small black circle peeking from beneath the collar of her shirt. She squinted to better make out the blemish, but this wasn't a birthmark or a mole. It was a tattoo of a slanted letter *G*—just like Robin's—except this one was over the woman's heart.

"Welcome, I'm Dr. Pound," the woman said, extending a hand. "I'll be your marriage coach this weekend."

Pound. Jenny knew the name, but she couldn't remember from where. She sank onto the white velvet love seat, and Curt waited for the woman to take her chair across from them before he sat.

"Thank you both for coming." Dr. Pound smiled and picked up a journal and an ink pen as Jenny suddenly placed the name.

Dr. Lydia Pound. This was the woman who'd been assigned to Edenberg Elementary as the curriculum coordinator. Jenny recognized her from the email Nichole had screenshotted and sent her at one point during this long week. It was also the name Emmy had repeated on her first day of school. *Dr. Pound, like pound cake.*

"You're a coach?" Curt asked. "I thought this was therapy."

Jenny studied the woman, who was about her age but had a streak of gray running down the right side of her part and into the tight bun at the top of her head.

The woman scrunched her nose just enough that Jenny could read the distaste. "I consider that term an outdated one for the kind of comprehensive care I give my clients. I'm not only helping you with your emotional or psychological needs. I'm doing it all."

Jenny's mouth turned up at this woman's confidence. "Don't you work at my kids' school, too? Developing curriculum?"

Her eyes crinkled at the edges. "One of my great delights is working with the students there, but I'm only on campus part-time for now. About ten hours a week while we assess texts. I devote the rest of my time to Genetive." She placed glasses on the bridge of her nose and examined a file. "I see from the notes that you've experienced a bit of a hiccup in your marriage?"

Curt coughed into his hand.

"It's been a rather long hiccup," Jenny answered for them.

"Good, well, that's the first step toward any healing: naming the problem."

Jenny tamped down a mirthless laugh. Her husband's affair—that was the problem.

"Jenny, let's start with you. The questionnaire you completed says that you're hoping to work through insecurities surrounding your career."

She tried to peek at the file that Dr. Pound held, but the woman raised it out of sight and waited. Jenny knew she hadn't written *that* on any forms.

"Sure, insecurities," Jenny said, treading lightly.

"And, Curtis—is that the name you go by?"

"Curt," he answered, clearing his throat.

"I see. Well, Curt, it says on your questionnaire that you are hoping to work on your marriage."

He nodded.

Dr. Pound leaned forward, her elbows on her knees. Jenny glimpsed a hint of cleavage.

"You see the problem here?" Dr. Pound asked, looking between them.

Curt moved his hand so that his fingers touched the side of Jenny's leg. "We don't have the same goals," he answered.

Jenny glanced at him, disturbed by how succinctly he'd verbalized the issue—part of it anyway. She turned back to the woman who was supposedly the professional in the room. "You do know he had an affair?"

"It didn't mean anything," Curt said, the same phrase echoing past arguments.

Dr. Pound paused for a few beats. "Jenny, do you agree that every conflict has two sides?"

"I suppose, but—"

Dr. Pound held up a hand. "Then, in the next forty-five minutes, let's put aside thoughts of your career, and together, let's unpack the blame and responsibility on both sides of this marriage. I believe that if we do this work, then your career will readily fall into place." The woman made eye contact for several seconds, waiting for each of them to give her a nod or any other indication that they were ready to unpack their baggage.

"I'm ready," Curt said, sitting up straight.

Jenny kept her face neutral even as she internally cursed her husband. He was ready to think about how *she* shared in the blame of *his* affair?

The doctor stood. "Now, some may think Genetive methods unconventional, but I'd appreciate an open mind as we embark on this undertaking together."

Jenny inhaled. She knew she had to play along, had to make it look like she wanted to be here, like she was ready to learn. "Yes, of course."

"Good. Then, Curt, you stay right here. Another coach will be with you shortly. Jenny, please. Come with me."

Genetive Inc. is a company that offers a variety of leadership workshops, seminars, and retreats to empower men--and women!--to reach their full potential. We also understand that some individuals may need help beyond our basic offerings.

For those participants, we provide an array of groundbreaking treatments and therapeutic exercises.

- Painting Auras
    * We believe art has the power to transform the way we see the world and ourselves. In these workshops, we'll put brush to canvas to capture insights only our souls can see.

- Electroshock Therapy
    * Using tiny electrodes, we harness microscopic shocks to stimulate underdeveloped or underutilized parts of your brain. This is a far cry from the film depictions of outdated practices. Ask about this therapy as a couples package.

- Genetic Mapping
    * The debate between nature and nurture remains ongoing, and here at Genetive, we seek to find balance between the two. Knowing your genetic past will enable you to know where you belong in the future of society. We also offer genetic counseling as you make reproductive decisions. Inquire today!

- Life Coaching
    * At each of our retreats, participants will be paired with a life coach who helps determine their sched-

ule and course load. At times, our coaches may provide hypnosis and talk therapy as well.

- Hypnosis & Talk Therapy
  * Here at Genetive Inc. we believe that no one is ever
    finished working through their subconscious fears
    and desires. Come ready to meet your inner self
    through hypnosis and guided conversations.

We have all this and more! In the near future, we plan to offer
the option to live on-site in our state-of-the-art cottages, so you
and your loved ones can experience Genetive Inc. year-round.
Click _here_ to find out more.

BEVERLY

ONE WEEK POSTMORTEM
THE NIGHT OF THE FIRE

The night before the flood, the kids trotted off to their cabins a bit more subdued than usual, their yawns nudging their bodies toward sleep. The sky overhead was beginning to cloud. Several inches of rain were expected, and the weatherman said it should stay steady through the night. There'd been no flash flood warnings issued. Let me say that again: no one expected a flood, least of all us.

That was why we were all shocked when around 3 a.m., thick drops began pelting the roof. Thunder rolled in, and when we heard the pop of a transformer struck by lightning, George took Max to check on the cabins and make sure they had enough flashlights. By 4 a.m. I debated whether or not to bring the kids to the big house, but the mud was getting thick and the waters were rising around the property. George said we should load up the campers and send them on their way before it got to be too difficult to leave and concerned families began calling.

Let's load them up. Just in case.

In case of what?

In case the waters start to rise, my husband answered.

I trusted him to know best.

What he didn't tell me—what I didn't find out until an argument a few months before I died—was that he didn't want the expense of keeping more than three hundred kids through the weekend or the headache of calling each parent. He'd completed his research, it was the last camp of the summer, and he wanted them gone. To that end, he was methodical as he determined the order in which to load the children along with the adults who'd volunteered to accompany them to the camp as sponsors.

The paying children and adults went on the first two buses, the partial scholarships on the next two, and the full scholarship kids went last. That was the hierarchy George had decided upon, so if something happened to the final buses, he wouldn't have to deal with parents who could afford lawsuits. Those most valuable left first; those least valuable, last.

Of course, all of this came out years too late in a heated argument, and still my husband didn't believe he was to blame.

It was the weather.

It was the potential expense.

It was the damn bus driver.

It was anything except him and his decision.

The first bus left by 5 a.m. with a packed breakfast of kolaches and orange juice. I stood in my rain boots and kissed the top of each little poncho-wearing head as they boarded the bus. Sleepy smiles shone at the adventure they were having. I was sorry they hadn't gotten to stay for one last morning meal, but it was best that they got on the road, especially for those with hours of travel ahead of them.

"Watch for Our Lady of the Guadalupe," I told a few of them with a grin, and they smiled back, unafraid. The second, third, and fourth buses loaded and exited the gate until only one group remained: our children most in financial need.

George had convinced their parents, guardians, and school

administrators that our camp would be a perfect place for lucky children to spend a week. He'd also worked with missionaries to a Muscogee tribe in Oklahoma, asking them to send their best and brightest, all expenses paid to spend time among *civilized* society without the threat of overtly religious indoctrination that some of their parents feared.

I know what he really wanted: a new sampling of subjects he considered lower on the social hierarchy as well as a reason to keep donations flowing in. Now, thinking about how I trusted his decision in all things, how I allowed him to use these children as pawns in dozens of twisted scenarios, sets a fire in my bones.

After the last bus was boarded, the driver closed the door. We could see the water lapping at the bridge as the vehicle took off down the paved road toward the edge of our property. George reassured me that he'd been watching the river levels all morning. The kids would be fine.

I wish I believed that he was innocent, that he had no idea. After all, he wasn't a coldhearted killer. At least, not back then. Now, I'm not so sure.

We headed inside to make calls to cancel the shift workers who hadn't arrived, but before we picked up the handheld, we heard something that sounded like the crashing of a waterfall.

I took off at a run, Max and George following right behind. From a distance, I could see the water pounding the sodden earth, rushing over the banks in three-foot swells. The screams of terrified children emerged from the direction of the river, but I couldn't see them anywhere.

George signaled for me and Max to climb into one of the golf carts with him before barreling toward the bridge over the Guadalupe.

When we arrived, I soon realized where the cries were coming from: the bus full of children was already overturned. I counted six heads bobbing above water, their expressions fran-

tic. One of the chaperones stood on the side of the yellow rect-
angle, reaching out an arm to try and grab one of the youngest.
Two more children were downstream, hanging on to branches
overhead.

I hurried toward the river. George took off his shirt and
waded into the water. When Max did the same, my heart
jumped inside my chest, and I grabbed his arm hard enough
to leave a bruise. My child was not going to join those in the
water. *Him* I would not sacrifice.

"Go back and call for help," I insisted.

I watched my son consider for several moments, but then
George, knee-deep, turned around and motioned him to the
golf cart.

"Do what your mother says!" George screamed, and I'd
never been so thankful for my husband's commanding voice
as I was in that moment.

Max drove back toward the big house to call for emergency
services while I kept counting the children. I could only find
five now, and my throat constricted as I thought of so many of
them trapped, their lungs hungry for air.

George waded to the center of the river and climbed on top
of the bus, which was acting as a sort of boulder in the midst of
the rapids. I was still at the edge of the devastation, but I got as
close as I could to the child nearest me, stumbling over broken
tree limbs to reach her as she clung to leaves, branches, anything she could find. A child just beyond her had already let go.

My eyes darted from the water around my calves to the
screaming child.

"Hang on!" I yelled at her.

As I approached, I finally saw her face, her eyes wide and
desperate. It was Winnie, an eight-year-old smaller than she
should have been with a fluff of dark hair atop her head. She'd
signed up for my art classes instead of the baking lessons that
most of the girls her age loved, and I'd seen her come alive as

she held a brush in her fingers for the first time. "Don't move, Winnie. Stay still."

I hadn't climbed trees in years, but going up and over this child was the only chance I had to pull her from where she balanced precipitously over the swift water. I laid myself horizontally along the sturdiest branch I could find, and like a caterpillar hugging a leaf, I scooted a few inches at a time toward her.

"Hold on, sweetheart. That's right. Hold on."

I must've been only four feet from her when the bus broke loose and came hurtling toward us. The last thing I saw of Winnie was her pleading eyes as the bus knocked her loose and sucked her under. George and the chaperone fell from the hood and into the current. I didn't even hear her scream as the water gulped her down.

27

NICHOLE

The image of Robin's lank limbs and hanging head were imprinted on Nichole's mind. Questions rushed like stampeding cattle, hurried and heavy laden.

Where was Robin?

Why had no one intervened?

And, perhaps as importantly, was Nichole next?

She blinked several times as George called her name and once again invited her to share. Nichole had to say something—anything—to stay upright and conscious.

Nichole cleared her throat and opened her mouth. "I saw... I saw my...my sister's face during the...the session."

"A breakthrough." George locked eyes with each person in the room. "Do you all see why this work is so crucial?"

Heads nodded and eyes glistened.

With the encouragement, Nichole decided to lie, stammering only once as she detailed how her sister had spoken, her voice clear and distinct as she encouraged her to move on.

The fabrication seemed to do the job because when she finished, George released them from the room, reminding the attendees to check their schedules in the next few minutes for "any potential changes."

Nichole couldn't quite shake the final effects of the hypnosis as she stood and hurried out of the space as quickly as her faulty legs would carry her. She had to find Robin, had to ask her why George had contacted Christina. In order to do that, she needed to figure out where Robin had been taken; whatever the Blue Room might be, Nichole assumed it wasn't a happy place.

She passed several other attendees dressed in a variety of clothing—a painters smock, a workout ensemble, a white robe—and she was relieved to see Max coming from the direction of the library. She tried to keep her face neutral as she explained what happened and asked about the location of the Blue Room.

Max's expression shifted as Nichole spoke, his mouth puckering slowly as if he was eating a sour lemon bite by bite. "Yes, of course, I can check on my wife. I'm sure she just needed a bit of time to rest."

If that was the case, George could've sent her to her room. But no, Robin had been manhandled by a giant member of the staff and dragged out of the session.

Nichole met eyes with Max and didn't flinch. "I need you to tell me where the Blue Room is. I'd like to see her for myself."

Max considered. "Really, there's no need. I can—"

She put up a hand and tried to use the authority of her teacher voice with this man whom she'd known from a distance for most of her life. "Look, I know Robin and I have been disconnected for a while, but she was my sister's best friend. Robin was speaking about Christina when she was..."

Nichole stopped midsentence, realizing she'd said her sister's name out loud without freezing or crying. Damn it. Had that psychobabble with George somehow worked?

"I need to see Robin," Nichole finished.

Max lifted his chin as he processed this request and seemed to decide it was harmless enough. "Follow me."

He led Nichole past the library and down a long hallway that spun off to the right. They strode past several rooms with closed doors, an art studio with gathered participants, and a nurse's station before stopping in front of a door clearly labeled *The Blue Room.*

Max placed one hand on the doorknob and took out a key card with the other. "We call this the Blue Room because we encourage people to use it when they're feeling blue. It's a bit silly, but it's not easy to forget."

Nichole assumed that if this was true, then a giant man wouldn't have needed to sedate Robin to take her there.

"Not that we advertise it as such," Max continued. "But when someone comes here—or is brought here—our medical aides conduct an assessment to see if they can provide anything to help."

"Like a sedative?"

"Or a conversation. It's different with each patient."

He opened the door, and inside, Robin was lying on a cot, facing the wall. The room was sky blue with white whisps of clouds painted on the ceiling. It was rather peaceful.

"Darling, I heard what happened," Max addressed his wife. "How are you feeling?"

Robin didn't move a muscle, and Nichole wondered for a moment if she was sleeping.

Max walked over and touched her shoulder, and she flinched.

"Leave me alone," Robin said, her words nasally and slurred.

"You have another visitor," Max told her, seemingly unsurprised that his attention was unwelcome.

Robin turned to look over her shoulder and saw Nichole. She struggled to sit up, as if her head was a bit swimmy, and put her arms out like a child who wanted to be lifted. Nichole bent forward and hugged her.

"I'm so sorry," Robin said, beginning to cry into her shoulder. "I'm so sorry."

"I can see that you've had a bit of medicine, but that should fix you right up." Max took a step away from the women. "I'll leave you two alone. Robin, feel free to come out whenever you're ready. I'll let Father know that he doesn't need to check on you."

When he was gone, Nichole nudged Robin away from her, so she could get a good look. "Are you okay? Are you hurt?"

"They gave me something," she said, flopping back onto the cot.

"What did they give you?"

"Calming Concoction," she said, slurring the words so it sounded more like *Cal-ling Cock-sun*. "It's George's special pills. Just for the ladies."

A jolt of anger rushed into Nichole's stomach, but she kept her voice steady so as not to alarm Robin. "For when you get emotional?"

"Hysterical," she said, a light chuckle escaping. "You know they used to believe the womb moved?"

"And that women's ovaries shriveled up if you read books. Yes, I've heard that." Nichole glanced around, realizing that no one was holding them prisoner and wondering if that somehow made things worse. If you could technically escape at any moment, then wasn't it really your choice to stay? And if you stayed, didn't that mean you knew you really belonged here?

"Do you think you can walk if I help?"

Robin's eyes lit up. "Do you want some pills? We can ask the nice doctors. Then you'll never need to think about your sister…" Her face turned down as suddenly as it had lifted. "Beverly said Christina and George… I didn't tell you because I wanted you to come, to help me… I'm sorry." She began weeping softly into her hands.

Nichole's heart beat faster, but she knew she had to get Robin out of here—if for no other reason than to keep the medical personnel from giving her more of whatever she was on.

"On the count of three, we're going to stand and put one foot in front of the other, okay?" She placed Robin's arm across her shoulder and counted. The first time didn't work, but the second time both of them were on their feet. "I'll take you to my room until you sober up."

"A good wife is a happy wife," Robin repeated again and again as the two of them made their way to the third floor.

28

JENNY

Jenny followed Dr. Pound down the hall and outdoors to the opposite side of the large mansion. "I know it's silly, but going this way is actually faster, especially with how often I'd be stopped."

So Dr. Pound was a popular figure around these parts.

"I noticed..." Jenny halted, uncertain as to how to bring up the tiny G she'd seen tattooed into Dr. Pound's skin.

"Yes?" Dr. Pound asked, her eyes bright with interest. "Don't be shy. Max told me that you might have some questions. He said you might even be interested in joining us here at Genetive in reaching your full potential as a wife and mother."

Jenny almost frowned at the mention of her children. *Let's keep them out of this*, she wanted to say. She swallowed back the words and smiled. "I was just wondering if I happened to see a small G on your...over your heart?"

"You are perceptive. Max said you used to be a journalist? At a high-profile news organization?"

Jenny nodded again, waiting for the woman to answer her question.

Instead, Dr. Pound reached out an arm and pulled open the

door. "We could use someone of your caliber around here. And as for what you noticed, I'll be happy to fill you in as soon as we sign some paperwork. How does that sound?"

Jenny knew from experience that this woman wasn't talking until Jenny signed whatever was put in front of her. Fine. As long as it wasn't actual legal documentation, she'd sign away her soul to figure out what was going on behind the scenes at this place—and the truth about Beverly's death.

They entered a solarium, lit only by sunlight and filled with plants. A group of three women she recognized from last night sat at a wrought iron table with a glass top. One of them was knitting, another was sketching a picture of a red flower blooming a few feet away, and the last was furiously scribbling in a journal.

"Hello, ladies," Dr. Pound greeted them.

"Lydia," one of them said with enthusiasm.

"Is this the new one?" the knitter—the woman she recognized from last night as the senator's wife—asked without looking straight at Jenny.

Jenny opened her mouth to introduce herself, but Dr. Pound placed a gentle hand on her forearm to silence her. "In this space, you're not allowed to speak unless spoken to. At least, not until you've reached the second tier."

Jenny disguised her surprise by casting her eyes to the floor in submission.

This must've pleased the knitting senator's wife. "Girl, what are your skills?"

Though no one had called her a girl in years, Jenny knew from context clues—and the fact that she was the youngest among these women by a decade—that they were speaking to her. This was her chance to win them over.

She tilted her chin upward but kept her expression demure. "I'm a writer," she said, intentionally not mentioning the reporter bit.

The scribbling woman halted her hand and stared at her with narrowed eyes. "What genre do you write in?"

"Nonfiction," Jenny answered.

The scribbler seemed relieved. "I'm a poet," she said, each word tinged with breathy hope. "I was recently published in *Ploughshares*."

"Oh. Wow. Congratulations." Jenny tried to tinge her words with envy even though she hadn't written a poem since high school English. The scribbler arched her shoulders and sat back to study Jenny. The hint of jealousy seemed the desired response.

"Jenny worked for the *L.A. Times*," Dr. Pound clarified. "She's interested in what we're achieving here." An ease settled across the woman's intense brow.

"Ah," the senator's wife said. "We could use someone like you."

"How so?" Jenny dared to ask, hoping to convey innocence and genuine interest in the question.

"Like any organization, we want accurate reporting on our goals and practices," the woman answered.

"Did you see that nasty review on that ridiculous blog?" the sketch artist asked.

"A bunch of hullaballoo because the attendee didn't like one of the sessions," the knitter stated. "Surely no one will listen to something that biased." Her tone didn't seem convinced.

"There, there." Dr. Pound motioned for them to settle. "We needn't worry about such things when we have a wise leader at the helm." She took a deep breath, held it for four counts, and released before extending a hand to them.

The women followed suit while Dr. Pound waited.

Jenny tried to join in too late, inhaling quickly, but no one seemed to notice.

"Now, you three seem busy as bees in springtime," Dr. Pound said, changing the subject.

"Oh, just completing our required active rest. We have water therapy later, but we wanted to get in a unit of productivity before we embarked on that journey."

Jenny understood the literal words these women were saying, but she could only guess at their meaning when strung together. Was this some kind of doublespeak? Were these euphemisms? Or coded language? Perhaps some form of groupthink?

"Good. Go in peace. We're off to do a signing," Dr. Pound informed them. "We'll see you all soon."

"Go in peace," the three of them echoed with bowed heads.

Dr. Pound led Jenny through the solarium and into a white room empty of everything except two chairs and a small desk on which sat a Zen sand garden with a tiny rake, a cassette tape, a small antique-looking tape player, and a stack of papers. "This is where I like to work when I'm not with patients or at the school. I think better here. A quiet mind is a blank slate, ready for supreme knowledge."

The last sentence sounded like some kind of mantra or proverb, but Jenny didn't recognize it.

Dr. Pound flipped through the pages on the desk as if making sure everything was in order and then reached into the lone drawer and pulled out a pen. "Before you get to tour the grounds or find out more about our mission here, we'd like to ensure privacy. Your signature on these forms says that you will not disclose any information you receive today."

"Didn't all of us attending the retreat already sign this?" Jenny asked as Dr. Pound turned the pages around so Jenny could read them.

"Not exactly. You signed an agreement saying that you wouldn't post about your experience on social media and that you wouldn't discuss the techniques used on property, but realistically, with the number of people coming through Genetive's doors, we can't enforce something like that. This document is more restrictive."

"May I take a moment to read it?" Jenny asked, trying to sound unconcerned as her pen hovered over the signature line. She was a journalist, ready and willing to get the story, but not if it meant she was going to get herself in some kind of trouble. She no longer had the backing of a news organization and all of their lawyers at her disposal.

"Certainly," Dr. Pound said as if this was a given. "I'll leave you to it." She turned and looked Jenny straight in the eyes. "We don't want you to do anything that would make you uncomfortable." She exited the room, leaving the door open behind her.

Jenny flipped through the pages, glancing over her shoulder to make sure Dr. Pound wasn't watching her from afar. Most of the document was legalese about not suing the organization if any of the following ensued during treatment or instruction: emotional trauma, mental anguish, paralysis, death. Whoa. Okay. She was also required to write her initials next to basic information that led her to believe she might soon be privy to at least the lowest level of information at Genetive Inc.

She signed everything and sat forward in her chair, picking up the handheld rake in the sand garden and combing through the grains. The cassette tape standing straight on its base caught her eye, and she examined the label.

Collateral: Robin Hoffman

Wait…what? She looked over her shoulder again and picked up the tape, turning it this way and that, looking for signs of the contents recorded inside. Of course, the object gave away nothing.

It only took a few seconds for her to decide to pick up the cassette and the tape player before closing the door and placing her back against it. She hurried to take out the tape that was inside—blank, it seemed—and drop in the labeled one. She pressed Rewind for a few seconds as she had on her Walkman as a child and then pressed Play.

Robin's faint voice came over the tinny speaker: "…has no idea that I was unfaithful to him. This is the secret I'm offering as collateral in order to keep my standing in this prestigious org—"

Jenny heard the clack of heels against the floor of the hallway, and pressed Stop. She pulled the cassette out of the player and shoved it in the pocket of her jeans. She put everything else back in order just as the door swung open.

"Everything all right in here?" Dr. Pound asked, a lilt in her voice. She walked behind her desk, running her eyes over the contents to ensure everything was as she'd left it.

To Jenny's relief, the woman seemed content. Jenny couldn't say the same for herself.

29

NICHOLE

After she settled Robin in her room and promised to check on her soon, Nichole met up with Wes for lunch. He looked way too relaxed for her liking.

"Hey, if you need to take a nap or anything, can you go back to your room this afternoon?" she asked.

He looked at her quizzically before lifting a shoulder. "Sure."

"It's just... I have a friend in my room who needs to sleep something off."

He frowned. "Jenny?"

She leaned forward to make sure no one was listening to them. "Robin. They gave her something—or she asked for it. I really don't know. But she needs to rest."

"Okay. Yeah, I can use my room."

Nichole tried to shift the subject. "Did you enjoy your sensory deprivation?"

"I fell asleep," he said sheepishly. "You?"

How to explain what had happened to her? And to Robin? Nichole was not someone who believed in things like hypnosis—or invasive drug therapy—but here she was, at the whim of both that morning.

"I'm a whole new person," she teased, evading the difficult job of explanation.

They ate lunch, which was admittedly an impressive spread consisting of sushi of all types—sashimi, nigiri, and maki—as well as a "build your own pho" bar and standard American fare. As they ate, they did some people-watching. Occasionally, one of them would motion at a person they recognized and lean over and whisper the name of the politician or actor in the other's ear.

After lunch, they checked their schedules, and Nichole was actually relieved to find that the rest of the afternoon would be spent in a variety of lectures along with most of the other retreat attendees. That would give Robin time to rest, and it was more Nichole's pace, like all those teachers' trainings she was required to attend. Boring PowerPoints and the endless droning of well-intentioned speakers—that, she could handle.

Nichole hurried to her room before the first meeting started. Robin was snoring lightly, which meant she was still breathing, so she left her alone.

In the first lecture, she sat next to Wes in the back row, laying her head against his shoulder. Maybe she would nap through this nonsense, her own form of sensory deprivation.

After a brief welcome and a repetitive chant—*I am Genetive, and Genetive is me*—George took the podium while Nichole's brain took a break. She came back to herself around the time he began to talk about discovering one's place in the world.

"It's important to find where you fit within the structure of society and to fulfill your purpose with confidence and kindness." George said the words as he stood on a slightly elevated stage that had been brought into the Great Room.

Nichole hadn't had a drink today, and while this shouldn't have been a problem—she wasn't an alcoholic, right?—she was feeling less than thrilled with her ability to abstain. Primarily because a headache was starting at her right temple, and a slight tremor was in her left hand. She tucked it inside her pocket.

"When I was invited as a guest lecturer at Harvard several years ago, I asked some of the best and brightest in our nation to map out the next ten years of their lives using emojis, words, and phrases that I provided. Do you know what I found?" George surveyed the room, and the audience remained riveted. Those adoring smiles were almost frightening.

"I found that seventy-six percent of the young men focused on work and career goals while seventy-eight percent of the young women incorporated some element of marriage or family into their timeline trajectories. Men are wired to succeed. We are built with a laser-like focus to earn, to perform, to dominate. That's how society made progress in the first era of mankind's existence. But women…" George shook his head in awe. "Women are the best part of society because they cultivate relationships and steer our moral compass. Their role, their purpose, their entire being is made to connect, to direct, to nurture, and to set an example."

Nichole noticed several men pat their wife's knee or place an arm around their shoulder. She glanced at Wes, whose eyes seemed heavy as he stared past George at the wall.

George continued. "This is why it takes one man and one woman in harmony to make a perfect family unit. That's why all of you are here: to become more perfect, to fulfill your God-given potential, your destiny." His gaze swept over his flock as he raised both hands, palms up. "But in order to fulfill your specific calling, you must understand your role in your family and in your community. On that note, I'd like to invite the men to join me in the study and the ladies to remain in this room, so we can talk more specifically and ask questions in the comfort of like-minded people."

"Don't make me go," Wes whispered, his tone somewhere

between teasing and pleading as he realized they were being separated.

"Don't make me stay," she countered, glancing around to find an escape. Each door was guarded by staff, and her mind turned to the big man and the Blue Room and the drugs coursing through Robin's veins. Sometimes Nichole did want to run from the sorrow that threatened to overwhelm, but she preferred to pick her mind-numbing poison, and the Blue Room concoction wasn't it.

BEVERLY

ONE WEEK POSTMORTEM
THE NIGHT OF THE FIRE

After the flood, life went quiet, like someone pressed Mute on all the laughter and squeals of delight I'd begun to associate with the summer sun and river breeze. I sensed a depression almost as deep as after I'd lost my baby beginning to coil around me. To cope, I started painting in earnest, trying my hand at a craft I'd admired for so long.

I knew I wasn't any good as a painter. I didn't have the technical skill like the Classical and Baroque artists I so admired. I didn't have the vision of the Impressionists I adored. I didn't have the confidence to attempt the abstract art that created its own sort of two-dimensional reality, and I didn't have the imagination to make up something entirely new. So I dabbled, painting this and that. Landscapes and very bad portraits, mostly.

Part of the problem with my art was the sinister atmosphere that wove its way into every painting. In Max's portrait, his eyes would turn downcast and heavy with purple rings underneath. In a landscape of our property, every blade of grass would be tinged with an eerie gray. I once piled fruit atop the table, thinking that would be a neutral subject, but in my version on the canvas, the fruit somehow ripened beyond use, the bananas splotched with large black welts, the apples bruised and battered.

I suppose if I'd been in therapy at that time, I would've realized that I couldn't help the direction my mind leaned. I'm sure a psychiatrist would've officially diagnosed me, handed me a prescription, and sent me on my way, but George was never one for outside help unless absolutely necessary. He believed, though didn't say publicly, that most talk therapy was mumbo jumbo, a weak person's excuse to air dirty laundry and blame other people. In his mind, the real problem lay in the way individuals failed to assert dominance over themselves and their emotions. He believed he could develop treatments to fix just that.

Still, George was affected. For that first year after the loss of the children to the river, he didn't do any of his research or write papers, though he still drove to the university to teach on Tuesdays and Thursdays, and he always attended Mass on Sundays, lighting candles for the children who'd died. Not that he blamed himself. *An accident, a terrible misfortune*, he would mumble if anyone ever dared to ask.

The media hovered for a couple of weeks, but other stories soon took prominence and the news cycle pressed onward. For Max's sake, I was glad the reporters were gone, but I did wonder every now and then how the families were faring without their children. I'd lost one myself, so I could imagine the depth of their sorrow, that hollow feeling in their chest as they opened their eyes each morning to a new day without their baby in it.

Periodically during that first year after the flood, I would catch George at his desk, staring into nothingness for minutes at a time. He wouldn't even respond when I was standing right in front of him. Sometimes I wondered if it wasn't just his condition, those episodes he'd always had. I wondered if he was traveling back to the time of our tragedy. I wondered if he was wrestling with demons I couldn't see.

Growing up, George had always experienced focal seizures,

but his parents never took him to the doctor, didn't want to admit that their boy might not be perfect. After the trauma of the flood, though, the episodes became increasingly problematic, George disappearing into himself for four or five hours rather than a minute or two here and there. That was when I made him see someone.

With these kinds of seizures there's no shaking—no *fits*, as my momma would've called them. It was just George staring into space or wandering the house with no destination in mind or spouting gibberish word salad, not answering to his name. Strangely, though, such episodes never occurred in public, as if his brain and body knew when he was safe enough to briefly collapse into nothingness.

I scheduled a physical for him, but of course once we were in the doctor's office, George acted as if he was completely fine. *No complaints.* When I mentioned the seizures, he would downplay the extent of the episodes. *Nothing I haven't dealt with before.*

He'd say some version of this every year until the episodes got so bad that I demanded a neurologist order an MRI, but by that time, we'd learned to live with the bouts of incoherent mumblings and even the voices he'd begun hearing during his episodes. Of course, the medication helped, but the disease never entirely disappeared. Not that anyone knew this, not even Max or Robin.

Sometimes George mentioned feeling a rush of endorphins after his episodes, and once or twice he said he'd heard a voice of inspiration, though at the time, I'd taken this to be metaphorical. I shouldn't have assumed.

When George began writing again, he penned grandiose ideas about social structure—ways in which society had gotten it right and where they'd gone terribly wrong. His prose and arguments were more convincing than they'd ever been, as if everything before the flood had been leading to the encapsulation of his ideas, ideas that would become Genetive's mission statement.

I feel like a fool now, but at the time, I thought my husband was a genius. I wouldn't have gone as far as to say that he was a prophetic voice for our generation. Such an idea was sacrilege to us good Catholics. But after studying so many family systems, his classroom and our camps included, he was now able to tap into that invisible thing that made people tick. He could dive into the subconscious of almost any given person to unearth their most intimate longings, and he could help people become the best version of themselves.

I saw the evidence myself as he began to take on patient after patient, working with them on experimental treatments in his home office until late in the night. When they finished a series of sessions with him, they were ecstatic at the change he'd wrought in them. They were eager to tell friends and family. Patients began flocking to our door.

Now, seeing with the kind of clarity that a death like mine can provide, I know that the tragedy at the river was the tipping point, not only for his seizures but also for the start of his madness. Too bad I didn't call it such back then. Back then, his ideas and practices were innovative and cutting-edge. I was wrong.

The year that he published his first book, George had his largest speaking engagement in front of more than a thousand people. A Fortune 500 corporation had hired him to teach a weekend workshop, and all upper-level management was required to attend. George knew this was his chance to get a foot in the door with the wealthiest and most influential people. That had always been his plan—get the rich on board first as fellow leaders, and later, we'd invite those less fortunate, less able.

I was standing backstage in the ballroom of the hotel when, minutes before he spoke, he went into one of his trances in public for the first time ever. I could see it come upon him. One second he was skimming his talking points, and the next he was staring out the window for one minute, two minutes, five minutes, motionless and uncomprehending.

He had medicine, but he hadn't taken it that morning, said it made him foggy and he needed to be sharp today.

I was at a loss. I finally filled a cup with water and tossed it on his face. It did nothing, but the episode must've run its course because a couple of minutes later he was back in the room with me. A rim of sweat had gathered along his hairline, and the toll the episode took on him was evident in his droopy lids and parched lips.

The first words he asked were in irritation. "Did you throw water on me?"

"No. I mean, yes. I was trying to bring you back," I told him.

He glanced at his watch. "Dammit. I'm going on in five." He ran a hand across his shirt and down the crease of his now-wet slacks as he frowned.

"Maybe we should tell them you're under the weather?" I grabbed a towel and dabbed at his suit jacket.

The look on his face at my suggestion was one I'd only ever seen once before, when I'd asked to see my daughter's body. Fear, shock, frustration.

"I cannot have people thinking I'm weak," he said, clenching his teeth.

"You're not weak. You have a medical condition. That's nothing to be ashamed—"

And that was when George got close, one finger pointing in the dead center of my face. "I am capable and in control. Do you understand?" The way he emphasized each word made me freeze.

Eventually, I nodded, frightened of him in a way I never had been. Confused by him, sure—that's normal in a marriage, isn't it? But frightened? No.

"Good." He cleared his throat and pocketed his notes. "Let's go out there and pretend that nothing happened. If we act as if the water spots aren't on my jacket, then they'll never notice. They're only concerned with my ideas and insights, as they should be."

And like a fool, I let him take my hand and lead me on.

30

JENNY

After Dr. Pound locked away the signed pages in the desk drawer, she invited Jenny to follow her through the short hall and solarium and onto the wide back lawn. Dr. Pound tapped on her device to update Jenny's schedule.

"I know you missed lunch. How are you doing?"

Jenny shrugged. She was willing to go without food if it allowed her more time getting to know these people and this place.

"Good. Everyone else is in a session now—including Curt—but I think showing you around is more important, especially if you're considering signing on." That smile was still in place as they walked toward the back patio. "You'll be exploring some of our three hundred acres with a very special tour guide: Mrs. Hoffman."

Jenny blinked. "Mrs. Hoffman?" She envisioned Beverly's shrouded figure.

"Yes," Dr. Pound said. "I'm sure Mrs. Hoffman will be a fantastic guide. Max selected her personally to show you around."

"Oh, yes, that's right," Jenny breathed. She wasn't sure if she'd ever be used to hearing Robin called *Mrs. Hoffman*. She wondered if it ever jarred Robin herself—but maybe not after what Jenny had heard on that tape cassette. Had Robin been hiding things all this time from her and Nichole? True, there hadn't been much time to fill them in, but she might've mentioned that the organization was holding collateral on her. But perhaps admitting that felt too shameful or dangerous since she was obviously beginning to doubt George, if not yet Genetive.

"Right this way," Dr. Pound said, motioning to the edge of the patio as Robin pulled up in front of them in some kind of hybrid golf cart, four-wheeler. Her face was pale and her eyes were speckled with mascara.

"I got the nicest ATV on the property," Robin said, saluting Dr. Pound with two fingers that shook like a vibrating string. Jenny noticed that Robin was wearing her pin with two stones. It was the first time she'd ever seen it on her.

"Very good, Robin. Jenny has been an eager guest. Please feel free to take her on a tour of most of the grounds, but…" Here, she gave Robin a knowing glance. "I would avoid going too far out."

"I understand," Robin said.

Jenny climbed into the vehicle next to Robin, and the two of them watched Dr. Pound stride away before Jenny spoke in a low voice. "Are you okay? You look…"

"Half-awake? It's because I am. The medical staff…they gave me something to calm me this morning. I had to force myself out of Nichole's bed."

"Nichole?"

"She found me and took me to her room to rest. I fell asleep and only woke when Max called my cell and told me that I was showing you around."

Jenny returned to the most pertinent information. "What do you mean that the staff *gave you something to calm you*?" Her mouth screwed up. "Did they drug you?"

"Not really. It's an herbal blend. Well, mostly. I don't know the details, but it definitely works."

"Did George order it?"

Robin met Jenny's concerned gaze. "I tried to keep Nichole from having to share during one of her treatments, and I...I accidentally said something that he didn't like."

Jenny thought of the cassette tape in her jean pocket. "What did you say?"

Robin took a deep breath. "I should've told you this earlier, but the week before Beverly died, she said that she knew that one of my oldest friends was somehow involved with George... and maybe with Genetive. She was talking about Christina."

The information hit Jenny like a kick to the gut. Christina? She would never get involved in something so...cultish. Would she? Jenny looked at Robin again, this woman she'd once so admired. If Robin had gotten sucked into this family and if George was somehow using his charisma to take over the town, why would Christina be immune?

"I just thought you should know," Robin said before revving the engine.

Jenny felt the rumble beneath her seat. "Where exactly are you taking me?"

"The place you're not supposed to go," Robin answered before flooring it. The two of them barreled off the path, bumping over splotches of grass and small mounds of raised earth. Robin had to raise her voice now to be heard. "Just don't assume anything until you've seen what I'm gonna show you. I haven't been able to figure out how the pieces fit together, but maybe with both of us..."

Jenny had always enjoyed hiking the Texas hill country, and even in the heat of summer, she appreciated the low hills and the scent of dirt in the air. The thick grass and trees scattered with Spanish moss was the landscape of her childhood. She remembered her first published piece of writing. It was in her sixth-grade yearbook, an account of her class trip to the famous—and infamous—trees around these parts: Baylor Street's Treaty Oak, the site of a Comanche and Tonkawa sacred meeting hundreds of years ago; the Baptist Oak in Goliad, marking the founding of the first ever Baptist church west of the Guadalupe; Seguin's Whipping Oak, where thieves received their lashings. The last one still made Jenny shudder.

Minutes—and what must've been a couple of miles—later, Robin pulled into a clearing. "We're here," she said as she shut off the engine.

The two of them crawled out of the ATV, and immediately Jenny began counting the structures surrounding them. There were a dozen cottages formed in a wide oval with a manicured space in the center filled with trees, picnic tables, and a small gazebo. It was picturesque.

"Who are these for?"

"No one's used them yet—well, except for Max and George when they stayed out here to oversee construction, but Genetive plans to start offering them to members later this year. The Reserves, they're calling them."

"And they're only for members?"

"Actually, they're only for the highest levels. Max has been trying to convince me to move out here."

Something about that final statement made Jenny's senses heighten. She hadn't been inside Max and Robin's home, but everyone knew that their house was one of the most beautiful in town: a white brick mansion on the outskirts of Edenberg, second only to George and Beverly's historical home downtown.

"So…these would be permanent residences? Like a compound?"

Robin hesitated, struggling to defend the organization she'd been a part of since its founding. "More like a…a planned community. Like a suburb."

"Except Genetive—or George—would own the property?"

Robin bit her lip and didn't answer.

Jenny could sense that the conversation had veered onto shaky ground. "So this is why George wasn't home with Beverly much this past summer. He was overseeing the building of these homes?"

"This is part of it. Follow me." She led Jenny down a path through the oak trees until they came to another clearing. Beyond it in the distance over a swell of ground was a one-story structure that looked like a massive metal box. It was nothing but clean lines, far more utilitarian than any other architecture she'd seen this weekend. The only thing keeping the metal walls from the sweltering Texas summer sun were the trees overshadowing the roof.

"That's The Ark," Robin said, pointing at the sleek—and bleak—structure.

"As in Noah's?"

"That's the one. This was the main thing that George was concerned about last summer. He wants to use it as a bunker to house a bunch of people. Just in case."

"In case of…"

"What he calls The Great End. Only the Leaders have access to those workshops, which are fairly new, I think. When Max mentioned the name of the seminars and then brought me out here…" Robin folded her arms around herself. "I don't know…this and Beverly and Christina, I had to tell someone. Even though I've personally gotten so much out of the women's classes, Genetive is…changing. Or, maybe I am."

"Maybe Beverly's death got your attention?" Jenny asked, trying to go easy on Robin.

Jenny squinted at the glare coming off the building despite the trees lining it on every side. She returned to a more practical concern. "Aren't bunkers usually underground?"

"That could flood out here, so this aboveground, airtight monstrosity was the next best thing."

"Why didn't you tell me about it?" Jenny asked, wondering at all of the things Robin had failed to share.

"I didn't actually think this was relevant to Beverly's death until Dr. Pound...at the funeral, she mentioned that Beverly hadn't been a fan of The Ark. Max had just brought me out here, or I wouldn't have even known what she was talking about."

Jenny studied her friend, waiting for her to say more about the good doctor.

Robin must've sensed a question. "What?"

"Do you know Dr. Pound well?"

Robin swallowed. "Not really. But...she has something... something important of mine."

Jenny fingered the cassette in her pocket and thought of her friend's voice coming through the tape. She decided to play her hand.

"Is this what she had?" Jenny asked, taking the tape out of her pocket.

Robin read the label and took it from Jenny's outstretched hand. "Oh, my God. How did you...?"

"It was in her office but had your name on it, so I took it. Figured it rightly belongs to you." Robin's eyes suddenly filled, and she hugged Jenny, who let her linger for a moment before pulling back. "Okay, tell me what's on it."

"Did you...did you listen?"

"A little."

Robin huffed out a breath. "It's my collateral if I...if I ever decide to leave."

"Leave Edenberg?"

"Leave Genetive. I thought it was silly, just an initiation into Learner Level, but now...it's so much worse." Robin glanced at Jenny for confirmation that this was indeed awful.

"It's incredibly invasive and morally despicable," Jenny told her.

Robin considered that for a moment before stepping back, throwing the tape at her feet, and stomping her heel into it.

Then, she stooped down and pulled out the thin black strands that held the recording of her voice and tore it into threads that blew in the breeze.

"It's not true. Any of it," Robin said, her voice going rigid. "When you move up to second rank, they take you in a room and make you write a confession, something no one knows. They call it collateral, like it's insurance in case you talk badly about Genetive to the media or something like that. I wrote this ridiculous story about an affair that I didn't have. I'm responsible for Lance and all his interventions and therapies, and two businesses on Main Street—when would I have time for an affair? They made me read my supposed confession into this cassette and said it would be stored somewhere safe..."

"Did Beverly know that Genetive was doing this?"

"No. Dr. Pound said that it was a new addition and that Beverly shouldn't be bothered with such things. I thought about telling her so many times, but in the end... I don't know... I guess I was afraid that Dr. Pound would release the tape. If I get kicked out, then I'll lose my businesses, my husband, my home...maybe even my son. If George has his way, he'll order Max to send him away to that boarding school. Without Beverly here..."

"But Max would know this wasn't real?"

Robin let out a shuddering breath. "I don't know my own husband anymore. I don't know what he would believe." She studied the ground, concern etching itself into her brow. "If it was in Dr. Pound's office...do you think she was getting ready to use it? Do you think she knows that I'm questioning Beverly's death?"

Jenny couldn't answer Robin's questions, and they both knew it.

That thought sat between them, and then Jenny looked back at the massive building in front of them. "Can we go inside?"

Robin held up a key card. "I swiped it off Max this morning

before session, but we can't stay long." She led Jenny through a thick metal door and into an entryway with three more sealed doors. "The design team just finished furnishing everything, so Max brought me a couple of weeks ago. He'd told me they were working on something big, but I had no idea. He's so proud of everything his dad is doing out here."

Robin took Jenny through the first door, flipping on the lights. "This is the only part of the property without any cameras or devices—well, this and George's office. He's paranoid, afraid someone will hack into the system and watch him."

Jenny squinted, wondering why this place in particular needed to be un-hackable as she walked into a simple kitchen. A connected room filled with bunk beds flanked a small dining area.

"Twenty pairs of bunks, and enough rations for forty people to live here for a full year without ever stepping foot outside," Robin stated.

"But why would George want something like this?"

"I think the more well-known he becomes, the more paranoid he gets. My personal theory is that he thinks he's the Messiah and someone will eventually come for him."

"That's...disconcerting," Jenny mumbled as she peeked into the sparse sleeping quarters.

"Max said that at first the only people who will have admittance to The Ark will be our family and the top tier of Genetive—those who've paid hundreds of thousands of dollars, if not millions, into the program." Robin flipped off the lights. "You need to see what's behind the other two doors."

They went back to the entryway and closed the first door firmly behind them.

"Which one should we try next?" Robin said, holding up the key card.

"The middle one," Jenny answered.

This second door led to living quarters that seemed much

more like a windowless apartment. There was even a faux fire-place with mementos and framed pictures, all of them of Mrs. Hoffman with various people, strewn around it. One with Robin. One with Max. Another with a group at an art gallery. A few others of her and George. Oddly, none of Beverly with her grandson. In fact, Jenny noticed, Lance was missing entirely from this wall.

Jenny tilted her head. "Looks like some kind of shrine to Beverly."

"Oh, my God," Robin said, picking up an item on the side table at the end of what looked like a never-used couch. "This is Beverly's locket."

The one I took photos of, Jenny added to herself.

Robin popped it open, but nothing was inside, which meant that the detectives—or George—had gotten rid of the Bible verses.

They peeked into a kitchenette that wasn't nearly as expansive as the one next door before wandering into the bedroom.

Jenny ran her fingers across a postcard that lay on the bedside table. It was a painting of a full-bosomed woman in a gold dress, holding a large peg in one hand and rearing back with a metal tool in the other. Beneath the peg was a man's sleeping head. She squinted to read the name of the artist and painting in the bottom corner. She held up the image by Artemisia Gentileschi. *Jael & Sisera.*

Robin stepped closer. "What does it say on the back?"

Jenny flipped it over and saw the postmark date. It was from June, three months before Beverly died.

They read together. *I know you were with her.*

Jenny cringed at the idea of George with any woman. "Do you think Beverly caught him cheating on her? With Dr. Pound?"

Robin squinted. "As far as I know, he never left town without Beverly by his side. And if it had been someone around here, everybody in Edenberg would know."

Jenny thought about her husband's own short-lived (in the scheme of things) indiscretion. "Maybe it was a one-time thing?"

"Maybe. But why?" Robin considered and then attempted to answer her own question. "Beverly was the perfect wife. Quiet and submissive, all the things that Genetive teaches we're supposed to be—at least when it comes to our husbands. In the real world, we're supposed to be calm, nurturing, and kick-ass at the same time."

Jenny sighed, setting the card back in the exact place from where she'd taken it. "Let's see what's behind the third door. I hope it's not severed heads."

Robin almost laughed, and Jenny realized that she hadn't seen a smile on her friend's face since she returned to Edenberg.

When they opened the third door, there were no severed heads, but there were enough weapons, guns, and ammunition to overtake a small town—or for forty or so people to defend themselves in case of the apocalypse. Having grown up in Texas, Jenny was no longer surprised by the sight of a gun, but the sheer volume threatened to overwhelm.

Jenny walked the line of guns of various sizes while Robin remained in the doorway, head down as if she was ashamed.

Jenny knew nothing—absolutely nothing—about this world. She could identify a shotgun, but these were far from shotguns. Some had short ends, which she guessed were rifles, and others had long, expansive muzzles and were most likely AK-something-or-others. These weapons were brand-new, of that she was fairly certain, and underneath them were rows of army green closed canisters with labels of ammunition. On the wall was a large diagram of the Hoffman property with entrances and high ground clearly marked.

Jenny picked up a notebook labeled "Inventory" lying on

top of one of the shelves. She flipped through the contents and saw a handwritten list that went on for pages. She put the notebook back on the shelf and spun around the room, letting her eyes take in the agents of destruction. They caught a poster that had been hung on the wall with tape. She moved closer to examine it.

"What's this?"

Robin came to her side. "That's the extent of George's art collection." She rolled her eyes and started to walk away. "He left art purchases to Beverly, but occasionally he would see something he liked and order a cheap reprint."

If this was the only piece of art hanging in this room and if art meant so much to his wife, this reprint must mean something important. "Do you know what it's called? Or who painted it?"

"It's Pieter Brugel the Elder." Robin reached the doorway. "And it's called *Last Judgment.*"

Goose bumps rose on Jenny's arms as she studied the image of strange creatures and a giant, eager mouth ready to devour the numerous dead. Above them, a Christ figure sat atop a rainbow, wielding both a vined flower and a sword. Jenny could imagine the person with whom George most identified in this painting.

George, the benevolent overlord using his power to extend mercy and execute judgment over the world he'd created.

This had to end.

31

NICHOLE

After the men followed George out of the room, the staff rearranged the chairs, and the senator's wife started speaking, her voice high-pitched and airy, as if she wasn't quite sure whether or not she really wanted to be heard. She began her lecture with a fun anecdote about dropping out of college to *marry my amazing husband*. Nichole tuned out sometime after the birth of the woman's fourth child.

Forty-five minutes into the lecture, she felt a tap on her shoulder and turned to see Robin. Gone were red-rimmed eyes and a foggy expression. This Robin wasn't exactly put together, but she looked almost...refreshed and rejuvenated.

"So sorry," Robin mouthed to the speaker, who was probably about to explain how cooking and cleaning up after her husband was the most important thing she'd ever done. "I'm going to need to borrow her," Robin said. She usually didn't have much of a Southern lilt, but she thickened her drawl now in this room of women. "Important business with Dr. Hoffman."

The women smiled knowingly. Nichole didn't like the looks they were giving her, as if she was the chosen one.

As they walked down the hall, Robin leading the way, Nichole spoke in a forced whisper.

"Are you okay? The last time I saw you, you were passed out on my bed."

Robin lifted a shoulder. "The stuff they gave me works fast, but it also wears off quick."

"Have you had it before?"

"Yeah, a few times. But usually by choice."

Nichole didn't want to dwell on that final sentiment. "Thank God you rescued me from whatever that was. I'd rather have a Pap smear and a root canal. At the same time."

Robin's mouth turned up on one side. "Don't thank me. The part where she's giving birth to her sixth child and feels at one with Mother Nature is something to remember." She walked a few more paces, glancing behind them to ensure they weren't being followed.

They turned a corner, and Jenny was waiting for them at a wooden door with branching trees carved into three elongated ovals running down the center. It looked like a more intricate version of the logo for Genetive Inc.

"Where are we?" Nichole asked.

"George's office."

Nichole froze. "Wait…aren't there cameras in there? Won't he know?"

"He won't allow cameras in his own office. He might see us going in, but I'm not sure if I care at this point." Robin spun around, her eyes steely. "We need answers."

Nichole bit her lip and nodded once, assenting.

Jenny tapped her hand nervously against her side and pressed her lips together. Nichole could read that expression as well as her own: Jenny was nervous and determined.

The two of them watched Robin wave a keycard in front of the lock before entering George's dark inner sanctum. Jenny found the light first, and when she flipped it on, Nichole took in the row of framed degrees, certifications, book covers, and family portraits hanging from wall to wall. In addition to being the size of her entire living room, kitchen and bedroom combined, the office was also sleek, elegant, and orderly. At one end, there was a separate restroom and a wet bar stocked with organic snacks and cold drinks of all kinds—though no alcohol. At the other end was a sitting area.

"How did you—" Nichole asked.

"I stole Max's master key this morning. I mean, I didn't really steal it. I'll give it back." Robin looked around to get her bearings. "Max is in session with the men, so if we hurry, I can get it back to our room before he knows it's gone. I figure if my father-in-law is hiding anything, it'll be in here." She glanced at her watch. "We have about a half hour before they pass out the covenants for everyone to sign."

"Covenants?" Nichole echoed.

"They're different for every couple, and they'll give it to the men to look over first. For the unmarrieds, it's mostly stuff about communication, but for the marrieds..." Robin didn't finish the statement.

Jenny stopped as she was about to pick up something from the desk. "What's the covenant for the married couples?"

"A sex covenant," Robin answered, her voice low. "Sex every day for a year."

"Sweet baby Jesus, save us," Nichole breathed out as she caught the look on Jenny's face. She knew pretty much everything about her friend's marriage, and she knew that wasn't happening.

"Max and I signed it a couple of years ago." Robin wrinkled her nose. "I thought it would help our marriage, and maybe it did—at first. But by the third month, sex became...I don't know...perfunctory? Although...Max had a good time."

Nichole smiled despite the bizarre conversation. Making that quip, Robin sounded more like herself than she had in years.

"If Curt knows what's good for him, he'll tear it to pieces," Jenny commented before changing the subject. "During lunch and the session, Robin took me to the outskirts of the property. George has built a bunker and a bunch of cottages for his followers."

Nichole frowned. "Wait...why didn't you come get me?"

"It wasn't on your schedule," Robin answered matter-of-factly.

"And breaking into George's office is on the schedule?"

Robin blinked as if just realizing what they were doing. Nichole could almost read the conflict on her face: What must it feel like for Robin to pull away from a way of thinking that had become so central to her life?

Jenny told Nichole about the reprinted artwork and the postcard with the message on the back—*I know you were with her.*

"Her?"

"No idea. Maybe Dr. Pound?" Jenny started toward a covered case at the far end of the space and lifted the edge of the fabric. Nichole helped fold back the cloth. Underneath was a model, tiny cutouts of houses and green trees and orange people.

"What is it?" Robin asked as she came to stand beside them.

It took only seconds for realization to dawn.

"It's Edenberg," Jenny mumbled.

"Like hell it is," Nichole said, tracing Main Street with her eyes. "The school's gone—and what is that?" She inched closer, trying to read the small print.

The Hoffman Institute of Primary Learning, read the tiny placard in front of what was currently the elementary school.

"That's why he bought the building," Jenny mused.

As they studied Main Street, they noticed that each building had been remodeled with the sharp edges and clean lines of modernization. Many of the business names had changed as well. Where Beverly's art gallery currently stood was now a miniature *Hoffman Cultural Center.* Where the *Edenberg Gazette* stood was now *Hoffman Media Corp.* Where the Lutheran church had stood for decades now was *Hoffman Spiritual Cen-*

ter. On and on it went. The only things unchanged were the diner, the cathedral, and the outskirts of town where most of Edenberg's citizens lived. Not that those people couldn't be replaced with a snap of George's fingers, it seemed.

"It's like that place in Oregon in the '80s," Jenny said. "Rajneeshpuram. Do you remember the podcast about it?"

"Where the cult took over the town?" Robin swallowed, looking as if she might be sick. "Yeah, I remember."

"This is insane," Nichole said, running her hands over her head as she staggered back from the display. "One man—or, one organization—can't change all of Edenberg."

"His family did found the town," Robin said, obviously torn.

"That was almost two centuries ago," Nichole countered. "It's time for us to be free of this man."

Robin checked her watch again. "Only fifteen minutes. Then we have to go." She turned to Jenny. "What else should we look for?"

"Nichole, you check inside his desk." Jenny wandered behind the uncluttered space and scanned the row of books lined up in alphabetical order. "Robin, do you see any authors here that...he talks about a lot...or that seem influential to him?"

Robin ran her eyes across the leather-bound volumes. "Uh... Aristotle. That's where he gets a lot of his ideas about women and men and hierarchy. *Politics* is a good place to start."

Jenny stood on tiptoe to reach it on the highest shelf. She held the thick text in her left hand and used her thumb to flip with her right. Occasionally, she would stop on a highlighted quote and read marked lines.

"*The courage of a man is shown in commanding, of a woman in obeying,*" Jenny read aloud.

A few more pages in and she saw another marked passage: *"Silence is a woman's glory."*

Nichole let out a quiet hoot. "Does that book come with a free muzzle for the woman in your life?"

"He...he never taught on those passages specifically...at least not from what I've heard," Robin said, almost defensively. "Although... I wonder if he shares these quotes during the men's sessions."

"Regardless, a few quotes aren't going to be enough to..." Before Jenny could finish her sentence, a single photograph fell out of one of the back pages of *Politics* and onto the floor.

Nichole stooped to pick it up and then dropped the image again as if it were on fire. Her heart thudded against her rib cage as the photograph landed face up on the desk. "Why... why would he have that?"

Jenny brushed her fingers over the glossy 4x6, stroking the edges of the woman's hair in the photo.

"Why would he have a photo of...whom?" Robin asked as she stepped forward.

"I don't understand," Jenny said, disbelief in her tone.

A knock sounded at the door, and the three women jumped in unison as Max stepped inside before shutting it abruptly behind him.

Nichole tucked the photo into the top of her shirt.

"Robin, what are you doing in here?" His eyebrows dipped. "Did you take my key card?"

Robin lied almost too easily. "I was showing Jenny and Nichole the plans...you know, for Edenberg? With Nichole teaching here and Jenny thinking about signing on...I thought that they might like to see the model."

Max turned to the model, yanking the fabric across the glass case as he went. Nichole could see that he wanted to believe his wife. He probably didn't want her to return to the Blue Room twice in one day. After all, what would his father say?

Max finally looked at the two other women. "Jenny, Nichole, I hope you enjoyed the tour, but my wife needs to return to our room to rest for a while. She's been distraught ever since my mother..."

Robin interrupted, lifting her eyes to meet his as if she was trying to find her courage. "Have the sessions ended?"

"Yes." Max was silent for a few seconds. Then he opened the door and stood against the wooden frame, signaling for them to exit. "In fact, it's almost time to transition participants to their next event. You two…" He pointed at Jenny and Nichole. "Jenny, you have a small-group discussion with Dr. Pound in a few minutes, and Nichole, you have a painting session."

As they filed back toward the main lobby with Max following behind them, Nichole peeled off. "I'm just going to run to the restroom first."

Max couldn't exactly argue with that. He gave a firm nod.

As soon as Nichole sat down inside the restroom stall, she removed the photo from its hiding place. She wasn't sure if her anxiety was from the lack of alcohol or from nerves.

The photo in her hand—the one that had been tucked inside George's favorite book—was the exact same image that she'd selected to run for Christina's obituary: there was her sister, smiling proudly on the day she'd been awarded the grant to fund her research on viral mutation. At the funeral, one of her sister's colleagues told her that he'd snapped the picture as Christina stood outside of the lab with the Gulf breeze tangling her shoulder-length hair. She was grinning like her entire life was ahead of her. Not a woman about to die.

Why did George have a photo of Christina? And was it somehow related to the message on the postcard that Jenny had found?

I know you were with her.

Nichole's worst fear was that this photo and Beverly's message were somehow connected. She swallowed hard against the bile in the back of her throat as she rested her head against the cool metal of the bathroom door.

She remembered the box under her bed, filled with the items

that Jenny had thought she might want to keep. Had Jenny looked through them? Or had she merely packed up things from her sister's desk that seemed noteworthy? It had to be the latter or Jenny would've said something. She needed to go home, unpack the contents of the box, and spread them out in front of her, reassuring herself that her sister had no connection to George or Genetive.

She stood in a liminal space, this knowing the past and being confronted with a new reality. Nichole wasn't sure she wanted to know the truth.

32

JENNY

Jenny fingered the thumb drive she'd confiscated from George's office as she made her way to her next session. She'd been discreet enough that she was fairly certain neither Robin nor Nichole had seen her take it. Not that she wanted to hide things from them, but she'd seen the devastation in Nichole's eyes when she'd found the photo of her sister.

Jenny's heart ached each time she thought about the loss that Nikki would never fully recover from. Jenny didn't have a sibling—Nichole was the closest she'd come to one—and she couldn't imagine losing the person who knew her best.

As for Robin, Jenny wouldn't tell her about the thumb drive. After watching Max's quiet control of his wife as he marched her to their room to lie down, she wanted the woman to have as much plausible deniability as possible.

"Jenny, so wonderful to see you again," Dr. Pound said, her voice steady as she motioned to the chairs in a half-moon around her. Four other women were going to be part of their small group discussion. "How was your tour?"

"Invigorating," Jenny said with a smile she hoped didn't look too fake. "Am I in the right place?" Jenny glanced at the other women, one of whom was the knitting senator's wife from the solarium.

"Oh, yes. We're about to start with a check-in. We've found that these more intimate conversations lead to greater enlightenment," Dr. Pound explained.

Jenny took a seat in the only open chair.

"This is Jenny Martin, everyone. She was on a tour of the grounds with Robin."

The other women's eyebrows lifted upward, signaling that this was a special honor.

One leaned forward eagerly and patted Jenny's knee. "Did you see the Reserves?"

Dr. Pound studied Jenny with uplifted eyebrows before answering on her behalf. "Robin didn't take her out that far."

Jenny didn't correct Dr. Pound. Instead, she decided to be vague and grateful. "The estate is lovely. I so appreciated Robin giving her time."

The senator's wife clasped her hands on her knees and spoke with a more demure tone. "We are anticipating even greater heights of understanding once they're finished and we can spend most of the year on-site. But, Jenny, how did you receive the honor of a tour at your first-ever Genetive event?"

Jenny's mouth opened, but she had no idea how to answer the question.

I'm researching the death of Beverly Hoffman. Her daughter-in-law—who actually seems almost as brainwashed as all of you—agreed to show me around because even though she somehow believes in this organization, she no longer trusts the founder.

Yeah, she couldn't say any of that.

Thankfully, Dr. Pound intervened again.

"As Dr. Hoffman has reminded us, those who are called will come. However, let's not spend time musing on the future when we could be talking about our present. I'll start us out: in our session today, we discussed how we as women are the backbone of the family." Dr. Pound made eye contact with each woman. "What exactly does that mean to you?"

A lady dressed in a purple pantsuit lifted a tentative hand, and Dr. Pound called on her.

"We trust our husbands to lead us, but they also lean on us to give them fortitude as they face the trials and temptations of the world."

"Very good," Dr. Pound said like a proud teacher. "I urge you. Do not deprive your families of the strength that you alone possess, ladies. Yes, this may mean repressing your own desires every now and again, but remember that any sacrifice you make is for the greater good of society. Your sacrifices bring about the health of the world. You don't want your husband leaving your home unsatisfied any more than you want your children leaving home on a rainy day without an umbrella."

Jenny was the kind of mom who was lucky if she could find an umbrella, let alone remind her kids to take one with them.

Dr. Pound took a pause and then repositioned herself on her stool. "Now, what questions do we have, ladies? Don't be shy. This is your time to share your struggles and learn from one another."

Jenny raised her hand.

Dr. Pound's eyes landed on her. "Yes?"

"When you say that we need to be sure our husbands never leave home *unsatisfied*, by that you mean..." Jenny waited.

"Well...we want our husbands satisfied in every way, but for today's unique hyper-erotic temptations, we especially need to know that he's satisfied sexually. It's a well-known fact that if a man isn't taken care of at least once every twenty-four hours, he cannot operate to his full potential. It's why we have so many men resorting to terrible crimes."

Jenny was speechless in the face of this pseudoscience, this nonsensical cause and effect.

A younger woman raised a hand and waited to be called on,

then she turned in her seat toward Jenny. "One of the most important discussions we have in these ladies-only sessions is the importance of fulfilling our husbands. Most of us don't have any trouble leaning in emotionally, but some of us struggle in...in other areas." This woman wore a pin with only one jewel, but she'd obviously mastered some of the talking points.

"Especially when you still have young children at home," another woman added.

"No strugglers or stragglers," the senator's wife said in a sing-song voice, her eyebrows rising.

"That's right, Mrs. Riley. Among men, there can be no strugglers or stragglers," Dr. Pound continued. "Some men struggle with their baser instincts because they're unfulfilled at home, and if one struggles for too long, he becomes a straggler, one who can no longer ascend to the top and become master of his own destiny."

Jenny tilted her head and leaned into the group, widening her eyes as if riveted. "So the frequency with which I sleep with my husband will determine how well he does in his career, his life." It was more a statement than a question. Jenny was hearing these women loud and clear.

"Quantity *and* quality," another woman piped up.

A few giggles issued from ladies around the room.

"That's not something Dr. Hoffman says," the senator's wife clarified. "It's just a little quip we've developed among us ladies." The woman studied Jenny, causing the hairs on the back of her neck to stand on end. "You haven't signed a covenant yet, have you, dear?"

"This is her first Genetive event," Dr. Pound answered on her behalf.

"Yes, of course." The senator's wife appeared relieved. "Well, welcome. We really should have first-time badges, shouldn't we, ladies?"

"It could say 'Genetive Virgin,'" another woman teased.

Dr. Pound chuckled. "Why don't you stay after, Jenny, and we can continue our chat?"

Despite the good-natured tone of the words, Jenny felt like a student in trouble with the principal.

"Remember, Genetive has given us the key, a secret that we—you and I—know and live, and that is what the rest of the world—" Dr. Pound paused for only a moment before the room sprang to life with a chorus of voices "—*will never know.*"

Jenny did not want to stay after. These women were creepy misogynists, somehow internalizing sexism until they believed themselves part of men's problems. She wanted to leave. She wanted to hurry to her room and plug in the thumb drive.

After the room emptied, Dr. Pound pushed two chairs to face one another. "Come," she said.

They sat as they had earlier that day in the counseling room, but this time without Curt by Jenny's side.

"Genetive offers powerful tools for women like us." Dr. Pound's mouth turned down with the gravity of her words. "But putting these tools to good use requires a bit of faith."

Jenny tried to read this woman. Her senses were usually sharp—it was what had made her so great at her job—but Dr. Pound had a poker face that matched the vague language she spouted.

"For example, when we were discussing the covenant and satisfying our spouses, I sensed resistance in you. Resistance should be resisted at all costs. Open yourself to the light of knowledge."

"Not resistance. Curiosity," Jenny said, hoping she sounded convincing. "Would it be all right if I ask you a question?"

"Certainly."

"Are you married?" Jenny wished she could find a gentler way to phrase it.

"Widowed," Dr. Pound said, her voice unwavering.

"I'm sorry. I shouldn't have—"

"It's been years, and ours wasn't a happy union. After he died, I went to school, earned my master's, got my license, and stumbled across George's—Dr. Hoffman's—teaching. Now my purpose is to help married couples avoid the mistakes we made."

"It's just..." Jenny thought for a few seconds about how to phrase her concerns. She wanted to stay on this woman's good side, but she also genuinely needed to know how an educated and accomplished person could fall into a place like this. "I have to admit that I'm getting a bit of an *us vs. them* vibe this weekend."

"What do you mean?"

"Like, the world is *them*, and the people here are *us*, the insiders who know the truth." Jenny kept herself from saying the word *cult*. She figured brainwashed people preferred to think of themselves as free spirits.

The woman's head tilted back as she let forth a melodious laugh. "Of course it sounds that way. Anything new and daring that appeals to a select group of individuals sounds a bit 'cultish.'"

Jenny's eyebrows rose at Dr. Pound's choice of language.

"Think about Google or Apple, the *cult*ure at those places. Think about the jargon that our own government uses when talking politics on Capitol Hill—part of our American *cult*ure. Anything and everything can seem a bit radical or exclusive if one stares at it too long. Think about Jesus. He started an entire movement that changed the world, but what did the religious leaders, what did society, think? They thought he was a radical whose ideas would die off with him."

Jenny swallowed hard at the comparison.

"The difference with Genetive is that we aren't trying to peddle a product or sneak our own agenda or even convince the masses."

They weren't?

"Our ideas are for the select few who will listen. If you give us a chance, Genetive—and Dr. Hoffman—will give you tools for everyday life, a way to see your potential and embrace it. And if it's not for you, we ask you to be honest and leave of your own accord."

Jenny thought again of the women who had been in that room and of the men whom George had taken with him earlier. She considered how to phrase her next question. "And who exactly does Dr. Hoffman want to embrace their potential?"

"Excuse me?"

"I don't mean to offend." Jenny took a breath and uncrossed her legs. "I look around these rooms, and all I see are a certain kind of people: upper-class, white, straight. Like me." She cleared her throat. "Is everyone…like me?"

"These are the people striving to be their best selves, to use the coaching and the therapeutic means we provide. We can't help everyone, but we help those who will listen. Take your friend—"

"Nichole?" Jenny asked.

"Yes, her. And her…partner?" Dr. Pound said the word as if it were somehow distasteful.

"Wes."

"All right. Nichole and Wes. We invite people like them on scholarship, so they can see the benefits an organization like this can provide."

Jenny felt heat rising up her neck and froze her expression. This woman's tone was placating at best, condescending at worst. Jenny breathed in calm, reminding herself she was here for information—even if that meant pretending to agree with whatever drivel Dr. Pound espoused.

"But Wes, he's…not like us, and we can all see it," Dr. Pound continued.

Jenny narrowed one eye. "And by that, you specifically mean…"

"Let's see, we could start with his income, his background."

"Because he's from Oklahoma?"

"No. His...ethnicity."

Jenny lifted her eyebrows, trying to appear inquisitive. She had no idea about his ethnicity. Wes was tan and had brown hair. So did Curt. What was this woman getting at?

"It was on his questionnaire. He's Native American."

"Interesting," Jenny said as if it actually was.

"It's not only that. He's also dating this woman—your friend…"

"Nichole," Jenny said a bit too loudly this time. She placed a hand on her chest and kept herself from clenching her teeth as she affixed a smile. "Sorry. We've known one another for a long time."

"Yes, well, she's a woman who is nearly forty and unwed. No children. No family to speak of. And…different than us in so many ways."

Jenny thought she might be sick but disguised it with the most bland expression she could muster.

"Unfortunately, neither of them is in a place to see how to overcome their current limitations and experience all they could become."

"So unfortunate," Jenny mumbled.

"If they would only try, they could be regenerated." Dr. Pound lowered her voice as if confiding an important secret. "That's what we do at Genetive. I can see that you and your husband are like us. Special. You have what it takes. So I'm going to let you in on a little insider secret."

Jenny was tempted to ask if it involved the stored ammunition several acres from here. Instead, she leaned into the woman's personal space as if riveted.

"I'd like to personally invite you—pending Dr. Hoffman's approval—to attend as many workshops and seminars as you can fit into your schedule in this next year. We can fast-track you up the levels if you so choose."

"What a lovely opportunity," Jenny said, tipping her voice up on the last word.

"We provide networking with the best in the field. Did you know that one of our members is the head of an imprint at a Big Five publishing house? And we have several actors, musicians, politicians. This weekend is only a tiny slice of our extensive database, though to be fair, most people are only Level One members. Still, so many influential people are intrigued by the lessons for living that Dr. Hoffman teaches. But you can only access that kind of material by committing to become a Listener. If you and your husband are interested, you can sign on before the weekend is out. I know George adores Curt's work, and he'd like him to officially become one of us. We would love to have a former Hollywood director—"

"Camera operator," Jenny corrected.

"And columnist—"

"Reporter," Jenny corrected again.

Dr. Pound waved away the amendments. "Just think about the opportunity. *Your victory is only one yes away.*"

The sentence sounded like a tagline from a bottle of whatever this woman must be on. "And how exactly does Dr. Hoffman—and Genetive Inc.—accomplish all of...*this*?"

She studied Jenny for a moment as if determining whether or not she was ready for the actual truth. "After my time with Dr. Hoffman—" her eyes began to well "—he changed my life, made me see the fullness of who I can be."

Jenny's eyes traveled again to the jewel-laden pin the woman wore. God, all of this and all she got was a stinking pin—well, that and a tattoo of George's initial. Before the other women had left the room, she'd caught a *G* embedded on the inside of one woman's wrist and another on a woman's ankle. Otherwise conservative women labeling themselves with Genetive's—or worse, George's—initial. It made goosebumps run down her arms. She squashed the question of where else these women might carry a G on their bodies, and her mind went to what could actually be another marker of this organization: the locket around Beverly's neck.

She phrased her question carefully as she pointed to the jeweled emblem on Dr. Pound's shoulder. "This pin you and several others wear, I assume it's a status symbol of your place in the organization?"

She fingered the pin on her shoulder and nodded.

"But Beverly, did she wear a pin?"

"The highest level—those who are at the apex of their enlightenment—wear a locket. Beverly was the only woman to reach this level thus far."

Jenny dared to reach a hand to place atop Dr. Pound's. "You are so…enlightened," she finished, borrowing the term. "You should be wearing a locket."

"With the unfortunate timing of Beverly's… Well, losing her was terrible for all of us. But Dr. Hoffman will need a woman to teach the new female clients, so perhaps…"

"And what do the owners of the lockets store inside? Photos of loved ones?"

"That's very personal." The woman narrowed her gaze. "But from what I understand, Beverly carried that which was closest to her heart." Dr. Pound shook her head slightly as if to stop herself from sharing anything else, perhaps remembering that she shouldn't disclose too much.

Jenny thought of those verses all about revenge. Had that been what the supposedly devout, rule-following co-founder of Genetive had on her mind at the end?

"I'm certain that Dr. Hoffman would be happy to answer any other questions you have. I'm guessing that he may personally participate in our coaching session tomorrow, to lead your reflection time." She clapped her hands together soundlessly. "I'm so excited for the journey you're about to embark upon."

"That's right," Jenny said, standing and placing one hand

in her pocket to feel for the thumb drive again. "I can't wait to begin."

Dr. Pound stood, hesitating for a moment. "I hope you don't think the invitation too forward, but a few of us ladies are gathering this evening for wine and chocolate in the solarium. Would you like to join us?"

"Wine? I thought this was a dry weekend?"

Dr. Pound lifted a shoulder as if to say, *Who's to know?*

Jenny tried to keep her eyes from widening. Of course she wanted to see these women in action, though she had no desire to sign up for anything…unless it allowed her more access to Genetive.

"I'd be honored," she said, trying to sound sincere.

"Good. Ten p.m. Be on time, or you'll miss the festivities."

BEVERLY

ONE WEEK POSTMORTEM
THE NIGHT OF THE FIRE

The day I held my grandson for the first time was one of the best days of my life. I teased Max that I finally knew the real reason I'd given birth to him: it was so he could make this perfect bundle, sleeping in my arms.

Robin and I had become fast friends by then. Perhaps she reminded me of the daughter I'd lost, of what could've been. Or perhaps I sensed we were kindred spirits because we were both married to determined men, though their goals were different. George wanted to run the world, and Max wanted to do whatever he could to make his father happy. Robin and I sensed we had to stick together, to be a unifying force in this family.

I was delighted that Robin let me stay in the room when Lance was born. She clenched Max's hand on one side and mine on the other.

At that time Robin was managing her little gift shop at the end of Main Street, a sweet store that sold home decor and knickknacks and a few kitchen supplies. It was quaint and kept her busy, but the store didn't bring in much money. That was all right, though, because they didn't need the cash.

While Robin worked, I kept Lance with me for a few hours

at a time three or four days a week. I loved every second with him. Once a week or so, just like when Max had been young, I would pack a diaper bag and take him into the city to visit galleries. I would unbuckle him from his carrier and hold him in one arm while I pushed the stroller with the other. Together, we studied the color and light in the pieces. By the time he was eight months old, he was reaching for the paintings, much to the docent's horror. I wasn't going to let him touch them, of course, but I wanted him to love this thing that I loved so much.

With Lance becoming the central interest of my life, I started reading all the parenting books that hadn't been published when Max was a baby. Every week I began anticipating what Lance would do next, watching for the next milestone.

That was perhaps why I was the first in the family to realize that Lance was a bit behind.

"Behind?" Robin asked as she unpacked the groceries she'd picked up on her way home.

"Just a little," I said as if I wasn't really concerned. "I think by now he should be crawling." He was ten months old. Some of the children in the church nursery were already standing and trying to take their first halting steps.

Robin let out a soft laugh. "If you weren't holding him all the time, he might try." She put a playful hand on my shoulder. "Where's his incentive when *BeeBee* will take you wherever you want to go and give you whatever you point at?"

We'd decided that *Grandma* or *Granny* was too old a name for someone with my energy, so I became *BeeBee*. George, who had little use for the child until he was older, was still just *Grandpa*. He didn't seem to notice. He was too busy planning an empire.

"All I'm saying is we should keep an eye on it," I concluded.

A couple of years later, when Lance started day school three times a week, the teachers noticed that he wasn't quite like the other children. On his semester evaluation forms they would write things like, *Doesn't yet know his colors* or *Sometimes aggressive with other students.*

I couldn't help but take these as a personal affront. Robin seemed much more levelheaded about it all.

"He's just unique. Was Max ever like this?"

I didn't answer directly, didn't want to tell her that Max had been ahead of many of his milestones, almost as if he'd gotten the memo that his mother had already been through rough times and his childhood needed to be a seamless one.

When Lance started kindergarten, trouble really started brewing. One of Robin's old friends, Nichole Miller—Ms. Miller to her young students—spoke to Robin about Lance's behavior, encouraging her to request a formal evaluation. *This doesn't mean that anything is wrong with Lance*, Nichole had said. *He may just need a bit of intervention to help him succeed in school.*

A few nights later at our weekly family dinner while Robin and I were discussing next steps, those were the words that triggered George. My grandson was in the other room, organizing his LEGO by color.

"What's this about Lance?" George asked.

I was taken aback, since my husband rarely even spoke our grandson's name. Sure, he put pictures of him online, the two of them smiling as if they were best buddies, but in our real day-to-day life, those moments were few and far between. Even though Lance would've followed his grandfather around from room to room, watching him work, if George had allowed him, my husband was more of the mindset that children should be seen and not heard. He probably would've preferred women fall in line with that way of thinking, too, but I wouldn't let him take things quite that far.

"The teacher is recommending that Lance be tested," I answered on Robin's behalf.

"Why? What's wrong with him?"

Robin teared up at the question.

"Nothing," I said, touching my husband's arm to still his anxiety. Perhaps he feared Lance would be like him. George despised his physical ailment more than anything. Or perhaps he was afraid of what people would think of his family if anyone appeared less than perfect.

Throughout dinner, Max was mostly silent, letting the rest of us make the decisions for his son.

Over the next few months Robin and I took Lance for numerous evaluations, writing check after check to get a diagnosis that concerned even my steady daughter-in-law: autism spectrum disorder.

"He's high functioning, but definitely on the spectrum," the clinician told Robin and me. We sat across from her at her meticulous desk while Lance wore the recommended headphones as he sat in the corner, drawing a map of a make-believe world. He loved all things building and structure. Lance was like his grandfather in that way.

"What does this mean for him?" Robin asked. "What do we do next?"

I already knew the answer. I'd been suspecting this for some time and had been reading up on the condition. I knew about regulating stimulation, camps for children with autism where they taught healthy social interactions, and regular therapy appointments with a trained clinician. It was 2019 and we'd caught it early. There was a lot to offer Lance, and I would have done anything for that child.

I dreaded telling George about the diagnosis, but after dinner that night, I steeled my nerves and relayed everything. After all, we'd need him to pay for the extra support. Thankfully, his second book had recently been received to even wider acclaim than his first, and Genetive was bringing in new influential clientele daily.

George didn't flinch as I told him the news. In fact, it frustrated me a little, his blank face. I almost wondered if he was having one of his episodes, but no, he was just staring into the distance as he considered what this might mean.

"We'll send him to a special school. He needs to be with his own kind," George finally said.

I found it ironic that George barely acknowledged his own limitations, the strange episodes he'd had his entire life, but he felt the need to place our grandson among other children he deemed deficient in some way.

This would become the standard line when speaking about anything related to Lance, and for years I was able to reassure George that the best place for our grandson was at home. For years I also kept Robin from learning what George wanted to do with Lance: to hide him from the rest of the world.

George liked to put people in boxes, to label them. I think it made him feel that the world was safer, more manageable, easier to control. I eventually came to hate him for it.

33

NICHOLE

Over the past year Nichole had become adept at temporarily forgetting. So for now, she pushed aside thoughts of her sister's photo, of Beverly's words on the back of that postcard. Her first goal was to get home, which might take some strategizing.

When she emerged from the restroom and back into the main hallway, she realized that everyone else had moved on to their next assignment. She grabbed her shoulder bag from the now-empty ballroom and checked the schedule on her tablet.

Painting as therapy. She was happy missing that, but she needed to figure out how to convince the staff to give her back her car keys and let her leave.

At that moment, her phone vibrated. She pulled it out and looked at the screen. Her ex. He'd called three times today—after months of silence. She pressed Decline. Her phone vibrated once more. Brian, again. Fine. She took a deep breath and answered.

"What do you want?" she said into the phone without preamble. The words might not have been the kindest way to speak to him after how everything ended, after how she'd been the one to cut the final thread of their relationship with such a pointed blade.

It had been mid-May, three months after Christina's death, when she'd broken up with him.

Until then, Brian had been incredible. He'd held her while she sobbed herself to sleep at night. He'd helped plan the funeral. When she'd returned to work two weeks later, he would wake her with a cup of coffee, pick out her clothes, and drive her to work. She couldn't exactly remember what happened once she got to her classroom, but she supposed she taught someone something.

Brian was a good boyfriend. Not perfect. He left his socks everywhere, and he was so stubborn that Nichole sometimes didn't tell him when she was going to do something she knew he wouldn't like. But Nichole hadn't expected things to end like they did.

Christina had died February 20. After that the fifteen longest weeks of Nichole's life had passed in a haze. When she finished the school year, she'd be staring into the void of a purposeless summer. Maybe that was why she'd said what she said.

They'd been out that Saturday, eating Tex-Mex and watching some silly rom-com she would've loved back when she could still laugh. But now the happiness on-screen only contrasted with how awful life really could be, and all she'd wanted to do when they got home was drink a glass of wine and crawl into bed. Unfortunately, after she'd put on a ratty T-shirt and running shorts, Brian had wanted to talk.

I found a grief counselor in San Antonio, he said gently while she stared into her wine.

Jenny checked in once a day and knew better than to say those kinds of things to her. Nichole turned her head to look at him blankly.

I just wonder if it might help. You're about to finish school for the summer, and I'll be at the office and I don't want you here alone. Wallowing.

Wallowing? In the death of her sister? The last living piece of her family? Sometimes she wondered if he actually heard the words he said.

I think I'm doing peachy for only three months out, she stated before taking another long sip.

That's not what I meant. He ran a hand through his hair. She never remembered him doing that before, but he did it all the time lately.

I'm going to bed, she said, taking the wine with her.

Brian stood to follow her.

Alone, she added.

Now I can't even sleep in our bed? Something about her tone must've made him snap. *God, Nichole. You cannot push away the one person who is here, the one person who cares about you.*

She stumbled a bit at the last few words, hitting her calf on the living room table. *Dammit,* she muttered under her breath. She would ignore his words. She had people who cared about her. Jenny. And…her colleagues at school. Okay, maybe that was a short list.

He followed her into the bedroom as she lumbered forward. *You drink a bottle of wine every night. You've stopped reading those cheesy romances you always loved. You don't run anymore. You don't turn off NPR when you're riding in my car. You haven't said a word about planning a trip with Jenny this summer. You aren't doing any of the things that make you…you.*

She set her glass down on the bedside table and turned to face him. *Maybe you're the reason I don't do any of those things. Maybe I can't move on because…you make me think of her.*

It wasn't untrue. She'd met Brian because of Christina, after all, and so many of her memories of the past few years involved both of them.

He frowned. *You can't push me away anymore.*

But I can, she said simply. *Because, honestly, it would be easier if you weren't here.*

And that was how it ended. She'd said something she didn't mean and couldn't—or wouldn't—take back.

He'd packed his things into an empty box, a laundry basket, and a duffel bag while she lay in bed buried in the comforter and let him leave.

After he was gone, she'd felt nothing, probably because she'd deadened all of her other emotions already.

Nichole hadn't seen or spoken to him since. Instead, she'd endured a lonely summer of men. Then, Beverly had died, and she'd started a new school year, and here she was—months without seeing or hearing from Brian. But now he was calling, and she'd answered without considering her words, saying the thing that was most instinctual—*What do you want?*

"Nichole?"

"Yes?"

"Thank God you're okay."

She was quiet for a few beats. She couldn't tell him that she wasn't okay, that she hadn't been okay for a long time.

"I'm fine," she managed. "Why wouldn't I be?"

"Listen," Brian said in a tone that he used when he wanted to calm her. "Don't be mad, but I've been following you on social media."

"Are you stalking me?"

"Kind of," he said. "I've been checking on you. With how things ended…you weren't okay. It was the only way I could think to keep tabs on you."

Nichole looked down at the phone in her trembling hand as if it had betrayed her. No, she was not going to accept his excuse as a reasonable answer. "You could've called me—or texted me," she told him. "I haven't heard from you since you left. I had no idea where you were staying, whether or not you'd started dating again." She let the allegations linger across the line, hoping he would offer some kind of answer.

"I've been staying at a tiny apartment near campus where a bunch of undergrads live. It's noisy, and I hate it." He sighed. "But...you...you seemed to need your space."

Nichole was trying to process everything Brian was saying. He'd been monitoring her? How often? She'd drunk-posted more than once, and she wasn't proud of it. He would've seen the seedy dives and the men.

"How's Wes?" he asked.

The heat rose to Nichole's cheeks. "How do you know about Wes?"

"He didn't tell you?"

"Tell me what?"

When Brian didn't answer, she took a deep breath, refusing the instinct to hurl the phone across the hall. "I cannot deal with this...with you right now."

Nichole looked around for someone, anyone. Where were the hovering workers when she actually needed some kind of interruption? No matter. She would follow her original plan. First, she would hang up on him. Second, she would find and collect her keys. Third, she would go home.

But then Brian continued his explanation, halting her plan. "Wes taught a continuing-ed course about how to start a small business. We met at a faculty mixer and hit it off. Went out for drinks a few times. Eventually, I told him about how things ended with us and how concerned I was. You kept posting about this one spot on the Riverwalk, so I asked Wes to bump into you, to check on you. I didn't think you'd appreciate seeing me there, since you never answered my calls."

"You didn't call."

"I did. Three or four times."

Had Nichole been in such a fog that she couldn't even remember her ex-boyfriend reaching out? No, Nichole refused to let herself feel anything but contempt for him in that moment. God, she just wanted a drink. Sour wine, metallic whiskey, she wasn't picky.

"So you basically pimped me out?"

"No." Brian sighed again. "It wasn't like that. Look, I just thought you should know in case the two of you are actually... dating. He posted that he was heading to a couples' retreat, which seemed really serious. He might be a nice enough guy, but I got the feeling he was hiding something. Like, he never wanted to talk about anything from his past."

"You deduced this from the few drinks you two had together?"

She could almost picture Brian's frustrated expression. "Yeah, actually."

Nichole rolled her eyes. "Is that all?"

"I just thought you should know. Don't you think it's strange that he didn't mention that we know each other?"

"Do I think it's strange that my new boyfriend..." They hadn't labeled things, but what the hell? "...that my new boyfriend wouldn't tell me that he kind of knows my old boyfriend? No, Brian, I don't think that's weird."

"Okay, but—"

Before he could finish, Nichole hung up. Bile rose in the back of her throat. She didn't have the bandwidth to process everything. She needed to leave.

As she rushed toward the staircase to head to her room and gather her things, she ran into a towering figure coming down the stairs.

"Nichole," George said, blocking her way. "You're missing your next session. Is everything all right?"

Nichole gulped back a sharp reply. "I need to leave. It's an emergency."

"Of course," he said, his brow furrowing as he folded his arms in front of him. "If you'll come this way, I can check you

out and get your keys back to you. I assume that your boyfriend..."

"He's staying." She averted her eyes, hoping he wouldn't ask
any more questions and would just hand her keys to her. That
was all she wanted. That and a stiff drink, and she would be
fine. Totally fine.

"All right, then. We'll just get you checked out, and you'll
be on your way." Dr. Hoffman nodded to a worker who appeared. "To the Exit Interview Room."

The young man nodded. "Right this way, ma'am."

Nichole folded her arms across her chest. An exit interview?
God.

"I really just need my keys," she said firmly.

"Certainly." Dr. Hoffman smiled. "And we'll give them to
you right after you answer a few questions."

Nichole exhaled and considered. She had no choice but to
do as he commanded.

34

JENNY

Jenny took the stairs two at a time as she hurried to her room after her tête-à-tête with Dr. Pound. Curt would likely be back soon, perhaps ready to discuss that awful covenant, but she had no intention of talking to him until she took care of the business at hand.

When she reached her room, Jenny locked the door behind her and pulled her computer from the center of her suitcase where she'd tucked it inside a cardigan. She opened it, logged in, and placed the flash drive inside. It took three seconds for the icon to appear.

There was one folder, titled *Maps.*

Jenny's heart fell. Maps were not going to get her far in the search for more information about Beverly's death, but she also wasn't going to return this drive to Dr. Hoffman's office without finding something, anything. She clicked.

Inside the Maps folder were two documents, both PDFs.

"Inductees" was the name of the first file, and after opening it, she was astounded at the page count: 1246. This was not the kind of map she'd expected.

As she scrolled through the pages of headshots and detailed

information, she realized that the first two thirds were current members. Next to the photographs—which looked more like mug shots than headshots—were the members' current rank in Genetive, the number of years served, and a list of networking connections as well as professional accolades.

Jenny recognized Senator Jim, his wife, and a handful of this weekend's attendees as well as the staff, ranging from the college-aged student who'd shown them to their room to Dr. Pound.

Jenny continued to scroll. There were only a handful of individuals who ranked as highly as George—the Essentials—but except for Beverly, they were all men.

A few names had been crossed out, including Beverly Hoffman's. Below her status, the word *Expired* blared in bright red.

As Jenny scanned the bios, she noticed other *expired* individuals—one was a player for the San Antonio Spurs and another was a news commentator for a Sunday morning show. Jenny knew neither of them were dead, so they must have opted out of whatever Genetive was trying to sell them.

At the bottom of each page was the approximated net worth of the individual—many of them in the seven-figure range—along with the amount they'd paid into the organization for trainings, seminars, retreats, and donations. Jenny's mouth fell open as she tallied the figures.

Genetive had raked in well over a hundred million dollars and thousands of volunteer hours since its inception, and these figures didn't even count George's book sales.

Of course, she knew the Hoffmans were wealthy, and Genetive was obviously successful. What struck her was how many people were giving their time to this place. How would they have room in their lives for anything other than their careers and Genetive? After seeing the cottages and the bunker, Jenny understood that this might be the point.

The last third or so of the document included lists of public figures and the kind of information one could only mine from extensive background checks. There was info on B-list actors, self-help gurus, mega-church pastors, politicians, Ivy-league professors, and federal judges. A handful were major celebrities, household names from blockbuster films or book series that had sold millions worldwide.

Realization dawned as she looked at the "Degrees of Separation" designation and saw names she'd recognized from earlier in the document. These were potential recruits, which meant this PDF was a map for the growth of Genetive's membership—and Dr. Hoffman's wealth and influence.

Jenny rubbed at her eyes before clicking on the second PDF, which was labeled "Grounds & Estate." This document was under fifty pages, the first dozen or so blueprints of the land and buildings, but after that were architectural renderings for future plans. Most of the ideas were standard, if still ornate, sketches for any large mansion in the hill country: an extensive wine cellar, a sprawling stable, a memorial garden.

The last few pages were photos of plaques that would be placed around the property. Several appeared to be in the names of donors, but one was for George's wife, which meant that either this document had been recently updated or he'd been anticipating her death. The thought made her heart race. Another plaque was for *The Children of the 1996 Guadalupe Flood*, which was somewhat surprising. But the final image on the last page was the most disconcerting, reading simply *For Christina*.

She studied the image, mouthing the two words to herself again. She could see the confusion on Nichole's face as she held the picture of her sister in Dr. Hoffman's office.

The door handle shook, and Jenny jumped.

"Hey, it's me," Curt called from the other side of the door. She'd forgotten that it was locked but was glad she'd had the forethought to keep him out. She did not feel like justifying her research to him.

"Just a minute," Jenny responded. She closed the files and copied them over to a folder on her desktop. She shut her computer, pocketed the drive, and opened the door.

Curt looked her up and down. "Where have you been all afternoon?"

She swallowed. "With Robin...and then, Dr. Pound. I came up here to lie down for a few minutes before dinner."

He scanned the room as if expecting her to have someone there with her. "We're supposed to do that Trauma Bonding Activity after we grab a bite."

Jenny was distracted by all she'd just learned, but she tried to act open to whatever was next on their agenda. "What's that?"

"I have no idea. I think we reenact the thing that caused us the most pain, something like that."

Jenny caught the fatigue in his voice and took a chance. "We don't have to go just because it's on the schedule."

Curt was quiet for several seconds before he met her gaze. "I know, but I came into this weekend willing to do whatever it takes to repair what I broke." He ran a hand across his brow as he sat on the bed and invited her to join him. "Listen, I've been thinking about something all afternoon. Can we talk? Without anyone watching us?"

Jenny took a sharp breath. She had no idea what was coming, and she didn't like not being able to anticipate what came next. This better not be about that sex covenant.

"I know your work is important to you," Curt began. "When you quit your job, at first I thought you might like staying home with the kids. I kept hoping you'd...I don't know...start acting like yourself again."

He paused, waiting for her to say something.

Her mouth went dry, but she knew she should try to meet him halfway—or at least that 10 percent that he'd requested at the start of the weekend. "I...something happened...that's why I quit."

His eyebrows rose. "I always thought that there must've been a good reason."

She opened her mouth to say more, but the words caught in her throat. She couldn't tell him what had happened. It was too horrific to relive and at the same time too shameful to admit that she'd been keeping this from him for so long.

When she didn't answer, he sighed. "I want to understand. It's just...it seems like you never got your footing... It's like you've been lost for the past few years, like you weren't sure which direction to aim."

She blinked back tears and tried to do what she'd heard once in a couple's therapy podcast: repeat back to him what she was hearing. "I think what you're saying is that I was... I've been struggling to find my...purpose." Her words sped up as she added, "But that's no excuse for what you did and how you..."

He put a hand on her cheek. "I'm more sorry than I can say." She could hear tears in her husband's voice as he leaned his forehead against her own. "Today, when the men were together, most of the stuff that George was saying wasn't for me. All about the man's role as the head of the home, how we should fulfill our job as the breadwinners so our wives can stay at home. And then he got into sex..."

Jenny's spine went rigid.

"He passed out a document that we're supposed to sign, saying that we'll have sex every day for a year."

She could feel the heat rising in her cheeks. Anger, not passion. She couldn't believe her own husband was about to suggest such an archaic—

"It's okay." He stopped her as his hand found hers. "I threw it away. But listening to him made me realize that I've been pushing you instead of letting you decide what you really want. Since I started working here, I've been thinking that George's tools would help me heighten my self-awareness and develop my emotional maturity, and maybe they have. But after today

I'm starting to wonder if his ideas about marriage are kind of… *off*." He sighed. "All that to say, this afternoon while he spoke, I was thinking…about us. Not about the kids or about how things used to be, but about *us*. Now." He removed his hand and looked at her with steady eyes. "Jenny, you gave me an ultimatum, so I sold my business and I moved to your hometown with you and the kids. I think you know how badly I want this to work, but I haven't asked what you want." He breathed deeply. "So I'm asking you: What do you want?"

She froze at the question. She didn't know how to answer him.

She supposed, like most people, she wanted too much and too little. She wanted a meaningful career and a balanced partnership in raising their kids. She wanted romance and passion and friendship and shared secrets. She wanted the two of them to kiss Emmy and Austen good-night before crawling into bed next to each other and making love. She wanted to talk and hold hands. She wanted to lie in his lap while she read a novel and he scrolled through camera gear deals. She wanted her marriage to be like it once had been.

She suddenly realized she'd said the last part out loud, so she repeated the words, louder this time.

"I want us to be like we once were," Jenny told him.

"That's what I was afraid of." He wiped at his eyes with the back of his hand.

"What do you mean? Isn't that what you've been saying?"

He stood and looked down at her. "We can't go back. You've seen me at my worst. I was at my worst when I even considered cheating on you. And then after I actually met her…"

"Tracy," Jenny said, putting the name in the room with them.

"With all of that, we can't be like we once were. Our marriage is different, and in some ways, it always will be. I don't know if you can be happy with what we are now."

He was right. He knew her too well.

"We'll leave as soon as we can tomorrow," Curt said. "I'm not going to keep forcing myself on you, but I'm not just walking away. I'll find a little place in town where I can keep the kids half the time. Maybe that will give you space to decide if you want to work toward something new. If not, we'll need to talk about next steps."

Jenny knew the word her husband wasn't saying, the word they'd sworn never to say when they married. *Divorce.* That was next steps.

35

NICHOLE

For her exit interview, Nichole was led outside to a one-room studio space that could've operated as a pool house. Instead, there were two wingback chairs facing one another in front of a fireplace that had been lit despite the warm evening air. A mahogany clock and several knickknacks ran the length of the mantel.

The room would've looked cozy if Nichole's head wasn't pounding and if she wasn't aching to leave this place. A staff member motioned for her to sit before bringing her a cup of water.

Minutes later, when George arrived, he'd changed into jeans and a button-down work shirt. He looked almost...normal.

She started to stand, hoping to signal that she was ready to go and this meeting was unnecessary, but George stopped her.

"Please, stay seated," he said, a sad smile playing about his lips. "I know you're ready to be on your way, but we like to take a few minutes to check in with all of our guests before they leave one of our retreats. Since you'll be missing our Reflection Session with your coach tomorrow, I thought I'd lead you through it now."

"We really don't need to," Nichole said. "I'm not feeling well."

He narrowed his eyes, studying her. "I understand, but we must do this." There was something in his tone—a threat or a demand—that made her back off.

She sipped at her water and forced herself to swallow the liquid past the lump in her throat.

"Good. So, Nichole—or do you prefer Nikki?" he asked as he sat across from her, his face open and ready for whatever she wanted to tell him.

With the wrinkles around his eyes and his salt-and-pepper hair, he came across as approachable, and with a notepad and pen in hand, he looked every inch the doctor who held all the answers. Even though Nichole was immune to his charisma after finding the photo of her sister in his office, she could see how the intensity of his gaze—one that said she was the only person in the world worth listening to in that moment—might appeal to others. Others like Christina?

"Nichole is fine," she told him.

"Nichole, thank you. I apologize for not knowing, but this is the first time we've really had a chance to chat one-on-one." He looked down at his notebook as if consulting a list of questions. "All right. Let's begin. What do you feel was the most beneficial part of your experience this weekend?"

Leaving?

"Um...the food was delicious," she answered.

He chuckled slightly. "We do have a rotation of amazing chefs, many of whom come out for several weekends a year even though they run Michelin-starred and James Beard Award–winning restaurants."

She raised her eyebrows as if this was interesting information.

"Is there any particular reason you'd like to give for not staying until the end of the retreat?" He glanced at her over the glasses perched on the end of his nose.

She shrugged one shoulder.

George settled into the high-backed chair. "Were you offended by anything that was said since you arrived?"

"No," she answered. "I actually…" She hated admitting this, but something about his stare was pulling her into his orbit.

He put his pen down and crossed his legs, waiting.

"I feel…different after the hypnosis…better…" She looked him in the eye. "But you should tell people what to expect beforehand."

"I understand. We don't announce hypnosis because sometimes it's off-putting, but if you look through the introductory material, you'll see that this is a standard practice at our retreats."

She didn't tell him that the introductory material was most likely on the floor of her car, but he seemed to realize as much.

"I assure you that you were not at any risk during the session. Hypnosis merely offers suggestions; even the best practitioners cannot force you to do something that goes against your character." He was quiet, allowing her to process what he'd told her.

She gave him a quick nod, her mind returning to her sister. She wished she could ask him about Christina, how he knew her, what he might've done to her, but she couldn't form the words.

Dr. Hoffman jotted something down before looking back to her. "Anything else you'd like to put on record before signing our contract?"

"What contract?"

"Oh, just a formality, reiterating that you won't discuss this weekend in any kind of public arena. Social media, news outlets, that kind of thing." He exhaled. "We take great pains to make each person's experience at Genetive one of a kind, so we can't exactly shout our methods from the rooftops."

"Sure," she sighed. "Give it to me and I'll sign it."

"Very good." He put his notepad on the floor next to him

and leaned forward. "I did want to let you know that we are aware you had a bit of a struggle following the rules this weekend."

She stared back at him. This was absurd. She was an almost-forty-year-old woman. If she wanted to sleep in the same room as her boyfriend, she most certainly would.

"Ms. Miller, these rules are in place not to inhibit you—"

Her brow furrowed and her mouth turned down.

He caught the look and put out two hands. "I know that your generation has different ideas about morality, and I'm not here to comment on the choices you make."

"Are you sure?" she asked. Up to this point, she'd been contained and cordial. She couldn't keep up that facade for much longer. Her heart was beginning to beat a hard rhythm inside her chest. "Because it sounds like you're very much commenting—and holding my keys hostage. I want to leave. Now."

"I'm aware." George smiled his insipid smile. "But we cannot abide theft."

Nichole suddenly realized that he wasn't talking about morality as a question of whether or not she'd slept in the same room as Wes.

"I will gladly hand over your keys if you'll first return what belongs to me."

Nichole met George's unflinching gaze.

He held out a hand. "I'd very much appreciate it if you gave me back the photo you found in my office earlier."

She shook her head one time, back and forth, as she clenched her lips and kept her eyes fixed on his.

"Ms. Miller, I realize that the photo is of your deceased sister, but it has special significance to me as well." His eyes darkened for the first time. "It is essential that you hand over that photograph. If you don't..." He glared at her. "Things might happen."

It was his tone; that was what finally did it.

Nichole shot out of her chair and bent forward, her head jutting into his personal space, her eyes wide with anger. If she could breathe fire, she would have. Instead, she growled each word slowly into his face.

"Why the fuck do you have a picture of my sister?"

George shrank back. That was a good choice on his part.

"She was…" He started and then stopped, composing himself. "She was important to me."

Nichole's stomach turned. "You know what this looks like, don't you? An affair—taking advantage of a woman decades younger than you?—this could ruin you and your beloved Genetive. If I went to the media…" Nichole couldn't think how to finish the sentence, so hot was the rage bubbling inside her.

She reached for the thing nearest her right hand on the mantel and hurled it at him. A framed photo of his wife hit him in the center of his forehead. He jolted back at the strike and brought his fingers to the wound.

She saw a welt already forming. A line of blood trickled down his nose. This was no longer the composed, charismatic Dr. George Hoffman everyone knew and loved. He could be broken.

Instead of throwing the photo back at her, he picked up his notebook and held the pages to his forehead to soak up the blood.

Nichole stood with her back straight. "If you ever so much as say my sister's name again, I will kill you."

"Is that a threat?" he asked, one side of his mouth upturned and his words too singsong for her liking.

"No. I will do it. In fact, I'll do it now if you want. Just say her name."

As she said the words, she reached for the next thing closest to her, the clock this time.

He put up a hand to stop her. Then, he took his phone out of his pocket, pressed a few buttons, and told someone on the other end of the line to bring around her car.

Nichole turned and walked to the door, but as she reached for the doorknob, she looked back at him one last time. He was staring into the fire. He'd removed his notebook from his bloody brow and he now sat unmoving, letting the blood drip down his face.

"Goodbye, Doctor," she said, her teeth clenched.

He stopped staring into the fire, and his eyes met hers.

"Christina?" he asked, his tone almost childlike. "Is that you?"

In that moment she knew only one thing: she hated him, and she would somehow destroy him.

She bit the inside of her cheek and tasted blood. Then, she backed away from him and turned and ran.

BEVERLY

ONE WEEK POSTMORTEM
THE NIGHT OF THE FIRE

By the day I died, I was fully enlightened, perhaps even close to regenerated, but not in the way the other women of Genetive might expect.

I'm ashamed that it took almost a lifetime for me to lose all faith in my husband. The flood should've severed our tie, knowing that he sacrificed those children to save a few dollars. The comments about sending our grandson away should've also broken our bond, but it didn't.

I'm sure some therapists—not those we trained—would've labeled me as codependent, would've said our trauma bond had been forged with untenable fires that would take serious time and intervention to melt. But I didn't speak to any professional willing to tell me the truth: that my so-called love for my husband was unjustified and unhealthy.

As the heat roiled in the June before my death, I began waking up in the middle of the night, sensing the presence of someone at the end of my bed. I would call for George, but he never answered. During the day, my head pounded, and nausea set in. When the pictures on my wall began to move, I knew something must be terribly wrong.

I reminded myself that some of the best artists were crazy—

Van Gogh, Munch, Rothko. If I was descending into madness, I was in good company. Sometimes I even wondered if maybe I was about to get a hit of artistic genius, but when I tried to paint again, I soon realized that I had the same uninspired brushstrokes.

The headaches and hallucinations came on shortly after things began breaking in our house. George was overseeing a top-secret building plan out at the property, so I had to deal with our residence downtown.

First, it was our dryer, which was an easy fix. I ordered a new one online and someone came and hauled the old one away. It made me think of the days when my mother still hung all of our clothes on the line to dry, how my Sunday dress always smelled like soap and sunshine. Now I could make a call or a few clicks and have what I needed delivered to my door.

Next, our water heater died, and I managed to hire a company to come out. The owner of the company himself made the visit and fixed it right up.

A week later the AC unit went out, and in a Texas summer, that will never do. I figured since things happen in threes, everything should be fine for a while. And it was.

Except for the fact that my body was breaking down.

I'd been prone to migraines ever since the flood, but I could usually take a pain reliever and continue my day. Not so with these new ones. These felt like someone had clamped my temples in a vise and squeezed until the breaking point.

Medicine didn't touch this kind of pain, and the only remedy I could find was cool compresses in a pitch-black room. I asked Max to come over and install blackout curtains, and those helped. Poor boy, he seemed so concerned. I told him not to bother Robin with my condition, and when she called or arrived to check on me, I could rally for an hour or two.

In fact, after twelve hours in bed, I could usually get up the next morning and make my way to the kitchen to cook breakfast. Or, if George happened to be home, I could sit with him on the back porch for a few minutes and talk about workshop material. I even tried to venture out to Robin's once or twice, but I inevitably had to turn around because of the nausea that would overtake me.

I was hoping to get over all of it without having to see the doctor. My daughter's birth had ruined medical professionals for me, and when I did manage to go in and tell the wrinkled man in the white lab coat about my symptoms, he patted me on the leg and reminded me once again, *You're postmenopausal. It's just migraines. These things happen sometimes.*

I tried reminding the doctor that only a few weeks earlier I'd been leading women's seminars at my husband's retreats. I had not been lying prone in bed, wishing I could tear my own head off my shoulders.

He wrote me a prescription but seemed more concerned with George and his top secret construction project on our property. I knew it was a bunker. I'd actually dared to tell George what I thought about the idea the last time he'd been home, and we'd fought.

I soldiered on, took medicine that didn't touch the pain, lay in my darkened room, prayed for healing. I hadn't ever been very spiritual, though I didn't share as much with the priest at my weekly confession. Don't get me wrong: I appreciate a good sermon and a passage of Scripture well-read, but I do not want to think about angels and demons and the stuff that goes bump in the night. If all that was true, what other awful things might also be true? No, denial was a friendly companion.

That was why the first time I felt the figure at the end of my bed, hovering and crouching silently like the gargoyle in Fuseli's *The Nightmare*, I sat up to inspect my surroundings rather than cower in fear. The presence disappeared, but as soon my head rested on the pillow again, I felt it there in the room with me.

Nonsense, I would think before rolling over and telling myself to go back to sleep. I didn't sleep, not with that feeling of being watched, but I shut my eyes tight and tried my hardest.

Of course, I didn't tell anyone at first. A lady's business is her business. I thought about saying something to George, but we weren't communicating well as of late, and his time was consumed with problems out on our land.

I could've said something to Max or Robin, but they would've only worried—and perhaps made me an appointment with a psychiatrist.

But it kept happening. That dark, ominous figure with no actual features hovering at my feet night after night.

Then, I noticed the plants. I'd always had a bit of a black thumb, but I still enjoyed trying to make things grow. For Christmas, Robin had ordered me a countertop herb garden that claimed to be foolproof. And it was for the first few months, but then, sometime after the headaches and the dark presence, my rosemary and basil started to die.

George said I'd probably forgotten to water them. But I knew I hadn't. I'd even written down a watering schedule for my herbs and the white orchid Max gave me for my birthday years earlier because I wanted so badly to keep them alive.

The wilted leaves were in the trash when the red lights began flickering in my print of John Singer Sargent's *A Dinner Table at Night*. When the woman in the painting began talking to me, I knew I needed help. Not that she was saying anything terrible. In fact, the lady in the gorgeous black dress was quite friendly, telling me about the wine she was drinking and who'd gifted her the gold necklace.

I phoned the doctor the next morning. I couldn't bring myself to tell him everything, but he continued to insist it was only migraines—the hallucinating kind, apparently. He had his office staff schedule an MRI, and he told me he'd refer me to a neurologist if anything concerning came back in the imaging.

"You're fine," the good doctor said. "Just need a bit more rest."

By the time the date for the MRI arrived, I was dead. So that took care of that.

PART THREE

"As he looked at the fire,
I thought I saw a cunning expression,
followed by a half-laugh,
come into his face."

—*Great Expectations*,
Charles Dickens

"At last both slept:
the fire and the candle went out."

—*Jane Eyre*,
Charlotte Brontë

36

JENNY

Curt fell asleep early that night, as he always did when life got emotional. Jenny was glad. She wouldn't need to make excuses for why she was joining women she didn't like at a wine and chocolate event at 10 p.m.

Though she was emotionally spent as well, she knew this was a chance to see inside, to listen to these women in their element, to find out if any of them had known the real Beverly Hoffman.

The solarium was bright and bustling when she entered. At least twenty women were buzzing around a long table filled with chocolates and pastries, though their tiny plates held only slivers of chocolate with nibbles bitten out of them. Each woman held a goblet of wine in one hand.

"You came!" Dr. Pound proclaimed above the hum of voices. She was cheerier, more relaxed than earlier in the day.

"I did!" Jenny said, trying to mimic her levity as attendees turned their heads to study her. "Hello, Dr. Pound."

Dr. Pound poured a drink and waved away the formal name. "Call me Lydia."

"Is this the new girl?" A woman she didn't recognize came

over to Jenny while addressing Lydia. The woman's mascara was smeared, creating a black crescent under one eye.

"It is." Dr. Pound handed Jenny a glass. "Judith Howell Martin, everyone. She's a journalist and can add her expertise to represent our little organization in the best light."

"There, there," one of them said, lifting her wine in a make-shift toast to Jenny.

It was the first time this Genetive phrase had been used in reference to herself, and Jenny felt a flush of pride, one that she quickly stamped out. Of course she didn't want these people toasting her.

Jenny glanced around for Robin, but she wasn't here. "I thought that Robin would be—"

Dr. Pound cut her off with a too-bright smile. "Max said she's staying in this evening. With him."

Jenny maintained a relaxed expression even though the statement bothered her. Dr. Pound lifted a hand, and a hush settled over the room. Jenny realized that they were waiting for some kind of response from her.

"Oh, well, thank you for having me. This weekend has been such…an eye-opening experience. I'm so interested in finding out more about Genetive."

The senator's wife laughed. "Oh, honey, this isn't Genetive."

Dr. Pound shot her a look and put a hand on the woman's upper back, taking her plate but leaving her the wine.

Jenny wasn't following. Her face must've said as much.

"Don't eat the white chocolate," Dr. Pound whispered in Jenny's ear. "It has a bit of an extra ingredient. We try not to let Mrs. Riley have too much." She turned back to the others and spoke more loudly this time. "Our dear senator's wife means that this is more than Genetive. We women have our own organization that falls under the wide Genetive umbrella. It's a little something that George asked me to found."

Jenny took a sip of red wine. "Oh, so Beverly helped?"

The question was asked innocently enough, but Dr. Pound

ignored the inquiry. Jenny had begun to notice that this seemed to be the response she gave when she preferred not to answer.

"Beverly wasn't interested," the senator's wife said as she tipped forward. "We call ourselves GEMS. It stands for a Generation of Engaged Mothers and Sisters."

"Ah." Jenny took another sip of wine to keep herself from showing her concern over the nomenclature. "So what exactly does this arm of the organization do?"

Several ladies turned back to their own conversations, no longer interested in hearing again what Jenny expected to be the mission statement.

"We're primarily here to encourage female advancement, which sometimes includes career networking." Dr. Pound scanned the room. "Let me introduce you to an editor for the *Texas Weekly*. You're interested in getting back to a larger media outlet, aren't you?"

Dr. Pound didn't wait for an answer as she led Jenny to the corner, introducing her to a small group of women.

"This is Lila Pointer, the editor in chief. Here's also Kylie Ranger, head of Ranger Clothing. And Poppy Brenner, a stay-at-home mother of four. We value all jobs equally."

Jenny tilted her head, noticing how Poppy's face darkened under the assessment. She got the feeling that Dr. Pound's statement was more of a talking point than actual reality.

"You know, we've been thirsty for some young blood around here," Lila Pointer said playfully.

"That's right," Kylie Ranger teased. "All of us old ladies can be terribly dull."

Jenny wasn't sure how much youth she could bring at forty, and she also wouldn't have called the tailored fifty-something an *old lady*.

"We're not old. We're seasoned," the senator's wife, having trailed behind them, corrected.

The tight circle laughed. A sisterhood sounded nice on the surface. But, Jenny wondered, what lurked beneath the simple-sounding name of the GEMS? What kind of *engagement* were these *mothers* and *sisters* hoping for? From everything she'd seen of the weekend, they mostly wanted to do whatever their husbands told them to do.

"We do have younger members, some even unmarried and in their early twenties, just at the start of their careers and lives," Dr. Pound clarified. "But most of them prefer to do online workshops and seminars. All that will change once we're finished with the Reserves. We can be so much more involved when we live on-site most of the year. We plan to host families' and girls' weekends and boys' hunting expeditions. We may even offer a few singles' events to help the right kind of woman find the right kind of man. It will be so lovely and lively. That's the tone George and I are going for."

Jenny caught the *George and I*. It smacked of an intimacy she didn't think Beverly would've liked.

"We already have many men—rising professionals—interested in Dr. Hoffman's ideas," Kylie Ranger added. "If we can get young women involved, we can build families into the program. Slowly, we can transform a generation. Wouldn't that be something?"

The hunger for fame or notoriety—or perhaps even a genuine desire to better people's lives—was evident in all of their voices.

"It would be...something," Jenny agreed, considering how she could shift the conversation to what she really needed to know. "If I was interested—and if my husband was supportive—how might I join this part of the organization?"

Conversations quieted around Jenny again as if everyone had kept an ear on the new girl's questions.

"Are you saying that you'd be interested in becoming part of the GEMS?" Dr. Pound blinked as the others congregated around her.

Had this been the moment they'd been waiting for? Were they going to rush her into some sort of initiation?

"It's really rather simple," Dr. Pound said, stepping even closer to her. The circled bodies pressed forward at the same time. "You take an oath and the mark."

"The mark?" Jenny's Sunday school lessons as a child at First Baptist rushed back at her. She could almost see a giant *666* across her forehead.

"It's nothing, really." A forty-something woman stepped forward, pulling her hair away and turning around to show a one-inch G marked into her shoulder.

Of course. The mark was the slanted tattoo. "And the G stands for GEMS?"

"It can represent so many things," Dr. Pound answered. "GEMS, yes. But also Goodness, God, Genetive..."

"George?" Jenny dared to ask.

The women tittered.

"No, never," Dr. Pound said. "We would never brand ourselves with a man's name. We are a women's organization."

"I see," Jenny said. "So an oath and this little...mark."

"A tattoo, really," another woman cut in. "We aren't barbaric enough to brand ourselves."

"Would I be required to do anything else?"

Dr. Pound lifted a shoulder. "Nothing else, except dedicate yourself to the teachings and the way of life that we promote, which it seems you're eager to do."

The senator's wife stepped forward, sloshing her glass, as she teased. "You know, just sign your life away."

The other women laughed again, raising their glasses to this assessment of their commitment.

Dr. Pound touched Jenny's arm almost affectionately. "Really, though. We're here to support one another, to encourage one another to be the best women, wives, and mothers we can be. A sisterhood of conservative minds and voices, ready to take back this nation one city at a time."

Is that all? Jenny thought as she raised her glass for one last sip.

37

NICHOLE

Nichole had heard the story a thousand times, how she was a gift for her sister.

We didn't know if we wanted more kids, her mom had said matter-of-factly on numerous occasions. *But Christina begged for a baby sister as soon as she could talk. We brought you home just to calm her down.*

Her mother would laugh and hug both of her girls tight as Christina smiled down at Nichole, mouthing the words, *You are mine.* Nichole would snuggle closer to her sister. That was fine by her.

Nichole wasn't sure how fast she drove home from the retreat, but she made it there in record time. The first thing she did was pour herself a bourbon that she downed in three seconds. Then she poured another, went to her room, and knelt by the side of her bed, ready to face whatever her sister had left behind.

"Please don't be George, please don't be George," she mumbled to herself as she slid the cardboard box out from where she'd hidden it all those months ago. Though she wasn't quite sure what she meant by these words—her sister would never, *never*, be involved with someone like him—she lifted them like a prayer.

She took a deep breath, wishing Jenny were here to help.

But no, she needed to face her sister's past on her own before she dragged someone else into the mess.

The trembling in her hand had stopped. She took one more sip of bourbon and pulled back the cardboard.

At the very top of the box was a large stack of mail that had been forwarded to her after her sister's death. For weeks she'd received odds and ends of her sister's life—advertisements, cell phone bills, bank statements—until Brian had taken a half day to notify the businesses of Christina's death. Every time she'd gotten anything with her sister's name as the addressee, without thinking, she'd shoved it in the box to deal with later.

After that the box was mostly filled with papers, some with typed writing and others handwritten, but there were a few things she was surprised to see: a ticket stub from *The Marriage of Figaro* at the Galveston Opera House, a printed acceptance email from a scientific journal, a perfectly pressed flower. Her sister had always been neat, almost to the point of minimalism, so if these things hadn't been thrown away, then they'd meant something to her.

Nichole pulled out drafts of several academic papers with her sister's handwriting scribbled in the margins. Then she lifted a notebook, empty except for a few pages of research notes. Underneath that was—oh, God.

She reached for her bourbon, but it was empty. Nichole placed both hands on the floor to steady herself because there in her sister's box was a copy of Dr. Hoffman's first book, *Sphere of Influence*. Nichole closed her eyes as she forced herself to open the cover.

To My Christina was written on the inside, Dr. Hoffman's signed name beneath the message.

No, this could not be happening. Her sister wasn't romantically involved with anyone. She never had been. Nichole had figured her sister was like a nun, except that science was the savior to whom she'd devoted her life.

She removed another few items: a book about the history of Galveston, birthday cards, and a name badge for a science symposium. And then, almost at the very bottom of the box, was something both familiar and disconcerting.

A postcard. On the front of this one was the name of the painting: *Mother with Children* by Gustav Klimt. The image was painted mostly in strokes of brown except for three sleeping faces: the mother leaning her head into a pink-lipped infant and another rosy-cheeked child leaning against his mother's cloak. Cocoon-like, all three figures were wrapped together in a kind of dormancy.

As Nichole flipped over the card, she realized she'd shut her eyes tight against what might be written on the back. She exhaled with puffed cheeks and forced herself to start at the top.

There was a date marked a week before Christina died in Beverly's handwriting. The note started simply with Christina's name followed by the first line of the message: *I hired a P.I. months ago when I began to suspect something was amiss.*

Nichole almost dropped the card. This couldn't be happening. Her sister would never do something like this. She closed her eyes tight against fears of the encroaching reality before forcing herself to read on.

My one regret is that I didn't doubt my husband sooner. I haven't yet told him that I know what he did, but I plan to tell him.

Nichole realized she was holding her breath and inhaled before continuing.

Please know I never stopped loving you, and I never will. You are always and forever my daughter. As soon as I've told George, I'll arrange a trip to see you. I've missed so much of your life already.
Love,
Beverly

Nichole did drop the postcard then, the pieces of her sister's involvement with the Hoffmans dissolving and reforming into a crystallized truth.

Christina hadn't been George's lover. Or his disciple.

And this wasn't some kind of revenge message from a wronged wife.

This was Beverly introducing herself to Christina as her biological mother.

Nichole exhaled with a shudder, releasing the tension she'd been carrying. She inhaled a new concern: her sister was the child of George and Beverly Hoffman. But how? And why had she been given up?

Nichole lifted the last item out of the box: an envelope with a broken seal. Inside was her sister's amended birth certificate and a folded note. Nichole remembered seeing the document when she'd been doing a family tree project in middle school, and in the place of mother and father had been their parents' names. It had never been a secret that both of them were adopted. Her mother had sat Nichole down when she was four years old and explained the entire thing without preamble or emotion, like a surgeon telling someone how to make an incision.

When Christina had asked their mother about the wrong names on the birth certificate, her mother had changed the subject a couple of times before admitting that in Texas, sealed adoptions changed the names of the parents to the adoptive ones. *You can order the real one when you're eighteen, if you like*, she'd said before leaving the room.

Christina must've waited until her forties, ordering this new certificate shortly before she died. Probably sometime after she began to suspect her true lineage. Otherwise, she would've told Nichole. She was sure of it.

Nichole unfolded the other piece of paper inside the envelope and saw that it was a note written in her sister's handwriting, responding to Beverly.

Beverly,

I hope you are well. The news I received from Dr. Hoffman a few weeks ago has been very difficult to process. Not knowing my birth parents was something I'd made peace with long ago, but now understanding that a man like him—someone who stands for so much that I oppose—is my real father is difficult, to say the least. It's been upsetting to the point that I have been seeking treatment for anxiety in these last few weeks. I will need time before I'm able to share this news with anyone, much less...

But the letter was unfinished. Her sister had died with the burden of this news.

If Beverly had sent a PI to tail George, suspecting her husband was up to something, then George must've gone to see Christina in person. She was sure her reserved sister wouldn't have wanted that. She must've been in such pain, and she hadn't told Nichole about any of it. Not while she had the chance.

Hardly knowing what she was doing, Nichole began to pack the items back into the box, wishing she could unsee what she'd found and yet relieved that it hadn't been an affair. As she came to the stack of mail, her eyes fell again on the cell phone bills.

She hesitated only a moment before ripping them open one at a time until she arrived at the list of phone numbers called or answered the month of her sister's death. She scanned the numbers, looking for Edenberg's area code. Sure enough, there was a number that Nichole didn't recognize but had the same first three digits as her own.

She scrambled for her phone, picked it up, and dialed. It rang once, twice, three times. After the fourth ring, it went to voice mail.

You have reached the voice-mail box of Dr. George Hoffman, the message began, robotic until George's voice stated his name clearly.

Her stomach churned with the realization that her sister had been speaking with this man, and then her mind turned to something even more terrifying... It couldn't be.

Again, she ran a finger down the list of phone numbers until she arrived at the very last one. There, at the bottom, was George's number, answered around midnight on the day of Christina's death. The call had lasted no more than two minutes, but these two minutes were the same time that the police suspected her car to have careened off the edge of the Seawall and into the warm embrace of the murky water below.

Grief threatened to overwhelm Nichole. She struggled to breathe as she stood and stumbled to her bed, where she fell into her comforter. The tears came then. Raw and real and intense enough to drown her.

In the next hour two facts would replay in her mind, swirling together into a vortex of rage: 1. Christina received a call from George. 2. Christina drove off the edge of the Seawall.

In Nichole's mind, this meant that the intrepid Dr. Hoffman was responsible for her sister's death.

Christina may have been distraught. Or distracted. Her sister had been supposedly celebrating that night, yes, but she'd also never been great at processing emotions, especially conflicting ones. What if she'd driven off the Seawall in a moment of distraction? Or worse...intentionally? What if...

No, Nichole knew she couldn't go there. She might never get out of bed again if she did. But maybe she didn't want to get out of bed anyway.

She fell into a grief-induced sleep. She didn't wake until hours later when Wes used a key to let himself into her house, sat by the side of the bed, and stroked her hair.

"Hey, I'm here," he said as she woke up, her eyes swollen.

"Go away," she muttered before rolling away from him.

"No," he stated simply.

"Go away," she said again. "You lied to me."

"Brian called and told me that he talked to you. I swear I was planning to tell you." Wes placed a tender hand on her back. "Don't pull away from me, Nichole. I know I should've told you that I knew your ex, but honestly, as soon as I met you, I didn't want to risk you walking away if I mentioned his name."

"Is that how you knew so much about me? Your buddy Brian filled you in on everything?"

"You told me those things the night we met. You have to believe me."

Nichole didn't move, so he inched closer. His voice was soothing, and she wanted to believe him. Her sister's face with different expressions kept appearing in her mind: one moment, angry; the next, confused; then, terrified. She needed the thoughts to stop, so she rolled over and looked Wes in the eyes. His were almost as tired and confused as her own.

She burrowed into his chest and cried, knowing she had no choice but to trust him. She desperately needed someone right now, and he was here.

BEVERLY

ONE WEEK POSTMORTEM
THE NIGHT OF THE FIRE

I told you that I'd tell the truth, and I have. But I may have also left out a couple of the most important parts—lies of omission, if you will.

My husband kept his own lie of omission for years, never telling me how he'd intervened when he thought our daughter might be less than he'd imagined. Because, you see, that was why he gave her away.

When the medical personnel told George that our daughter's APGAR score was low, that she likely had brain damage and physical disabilities, he decided that kind of life wasn't for us. No consulting me, no soul searching. My husband needs his reality to look a certain way, and that certain way is *perfect*. A special needs child didn't fit the bill.

I know it may seem far-fetched to think that one man could hide a child, but this was the late seventies, and even though a woman might be the one delivering the baby, she had very little say over her own body or the tiny infant that emerged from her womb.

After the nurses rushed our daughter away, George took matters into his own hands. Calls were made. Documents were signed. My child was given away like a discarded trinket or an unwanted doll.

What the medical professionals didn't know at the time was that an illness like Group B strep—which my daughter was born with—can cause all kinds of scary signs in the first few days after delivery. Decreased movement, breathing problems, seizures: the list is long and frightening.

Doctors didn't even know what to call it until the early '70s, and they didn't know the disease could be prevented with a routine test until the '90s. George might've been right in thinking that our daughter would be different than what he'd expected. These symptoms can stick around for the child's entire life. But sometimes they don't, and for our daughter, they didn't.

It wouldn't have mattered to me either way. All I wanted, for my entire life, was to hold, to love, to be with my darling girl. I wanted to go on the journey of parenting our daughter regardless of where that road led.

By the time our daughter was well a week later, by the time she was kicking her tiny feet and crying for milk, she'd been sent off to a neonatal facility in San Antonio, and George had taken care of all the documents that would legally sign our rights away. He was always good at convincing people to do things that were just left of ethical.

Of course, I didn't know any of this until just before Christina died. Knowing that might make it less surprising that I didn't survive too long after.

I'd already buried my child once; to bury her again, without ever having a chance to know her, that was what really killed me.

38

SUNDAY

JENNY

Jenny woke up the final morning of the retreat, eager to see her kids. Curt wasn't in bed or in the bathroom, so she assumed he was on the large back patio or roaming the grounds. It was probably better that way. Until she had an answer to give him, neither of them had much left to say.

That was why she was surprised when there was a pounding at the door to her room.

"Coming," she mumbled, stumbling out of bed and opening the door to find Robin holding a sheet of paper.

"Where's Curt?" Robin asked, her eyes darting past Jenny and into the room.

Jenny shrugged. "No idea. Where were you last night?"

"Max made me stay in our room all night, but I waited until after he fell asleep and stole his key again so I could go snooping." There was a smirk about Robin's lips that Jenny hadn't seen in a while, but the reference to Max forcing his wife to do anything made the hair on the back of Jenny's neck stand up.

"What do you mean Max *made* you stay in your room?"

Robin lifted a shoulder and walked across the threshold. "He brought me dinner and asked me not to leave, said that I didn't seem like myself. He's been saying that a lot lately."

Jenny clenched her fists in exasperation. Perhaps it was the dismantling of her own marriage causing her to reflect on the relationships around her, but she couldn't understand how her formerly strong-willed, adventurous friend could be with such a man. Robin must've sensed her question.

"I realize that we seem like a strange match, but we met as babies in the nursery at church—not that I paid him any attention until after we both came back from college, but... I don't know... I've known him my whole life. He was sweet and romantic before we had Lance, before he started getting involved in his dad's business." She lifted her eyes to the ceiling, and Jenny heard echoes of the same reasons Beverly might've given for first marrying George. *He seemed kind. He was there. It just happened.*

"Look," Robin continued. "If I'd thrown a fit last night, Max might've let me go to the GEMS thing, but I've been thinking..." She hesitated.

"Yes?" Jenny asked after a few seconds.

"I've been thinking that I might leave. Stop doing the get-togethers and workshops, take a break from all things Genetive. I thought they were helping me, but seeing things through your eyes—and Nichole's—I'm not sure anymore." Robin took a deep breath. "So last night...I snuck out and searched through Max's office. I didn't find much..." She held up a typed page. "Except for this. It's the autopsy—the real one, not the coroner's report that we saw."

Jenny took it from her, scanning the contents as she sat on the edge of the bed.

"Technically, Beverly did die by drowning, like the coroner's report said," Robin told her. "But she also had high levels of something called thallium in her body."

"What's thallium?" Jenny asked, already reaching for her phone.

"I looked it up online. You can inhale it, ingest it, absorb it through the skin. It was once used to kill rodents, but it was banned a while back."

"Oh, my God," Jenny breathed.

"I know. The report we saw was technically correct, like you thought. Death by hypoxia, or suffocation, but the thallium in her system definitely contributed to whatever kind of state she was in before she died. Plus, there's this." Robin pointed to a line on the page.

"Valproic acid?" Jenny read.

"It's some kind of anti-seizure medication. Her doctor didn't mention anything, though, so it could belong to George."

"Does he have seizures?"

Robin considered. "I actually have no idea."

Jenny ran her finger over the report more slowly this time. "Regardless, none of this explains how she ended up in the river."

"I know, but…" Robin said. "I mean, this helps, right? We can use this info to take him down."

Jenny looked at the ground for a few beats, thinking. "I'm not sure."

"Maybe…maybe he put the thallium in her food. Or, maybe he'd been slowly poisoning her."

Jenny bit her lip. They couldn't merely grasp at straws. They needed concrete proof.

"George cannot send Lance away, and he cannot continue running Genetive." Robin's tone was becoming desperate. "George has to be involved in Beverly's death. Somehow. I can feel it."

"Do you think that Beverly may have been…" Jenny swallowed, not wanting to say the word. "Would she have taken her own life?"

Robin shook her head. "No. I know Beverly. She was not suicidal."

"I understand, but the police—or a court—won't just take your word for it. And with all the other symptoms, they could say she was...unwell."

Robin ran a hand across her forehead in exasperation. "You could do an exposé about him and this organization."

"And say what? That he does some kooky therapy exercises and that women tattoo themselves? We don't have any hard proof that this man is dangerous."

Jenny gave her a concerned smile as Robin glanced at her own mark. "Talking about Beverly's medical condition isn't exactly journalism. I don't know anyone who would publish it, not with what we've got here." She put a hand on Robin's shoulder. "I'm sorry. We either have to give up, or we have to keep searching. We need to know why Beverly was at the river—and it would be great if we could find out how the thallium got in her system. If in the middle of all that, we can piece together George's involvement, we might have something on him. But until then..." She wanted to give Robin some hope, so she made a suggestion. "Check and see if there are any security cameras in the Hoffmans' house downtown. I can try to call and ask the detective if he's considered that angle."

They both knew the detective likely wouldn't call her back.

Robin sank to the edge of the bed.

"I was hoping this was it, that we could finish things, that we could bury him." Robin hit a clenched fist into her palm. "It makes me want to..."

Though she didn't finish the statement, Jenny could imagine a myriad of things that Robin might like to do to George and his beloved company.

"Listen, coming from investigative journalism, I've learned that these things can take months—"

"I can't wait months. Lance could be gone by then…" Robin said, her eyes filling with tears.

"We'll figure it out. We have to. There are suspicious things about this organization, about George, about Beverly's death. I promise that I won't let this go."

Robin's phone rang. "It's Max," she said, her tone disappointed.

"Answer it."

Robin sighed and picked it up. "Yeah?"

Jenny was again relieved to see that her marriage wasn't the only one in turmoil.

Robin answered in monosyllables for most of the conversation before telling him she'd be down in a few minutes. "Yes, I'll hurry," she said before she hung up.

"George is holding an impromptu press conference. He's invited reporters from a handful of newspapers and news crews out here before checkout time."

"Why would he—"

Robin cut in. "I assume that he's hungry for any kind of publicity. Maybe he knows we're suspicious, and he's trying to get ahead of it?"

Jenny looked down at the T-shirt she'd worn to bed. "I guess I should get dressed."

Robin gave a curt nod. "I'll see you downstairs."

39

NICHOLE

When Nichole woke up the next morning, she realized she was lying against Wes's chest. He must've fallen asleep fully clothed sometime after she'd cried herself to sleep. She didn't know if she wanted him here, but she also didn't want to be alone, didn't want to think about the postcard or the photo or her sister's connection to the Hoffmans.

She glanced at the clock.

Ten a.m. Jenny would be leaving the retreat in a couple of hours.

Nichole would wait until then to send Wes on his way. She tiptoed out of the bedroom and into the kitchen. As she made oatmeal, she thought about how this morning was reminiscent of the one when she'd found Beverly in the river almost a week ago.

"Hey, sleepy," he said, emerging from the bedroom a few minutes later. "Thanks for letting me stay last night."

Nichole didn't say anything as she took a glass out of the cabinet and filled it with orange juice and a splash of vodka. "It's fine," she said, her tone sharper than she intended.

"Can we talk about what happened?"

"Yes." She took a sip—or, rather, a gulp. "How did you get here?"

"Uber."

"Ah." She raised her eyebrows before diving straight into the real issue. "Why didn't you tell me you knew Brian? At least after that first night?"

He huffed out a breath. "I should've told you, but... I guess it seemed...it seemed awkward to meet you, hit it off, and then be like, *By the way, I know your ex*. As the days passed, it just didn't...I don't know, seem important." He sat on the edge of the coffee table across from her and clutched his chest with one hand. "But Nichole, this is me. You know me. I haven't lied to you about who I am."

Nichole thought of the first time she remembered actually hanging out with him—when she took him to the diner in town and he charmed her. She thought of how easily he had lied to Marge about scoping out a new location for one of his branches. At the time, it'd been charming, but now, maybe it was evidence.

"But you lie like it's second nature," she said to him.

"When?"

"Besides the way we met?"

"That was a unique situation. I thought I'd say hello, tell Brian that you seemed fine, and be on my way. I didn't know—"

"And what about when you told Marge you were looking to move your business here?"

"What? When did I..." He seemed to suddenly remember. "I mean, that was a silly thing. I was making excuses for you. Besides, I had been thinking of opening up a branch in one of the small towns around here. I'd already serviced the Hoff—" He ended the sentence too abruptly.

"Finish what you were going to say," Nichole demanded.

He shook his head. "I just meant that I'd done some work out here before."

"When?"

This was a small town. No businesses operated here without someone noticing, and certainly not lately without the Hoffmans' seal of approval. She'd lived in Edenberg for her entire life, except for a brief stint in the UT dorms, and the town was so small that there was one AC company everyone used. Also, one roofer, one tree guy, one plumber—and it wasn't him.

"Me and some of my guys put out flyers on Main Street a few months ago," he admitted.

"Where?" Nichole took another sip of her drink. Something was bothering her about what he was saying, and the drink was calming her mind enough to put the disparate pieces into place. "On Main Street? Where the Hoffmans live?"

He came toward her. "Look, we can talk about everything later. I should probably get home before—"

"No, wait. Our first real conversation—the morning after we met—you said you'd never been here." She squinted, thinking. "You said you'd never even heard of Edenberg, but now you're saying that you were putting up flyers? And only on Main Street? Something doesn't make sense." She stepped toward him, studying his set jaw, that mouth she loved. "What are you not telling me?"

Wes looked around as if deciding whether or not to make a dash for the door. He pinched the bridge of his nose and exhaled. "Okay, I may have done some work at the Hoffmans' house on Main Street. I'd heard of them, knew they were influential, knew they might be a good way into more business."

Nichole narrowed her eyes. "You're lying."

"No, I'm not," he grumbled, almost sounding like a petulant child.

"Your lip, it's doing that thing where it rises up, the same thing it does when you're teasing me, the same thing it did when you told Marge you were looking to move your business here. I just didn't know how to read you then."

He turned and stomped into the bedroom to gather his clothes. She grabbed her drink and followed him, watching as he stepped into his pants and pulled on his shirt. They stood facing one another for a full minute before she finally spoke.

"What is it?" Nichole rolled her eyes and raised a hand. "I've lost my sister, I just found out that she—" Nichole swallowed down the words she wasn't ready to say out loud. "I don't even know if I can trust you. Just—for God's sake—tell me what you're hiding."

Wes studied her, seeming to gauge how serious she was about wanting to know the truth. She was dead serious.

"Fine. I'll tell you, but you won't like it."

"Try me," she said.

He began, and he didn't stop until the glass in Nichole's hand fell to the floor and shattered into a dozen sharp edges.

BEVERLY

ONE WEEK POSTMORTEM
THE NIGHT OF THE FIRE

It's funny how we let people into our homes, trusting them to do the right thing, trusting that they aren't out to get us.

It was June. I'd stepped into my shower that morning, and the water was cold as ice. I washed my hair in two minutes flat and shimmied out from under the water as fast as my sixty-five-year-old knees would allow.

I thought it was lucky that there'd been flyers on my door recently, advertising half-off plumbing services. It was the same company that had pitched George to take over all of our plumbing needs out at the property. Someone was trying to run Paul's Plumbing Service out of business, and I figured since that man was in his eighties, it was probably time to try someone new.

Not that I needed the half-off deal. We'd had to count pennies in the early years of our marriage—before George's parents liked me and his career enough to pour out their blessings upon us—but in the past decade, we'd made millions. I considered calling Paul's Plumbing, but then I thought, why not give this new place a try? They'd been industrious enough to pass out flyers in our small town, and I secretly loved a deal.

So I rang them up, and within the hour, the owner himself

was at my door. I gave nothing away, but I knew him immediately. It was his eyes, almost the exact same shade of umber that had been staring back at me from the river that day, frantic and afraid. I didn't get to her in time, and she'd become a number, one of the fifteen children who'd drowned on the banks of the Guadalupe that fateful summer day.

Of course, I sent postcards to each of the family members of the children we'd lost. I selected photos specific to each family.

Bellini's *Virgin and Child*, Mary's face so exhausted and concerned.

Gauguin's *Children in the Pasture*, the landscape idyllic and serene.

Cassatt's *Mother's Kiss*, the mother holding tight to her naked child.

I thought that sending these images might somehow convey the depth of sympathy I felt for their loss, but I put too much faith in the art and in my own paltry words. Later, when I heard nothing back from any of them, I wondered if I'd done the right thing. Perhaps the images were insensitive or unwanted, even though my words and condolences had been sincere.

Now the same eyes of the girl I couldn't save, the eyes that had haunted me every day, stared back at me out of a grown man's face. This must be her brother—he seemed the right age. He'd come to balance the scales, this angel of death in coveralls.

I opened the door wider and let him into my home. The urge to apologize and to acknowledge the loss of his sister rose in my pounding chest. I wanted to weep and wail and beg him to forgive me. Instead, I did as I'd always done and kept myself together.

He didn't try to upsell me or tell me we needed a new unit. He asked if I could leave the house while he turned off the gas, and since I had errands to do, I told him that I didn't mind. I was actually surprised he hadn't pulled a knife on me. I had no idea he planned to kill me more slowly.

With only a two-hundred-dollar check, he was on his way. He never cashed that check. That was when I should've known that he hadn't come for payment, but to pay me and mine back for what I'd taken from him and his.

You see, unbeknownst to me, he'd left a sprinkling of thallium in my water heater and pipes. Now the liquid that came so readily to me each morning, afternoon, and evening—in my bathwater, in my tea, when I brushed my teeth—might carry the tiniest bit of the toxin into my system. It's funny the minuscule traces that can do such lasting damage.

I was being slowly poisoned, that young man made sure of it. Little by little, over the next few days, I started to experience aches and pains. Within weeks, I had migraines, fatigue, nausea. By the end of summer, strange things began happening. My plants died. I saw things. I even heard the figure in a painting speak to me.

I'll say this much for him: Wes is a patient man. And why shouldn't he be? After he'd waited nearly a lifetime to exact revenge, he could wait a few months for the thallium to do its worst...or, if it didn't work in the end, I suppose he could at least comfort himself in the fact that we'd suffered.

Or I had. Same difference.

I assume that the man expected George to be home, so we would both experience the effects, but my husband was overseeing the construction of the cottages and his bunker. He was convinced we would need it someday when the progressives tried to tax him to death or destroy America, whichever came first.

Good Lord, I still cannot believe how long I believed that my husband knew what he was talking about.

40

JENNY

George stood on a dais in the Great Room, a podium and microphone in front of him. A frenzy of media formed a half circle around him.

Jenny walked into the space and noted the expressions on the retreat attendees' faces. Dr. Pound, near the stage, caught Jenny's eye and offered a thin smile. The whole crowd seemed ready to be part of such an exciting moment in the history of Genetive, even if no one actually knew what this press conference entailed.

Jenny spotted her husband, wearing a suit and tie. He had on a headset, and she made her way to him.

"Is there some kind of announcement?" she asked.

Curt lowered his mouthpiece. "No idea. George found me on a walk early this morning and told me to set it all up. He won't tell anyone what this is about."

Max stepped beside his father and tapped gently on the microphone. "If I can have your attention. Those in the front, feel free to be seated. We'll begin in one minute and counting."

Reporters spoke into their microphones, preparing their audiences for news important enough to warrant open doors to this sprawling estate. Exactly sixty seconds after Max's announcement, George began to speak.

"Thank you all for coming on such short notice. I will be brief in my remarks, and I plan to address questions individually in coming weeks." As George said the words, his face remained somber. "As you all know, I lost my wife a few days ago, and I already miss her companionship and support. During this time, however, I've also had the opportunity to look back over my life and consider the legacy I want to leave.

"Genetive has made incredible strides since its formal launch, and that success is due entirely to the preparations my wife and I made in the early 2000s. We had a vision, one in which men and women across the nation—and eventually across the globe—would realize their proper place in society and reach their full potential within their own individual spheres of influence.

"We've seen senators reelected. We've seen actors break out on screen. We've seen companies rise out of the ashes. No one can say we haven't been effective."

Jenny couldn't help but grimace. Yes, people in their program may have accomplished things, but she was certain it wasn't because of Sharing Circles or Couples Yoga.

"But all this time, my wife and I had been hiding something significant, something that I'd like to share with you today."

Robin came up behind Jenny, startling her. George glanced their way for a brief moment before his eyes flitted back to the cameras.

"We had a daughter that we gave up for adoption when we were little more than children ourselves. While this child was not conceived out of wedlock, I am ashamed to say that we were unprepared for a responsibility of that magnitude. Beverly considered an abortion, but I forbade it."

Robin let out a gasp, but Jenny's eyes were riveted on George.

The reporters didn't seem to hear, their attention also fixed on Dr. Hoffman.

"When we had the baby, my wife was so distraught that she demanded we find a home better prepared to welcome such responsibility. That child was placed with a loving family who gave her a lifetime of care and nurture in this very town—her name was Christina Miller."

Robin gripped Jenny's arm, her fingers pressing into her flesh. "Is he—"

"Lying? Yes. Has to be." Jenny's gaze darted back and forth, scanning the room for Nichole. She could only imagine how hearing something like this would add to her friend's grief.

"While I do not regret our decision to give life to this child, I do regret allowing my wife to convince me that we were not ready for children, particularly since Christina Miller passed away in a tragic car accident a few months ago. The choices we made and the ensuing consequences run completely contrary to the traditional family values and the message of social responsibility that we promote here at Genetive.

"In coming days you may hear from Christina's adopted sister as well as from opponents of Genetive who want to discredit the phenomenal institution that we've built. I encourage you to do two things."

Here, George zeroed in on a camera that was obviously zooming in on him. "One, consider the source. And two, come to me. I'll be happy to answer any questions you might have. Thank you, and God bless."

Jenny's stomach roiled as she realized how much this would affect Nichole, and worse, how much George seemed to be relishing the attention.

41

NICHOLE

Nichole stooped to pick up the largest pieces of glass, but when Wes moved to do the same, she stopped him.

"I've got this," she said, a crispness in her voice.

He went for the broom as she skirted the worst of the fallout.

She could hardly believe that he'd told her the truth. It had to be the truth because why would he make up something so… horrifying?

What kind of person slowly poisons an elderly woman in her home? She realized she'd asked the question out loud.

Wes stopped sweeping. "When you say it like that, I can't believe…"

"And why? What have the Hoffmans done that's so…awful? Their teachings are strange, their practices are bizarre, but… I just don't understand why." She sat back on her knees and held the glass in her right hand.

"Do you remember when I told you we both have…had sisters?"

Nichole couldn't answer.

"My sister was younger. She was eight when she went to a camp one summer and never came home. The camp was in Edenberg."

Nichole sank onto the couch. "You're saying that the Hoffmans...the camp they ran...the one that flooded...your sister was there?"

"Her Muscogee name was Wynema, but we called her Winnie."

"Wait... Muscogee? But you said you're Creek."

"Creek is what the English called us."

"So, is your real name Wes?"

"Wes is my American name. My Muscogee name is Wahya. It means *wolf*."

Nichole looked at Wes with fresh eyes. He had lied, yes, but he was also a person who'd been wounded at an early age, the loss he'd suffered impacting the rest of his life.

"Beverly sent a postcard to my family—sent one to all of the families who'd lost children—and she told us how Winnie had hung on to the branches as long as she could. I guess she thought this would give us some kind of comfort, but instead..." Wes hung his head. "Then the bus broke loose and washed her away with the others. They found her body, and we brought her home, dug her grave by hand, and buried her. My parents were never the same, and I promised that I would make the people who were irresponsible enough to—" he spat the last words "—to cause her death, I would make them pay. I wasn't sure how long it would take, but I would find a way into their home."

"And kill them?"

"I wasn't sure. I'd thought of so many different ways to punish them, but once I was there and I actually had the chance to do it, I couldn't go through with it, at least not fully. I opened the pipes and those leading from the water heater, sprinkled enough thallium in them to cause damage, and then I waited."

"Were you interested in me because I was from Edenberg?"

"No, I swear." He put the broom down. "I know how this must sound, but I didn't even realize you were from the same small town as the Hoffmans until we started talking that first night."

Nichole threw away the shards and noticed that blood was springing to the surface of her palm, but she could barely feel it.

"I'll understand if you call the police," Wes told her. "I'll confess. Tell them what I did."

Nichole put her hand to her mouth and drew in the blood, tasting metal. She needed to think. She'd pushed thoughts of her sister down for too long, but now that she was faced with what Wes had done for his own sister, she realized she might actually understand him better than he could ever know.

George Hoffman was the reason Christina had died in emotional pain, pain she hadn't even shared with Nichole. He could very well also be the reason she drove off the Seawall that night, intentionally or by accident.

Nichole realized suddenly what she wanted to do. "I'm not going to call the police," she said, picking up the dustpan.

"You're not?" Wes seemed genuinely surprised.

"No." She leaned against the broom handle, considering. "I have an idea, but before I tell you, I need to know you're all in—whatever it is."

Wes stared at her, eye to eye, for several seconds before agreeing. "Deal. You say the word, and I'll do whatever you need done."

"No questions?"

He shook his head. "None."

"Good. Then let's clean up this mess."

But before she could do that, her phone blew up with texts and notifications. George's message, stated across local news stations, had reached her, loud and clear. He would take care of his name and reputation at all costs.

Knowing this made the spark of Nichole's rage from last night flame into a fury unlike any she'd ever known. There was only one way to put out the fire inside her.

42

Jenny was behind the bar at the wine room, pouring each of the three women a glass of something bubbly on the night of the annual Paddle Parade. With the rain from the weekend, levels were high enough for quite a spectacle this year.

"To Christina and Beverly," Robin said, raising her glass.

Nichole's smile was faint, but Jenny was relieved she was showing any emotion after fleeing the retreat and finding out everything about Christina.

Robin seemed to be wrestling with her own conflicting emotions about leaving Genetive—and possibly Max. All she would say for now is that she had decisions to make, and that in the end, she and her son would be all right. Nichole took a sip of her drink and spit it back into the cup before brushing her lips with the back of her hand. "What is that?"

"Sparkling nonalcoholic wine," Jenny answered with an upbeat tone. Last night, after Wes had fallen asleep and Jenny was back home watching Curt pack his bag, Nichole had called to tell her everything. At the end of the conversation, Nikki added that she'd poured out every bottle of alcohol in her house. She wanted to begin again, and to do so, she needed a clear head. Jenny would help her do just that.

Robin took a sip and smacked her tongue against the roof of her mouth. "Well, at least it's bubbly?"

Nichole lifted a glass. "To starting over."

The words meant more to each woman than they could say in that brief moment, so they simply nodded and took one more sip before screwing up their mouths. Jenny took the three glasses and poured them out behind the counter, refilling them with sparkling water instead.

"I'm thinking about pitching a piece to *Texas Monthly* about Genetive," Jenny said. "I know we don't have enough yet to take them down, but I think I can go with some sort of political ideology angle. I'm still figuring it out, but I have to start somewhere."

"I'll give you a full interview, no holds barred," Robin said.

"I thought you might."

"I only wish we had some concrete proof that he was involved in her death," Robin added.

"I know," Jenny mused. "Or, at least some way to stop his organization, his takeover of our town."

They finished their waters, and Robin went to the back to shut off the lights, calling out as she walked, "The worst part of this week is that in addition to losing Beverly, I feel like I let her down."

Christina, too, Jenny thought as she eyed Nichole.

"We didn't let anyone down," Nichole stated, her tone resolute. "Beverly and Christina know how hard we tried. I'm sure of it."

Jenny weighed her friend's words. Perhaps they knew. Or perhaps they didn't. Either way, George's subtle and dangerous influence would continue. As a reporter, she'd seen too much to believe any differently.

"Is Curt staying for the Paddle Parade?" Robin asked as she grabbed her purse and motioned them to the back door.

"Yeah, he's staying at a hotel, but we agreed to do this as a family tonight."

Things were far from fixed between Jenny and her husband, but they had a date scheduled. He also planned to leave Genetive as soon as his contract was up, and he'd mentioned looking into teaching film classes. She was starting to think that maybe, with enough time, she could forgive him.

Jenny turned to Nichole. "Is Wes coming?"

"I think so," Nichole answered easily. But there was a glimmer in her eye.

"What are you not saying?" Jenny asked.

Nichole looked up, feigning innocence. "Nothing. I'm just... happy?"

That was new.

A minute later, as the three of them passed through the back door and into the sticky night air, Jenny and Robin put their arms around Nichole's shoulders.

"We'll take happy," Jenny said.

43

NICHOLE

With sparklers in hand, Emmy and Austen and Lance ran around the blankets that the grown-ups had set up in consecutive squares overlooking the Paddle Parade route. Nichole waved at several of the children she'd taught over the years, and she thought about how each of their lives might change in coming years if she didn't act. This only steeled her resolve.

The Genetive float was first, covered in red and white roses. Blue lights had been woven in between the flowers, and in the tiny bow of the boat, Dr. Pound stood, waving and silencing the crowd as she passed.

What a fitting image: Genetive silencing the masses and taking center stage, ready to claim control. Nichole assumed that the quiet was in part because everyone was looking for George, but he was nowhere to be seen. Good.

That meant he'd likely received her message, asking him to meet her at his home during the parade. *I know everything*, she'd written, making up a lie that he was paranoid enough to believe. George hadn't replied, but she'd expected as much. He wanted to pretend he didn't care.

The atmosphere livened again as soon as the Genetive float was downriver, and Tejano beats replaced the patriotic tunes.

"I don't remember it being this loud," Jenny yelled into Nichole's ear at one point, but she was smiling. So was Nichole.

Wes sat next to her, drinking a beer as the crowd oohed and aahed at the ensuing floats. Nichole had the urge to steal the drink from him, to take one small sip, but she refrained.

Instead, she stood, antsy to get on with it. "This breeze is making me chilly. Gonna grab my jacket from my car."

Wes gave her a side glance. "I'll come with you."

It was early September, far from chilly, and Nichole didn't need a jacket, but she did need to leave. She had a dark errand to run. Not that she planned to be gone long enough to be incriminated, but even if she was, she knew Jenny and Robin would cover for her.

She and Wes had discussed everything and gathered the scant but necessary supplies the night before: a crowbar, matches, butane. Wes headed to his work truck and then drove out toward Genetive's property while she started back downtown.

After walking just a few blocks at a quick pace, Nichole reached her own destination: the Hoffman home on Main Street.

She slid on her gloves, took the crowbar from the nearest bush where she'd left it earlier in the evening, and crawled through a window in the back. Last night she'd spent an hour and a half learning this technique online, so she was quick and efficient. She shut the window behind her and headed to a crawlspace, mentally recalling the diagram of the house that Wes had drawn for her.

Are you sure you don't want to just do headquarters? Wes had asked, his head in his hands as he considered Nichole's plan. Not that he seemed to have moral qualms, since he'd been the one to place the poisonous thallium in the Hoffmans' home. *It'll be less suspicious if just one place catches fire.*

Do you want George to get away with essentially killing your sister? And mine? Nichole had shaken her head and insisted that she needed to know George's home downtown was gone as well. *I want him to have no reason and no place to stay. I want him to feel in his bones that this town doesn't want him here.*

What she hadn't told Wes was that she was planning for George to be inside once the inferno began.

Nichole wasn't nervous or frightened. She knew it was the right thing to do. They didn't need to kill anyone else. They just needed to ignite George and his dangerous organization.

It was exhausting, bearing witness to truths that no one else wanted to fight against. Except for Robin and Jenny. She'd almost let them in on her and Wes's plans but then thought of their children and knew she couldn't risk them getting caught. Nichole was willing to go down—if it came to that—but she wouldn't take them with her.

She could've knocked at the front door and waited for George to answer. She could've held him at knifepoint or gunpoint, but she didn't want to expend the energy. She didn't really even want to see the man she despised, but she needed to know he was there.

She crept down the hallway and spotted him in the den, sitting in his chair, staring into nothingness. In this frozen pose, he looked childlike, even vulnerable. This hadn't been what she'd expected.

She hesitated, wondering if she should approach him, but no, she would leave him be, doing whatever nonsensical meditation or self-hypnosis he was currently employing. If the fire happened to knock him out of his trance, well, so be it. She would cross that bridge over troubled waters if it ever came to it.

Now, in the dark house, Nichole hurried to the water heater and took several deep breaths before holding her own. She flipped the gas valve and backed out of the space and down the stairs. She went to the bathroom and poured out nail polish remover, rubbing alcohol, and two flasks filled with butane that she'd stuffed in her pockets. In the kitchen she tossed around napkins, paper towels, recipe cards, cookbooks, and wooden utensils. On her way out, she overturned items and opened bottles lining the table and countertops. George didn't budge, almost as if his mind was somewhere else entirely.

Nichole looked at the mess spilling across the kitchen floor one more time as she crawled back through the window, lit a match, and got the hell out of Dodge. She would head back for the end of the parade, and as the fireworks lit up the sky, she and the entire town could watch it burn.

BEVERLY

ONE WEEK POSTMORTEM
THE NIGHT OF THE FIRE

Since we've come to the end and the flames are starting to climb, it's time for my last confession.

No, not that kind. I never got a chance for the priest to give me my last rites, but I need you to know one final thing: I lied, okay. Not outright, mind you. I just did that thing that people sometimes do when they tell you the truth, but they "tell it slant" as our national poet Emily Dickinson once wrote. I've told you the real truth, mixed with a tad bit of fiction.

The slant truth is this: I died because of George, because he gave away my child, because he took land and turned it into a camp that killed innocent children, because he despised our grandson's differences while never admitting his own.

Some will say that I took part in his ideas, that I helped him build Genetive and everything else that now carries the Hoffman name. They aren't wrong.

After I found out about Christina and took a good look at the reality of my husband and the organization we'd built, I realized I was helping create dependent, obedient women. But I was also codependent and weak and needy. Like George says, each person needs to know his—or her—place in society and embrace it. Well, the little wife, doing his bidding, that was my place, and I was damn good at it until I suspected George of lying and hired a PI.

After a few weeks, I'd expected the PI to hand me photos of my husband sneaking around with another woman, perhaps even Dr. Pound. What I discovered about the loss of our first child—and the recent contact he'd made with her—was so much worse.

I have no idea what he hoped to gain from reestablishing this connection, but knowing my husband, I'm certain he was planning to use Christina just liked he'd used everyone else in our lives: used us until we were spent and dried-out husks of our true selves.

I sent her the postcard a week before she died. A week. Do you know what that does to a person? To have the thing you've mourned your entire life within reach, and then *bam*, it's stolen away again?

I spent the next few months growing sicker and mourning my girl. At moments I tried to rally. I tried to forgive George, but I couldn't find that kind of compassion in my soul. One day at the art gallery I tried to explain to Max what his father had done, but he refused to listen and grew argumentative any time I broached the subject. I tried to stick around for Robin, but I wondered if she would ever find her own strength if she was always depending on me.

And so I planned. It took me weeks to find the perfect art, to have the paintings printed on postcards, to send them to the three women who would care. I also changed the contents of the locket I wore around my neck from a picture of Lance to that list of verses spouting revenge. I hoped that might make it into the national newspapers along with my death, but I should've known that no one—not even reporters or detectives—would care about an old woman drowned in two inches of water, even if it was the wife of Dr. Hoffman.

So that's the slant truth.

The raw truth, however, is this: my husband didn't kill me, not in the most literal sense, but he did leave bruises on both my body and my soul when I confronted him, told him what I knew about our child, our Christina.

You know nothing, he spat at me the night before I died, gripping my arm tight enough to leave marks. *You're a simple woman with a simple mind. Just like all the rest.*

I do know, and the world will soon know, too, I told him.

No one will believe you. He grabbed me again, pushing me against the wall. He'd never laid a hand on me, but this seemed fitting, the culmination of all we'd become. *You have a good life with me, here. Take that and let it be enough.*

It was never enough, I hurled back at him. *Now I'm the one to fix what you've broken.* I thought about the postcards I'd sent. *I have a plan, one that can destroy you,* I spewed, praying the mail would reach its intended audience—women of Edenberg who might grow suspicious and seek to do the things I'd been too scared to do: destroy my husband and his ideas of perfection and power. If they were successful, they'd not only save this town, but also my son and my grandson.

I wanted to raise enough suspicion to cast doubt on my husband's innocence, but not enough to outright frame him. That would be too cliché, and with an exorbitantly expensive lawyer, he would wrangle out too easily. But if I was careful, if I sent just the right missives to just the right people, I figured Robin—and the friends she'd mentioned over the years—could take care of the rest. I'm so glad I got to see how it all worked out.

In the early-morning hours I took a handful of George's seizure medication and downed them with a fine glass of cabernet that Robin had given to me last Christmas.

What are you doing? he'd demanded, trying to seize me again. *Spit those out.*

This time I didn't obey. Instead, I ran. I was heading toward

Robin's house, picking up my pace as I thought about how if I made it all the way there, then perhaps I would have a few moments to tell her goodbye, to tell her about Christina. I was probably halfway out of my mind by then, but with the medication starting to do its work in my system, this final conversation had all seemed so reasonable.

As I neared the river, though, I paused. I thought of the Paddle Parades over the years, of how much this water had given and taken from me. I waded into the low water, stood in the center, and imagined the Virgin of the Guadalupe smiling down on me. My heart stuttered, and I fell face down.

The official cause of death: hypoxia, drowning. That was all George wanted reported, and why wouldn't the small-town authorities grant the wish of the grieving husband? It was just an accident after all.

I hoped, though never expected, that the detective and the coroners would do their jobs. I hoped for too much, forgetting that my husband has convinced wealthy, influential people to fork over millions for his mission, his lies. I'll say this about George: he knows how to work the system.

One week postmortem, as my spirit rests above the banks of this river, the Paddle Parade passes and the scent of a fire catches on the breeze. I think it might be time for me to go. I can feel myself fading in the best way.

So here's the deal: if you never hear from me again, then let's assume that the fire succeeded, that George and Genetive went up in flames, that my soul was finally able to find a bit of peace.

If you do hear from me—like out loud, audibly—you might want to have a quick-check in with your doctor of choice. These kinds of things can be catching.

44

NICHOLE

Nichole hurried back to the parade. For a moment she closed her eyes and her sister was there with her on the banks of the Guadalupe, an arm draped over her shoulder, singing along to Selena's "Dreaming of You," as the final float passed. This one was sponsored by Hill Country Farms and overflowing with every color of purple, Christina's favorite. Wild bergamot, coneflowers, and snapdragons spilled out of the flatboat as two men stood at either end.

These men were no longer lifting and lowering their oars. They stood motionless, except for the one who pointed at the fire rising behind the onlookers. One by one, adults and children realized that the parade was no longer the thing that should be holding their interest.

Jenny shouted, "Fire!" first, which Nichole thought fitting. Jenny always did want to report the news.

Nichole feigned panic. She needed to match the rest of the town.

She and Wes had made a two-fire deal. He would set light to the Hoffman property at the edge of town, while Nichole started the blaze at the Hoffmans' original house on Main Street.

The arrangements had been easier than she'd expected, though less simple than they would've been if not for all the recent rain. Still, Nichole relied on the weather and the prompt response of the firemen to keep the fire contained downtown. She was fine with a complete spread out at the Hoffman head-quarters. Let it blaze.

Other than starting the fire and ensuring its spread, arson wasn't a complicated process.

As Nichole helped corral all of the children and lead them to safety, she thought again of her last look into the Hoffmans' colonial home, particularly of George's face staring into noth-ing as she tossed the match inside.

Maybe Dr. Hoffman was tired of lying and decided to stay put. Maybe he'd absorbed the remaining thallium in the walls of his home. Maybe he'd become disoriented, confused, lost in his own memories. Maybe the paintings on the walls had begun to mutter his name. For whatever reason, George was at the bow of the ship as it sank into oblivion.

The firemen later said that his charred remains had held one thing: Beverly's locket. Nichole thought that was a sweet story, but it sounded too much like something he would've wanted said about him, so she refused to believe the tale.

Regardless, she was glad it happened the way it did. With George gone, with Genetive and the town it had planned to control in ruins, the good people of Edenberg could rebuild in peace.

As we all know, unfortunately, sometimes these things just happen.

EPILOGUE

JENNY

A FEW MONTHS LATER

Jenny sat at her desk in the office at home, reading again the account she'd written of George, Genetive, and Beverly Hoffman's death. Her deadline for *Texas Monthly* was the following week.

On most late-August nights out in the Texas hill country, the stars blaze, poking through the clouds and unencumbered by big-city lights, but in the middle of this night, the night of Beverly Hoffman's death, the clouds were heavy. In the town of Edenberg, streetlamps ran along Main Street, shining a yellow haze into the diner, the newspaper office, an array of boutiques, and the local wine room.

Wearing her favorite navy blue, calf-length cardigan and her standard black elastic-waisted knit pants, Beverly was running from all of that and more. She'd thrown a paisley silk scarf around her neck, because what Texas socialite of a certain age would leave the house without it?

Curt brought Jenny a cup of coffee. It was late and the kids were in bed. He kissed her gently on the forehead and whispered, "Thought you could use a pick-me-up."

Jenny took a sip and leaned forward, wondering how much she should include about what exactly Beverly was leaving behind. Maybe she should add more details about George Hoffman, about the flood, about all those children. She would keep working on it, all night if necessary. This piece had to be perfect. It was her foray back into real journalism.

She skipped down to the end of the story, to the part that had been giving her particular trouble, largely because the last hour of Beverly's life was still a mystery in many ways.

The next part—the details of Beverly Hoffman's death—are largely conjecture, built from pieces of scant evidence. Did she step one striped canvas shoe into the river as the wind picked up? Did she hear a crackling of leaves that sounded like footsteps, and shift her weight in the wrong direction? Did the knee she'd injured in a skiing accident begin to buckle? Did she move her head this way and that and peer into the darkness? She'd been myopic for so long, and she'd left her glasses at home, so if someone was there, she certainly wouldn't have seen them.

Cicadas and katydids continued their rhythmic song, and the moon was only half of itself that night as Beverly struggled past the earthen edge of the Guadalupe. When she reached her destination, she no doubt creaked into a sitting position and wiggled her bottom over the edge. With the pills in her system, she was growing drowsy, stumbling into the shallow water.

Only a little farther now, she might've thought as she looked at the other side, but before she could reach it, the darkness settled over her, shrouding her vision and forcing her to her knees.

Within seconds she was face down in the water, the blessed end washing over her, freeing her from her life sentence.

Jenny put her head in her hands. Was the ending too heavy-handed? Too biased? It was a feature, and features needed lots of color, but maybe she was overdoing it.

She'd pitched the piece with the headline "Texas Woman Takes All." The editor at *Texas Monthly* had loved the concept: a wronged woman whose child is stolen from her eventually takes matters into her own hands and sets things right at the very end of her life.

Of course, Jenny would leave Nichole out of things. She wouldn't mention how she'd noticed Nichole walking in the opposite direction of her car when she said she needed a jacket, how she'd left the kids with Curt while she followed Nichole to the Hoffmans' house, how she'd watched her friend light a match and throw it inside. She also wouldn't mention that around the same time, Nichole's boyfriend, Wes, had driven out to the Hoffman headquarters, flasks of butane and a box of matches in his trunk. No, she wouldn't mention any of that. To anyone. Ever.

In Jenny's story, the fire downtown started with a bad water heater, the same one that had acted up a couple of months before Beverly died. The burning at Genetive headquarters was an unfortunate case of faulty electrical wiring. Such a coincidence that they both went up in flames, but real life is stranger than fiction.

In Jenny's story, George was the eternal villain and Beverly, the woman who was vindicated in the end.

In Jenny's story, Genetive Inc. died along with its founders.

Like any good story, it was true. Mostly.

★ ★ ★ ★ ★

ACKNOWLEDGMENTS

This book is only possible because of Hayley Steed's early belief in my work. She was a fearless champion for four years, steering my writing and my career in the right direction. Thanks to Jill Marsal for taking the reins and giving me valuable insight over the past few months. Thanks also to Elinor Davies and everyone at Madeleine Milburn Literary Agency, Marsal Lyon Literary Agency, and Taryn Fagerness Agency.

I adore working with my editor extraordinaire, Leah Mol, whose writing-brain works parallel to mine, making the prose, plot, and characters stronger and more nuanced. Thanks to my publicist, Leah Morse, for spreading the word about this book. Thanks to copyeditor Kathleen Mancini, typesetter Tamieka Evans, proofreader Sophia Kostanski, and everyone at MIRA who worked hard to get this book into readers' hands.

Thanks to my first readers: my mom, Kathy Brock, and my friend Gina Johnson. You see my stories in their rawest forms and love them anyway. Thanks to my Kinkaid gals—Dr. Tara McDonald Johnson, Dr. Jenny Howell, and Dr. Robin Riehl—for reading and giving feedback. Thank you for letting me text you random questions about everything from title ideas to the darker side of human nature—oh, and for letting me steal your names. Continued thanks to Jonathan Eades, Alex Spencer, and Kate Lambert for your ongoing encouragement and support.

Thanks to my Thriller Writing Group—Allison Buccola, Jennifer Fawcett, and Olivia Day Wallace—for their feedback about what worked and what needed significant tweaking. Our monthly get-togethers help sustain me as a writer.

Thanks to Murder by the Book, Blue Willow, and Fabled for your support and for providing the most amazing book recommendations.

Thanks to Jessica Lee and Sarah Dean for shared laughter and tears, for late-night texts about everything from silly memes to the more serious side of life. Thanks to Brandi Lucher and Christi Green for drinks and prayers.

Thanks to my extensive family for swim time on Sunday afternoons and providing fodder for plots. Mom and Dad, you've known I was a writer for almost four decades, encouraging my efforts at each stage. Lindsay, Katie, and Cody, pieces of you are in every tight sibling relationship I write. Dylan and Daniel, I love y'all like brothers. And to my nieces—Rhea, Abby, and Sarah—and nephew, Isaac, it's so fun watching you grow into fabulous humans.

And finally, to those living in the Bird house: Macie, I love that you introduce me to new music and laugh with—and sometimes at—me. Sadie, I love that you're always drawing, reading, or asking questions. Never stop. Ruby, I love listening to you play piano and watching you make pizza with your daddy on Friday nights. And, Tim, let's see if we can drop the kids at Nana's, so we can pick up Gringo's and Phish Food before we go home and curl up on the couch to watch *The Bear*. It's been two decades, and I still like hanging out with you.

1. In many ways, this is a book about longtime friendships. How would you describe the friendships at the heart of this story? Did any of them remind you of relationships in your own life? Why or why not?

2. Beverly agrees to marry George on the night of her high school graduation. Why do you think she goes along with her husband's ideas for more than four and a half decades?

3. Whose perspective—Nichole's, Jenny's, or Beverly's—resonated with you the most? Why?

4. This is Kristen Bird's first book featuring a "ghostly" character perspective. How did you feel about being inside Beverly's head from this vantage point? Was it helpful to hear her perspective?

5. Dr. George Hoffman is obviously morally wrong, but he never technically takes part in illegal activity—at least nothing he can be accused of in a court of law. What did you find problematic about George and his ideology? In

the book, what makes it possible for these beliefs to flourish and for George to find followers?

6. Which parts of Genetive Inc. were most believable or recognizable?

7. How does the setting—the small hill country town of Edenberg, Texas—contribute to the story as a whole?

8. Moral ambiguity and gray areas are at the heart of much of this story. Which of the characters or moments of questionable morality were most disconcerting? Why?

9. How does the depiction of children in the story add to the overall tone of the book?

10. Beverly was a lifelong admirer of visual art. Which piece of art mentioned in the story struck you the most? Why?